illusion

also by j. s. cooper

illusion

j. s. cooper

GALLERY BOOKS

New York London Toronto Sydney New Delhi

G

Gallery Books
A Division of Simon & Schuster, Inc.
1230 Avenue of the Americas
New York, NY 10020

First Gallery Books trade paperback edition November 2014

GALLERY BOOKS and colophon are registered trademarks of Simon & Schuster, Inc.

For information about special discounts for bulk purchases, please contact Simon & Schuster Special Sales at 1-866-506-1949 or business@simonandschuster.com.

The Simon & Schuster Speakers Bureau can bring authors to your live event. For more information or to book an event, contact the Simon & Schuster Speakers Bureau at 1-866-248-3049 or visit our website at www.simonspeakers.com.

Interior design by Jaime Putorti
Cover photographs by Shutterstock

Manufactured in the United States of America

10 9 8 7 6 5 4 3 2

Library of Congress Cataloging-in-Publication Data

Cooper, J. S.
  Illusion / J. S. Cooper. — First Gallery Books trade paperback edition.
     pages cm.
   I. Title.
  PS3603.O5826365I55 2014
  813'.6—dc23   2014020508

ISBN 978-1-4767-9098-5
ISBN 978-1-4767-9103-6 (ebook)

The path to true love is never an easy one.
Dedicated to all those who keep on keeping on while searching
for the one.

acknowledgments

To Rebecca Friedman, the best agent I could have possibly asked for. The excitement you had for *Illusion* from the beginning has helped me bring this story to life. To my editor at Gallery Books, Abby Zidle, for making me laugh during the editing process, even though I wanted to cry. To Katrina Jaekley and Tanya Kay Skaggs, for always being there to listen and provide feedback during every book plot dilemma. To Elizabeth He, for being my friend and daily talking sponge. To Thao Mai, for always believing in me and supporting me: from hot prof to law school to writing—you've always been there backing me up. To Jessica Wood, for being my writing partner in crime. To my teacher in second form English class, thanks for reading my story aloud in class and making me believe I had a talent for writing.

All my love goes out to all the J. S. Cooper Indie Agents for providing me daily support and love. My thanks and appreciation go out to all the bloggers and readers who read and promote my books with exuberant fanfare. Your support and kindness are always in my heart.

Thanks and appreciation to my mum for telling me to follow my dreams after earning three degrees and deciding to quit my job to become a writer. Your support and love have made me very blessed. Thanks be to God for all my blessings. All I can hope is that my books continue to provide a respite and journey for my readers. I know that I'm taken on a journey with every book I write, and these stories give me a reason to smile every day.

prologue

"Bianca, where are you?" His voice sounded angry, and I shivered as I opened my eyes.

I stared at the large expanse of dark midnight blue sky through the tree branches and prayed that he wouldn't find me. I could see the white-sand beaches from my vantage point. The whole island looked so much smaller from up here. My limbs felt numb, but I was too scared to even move an inch. If he heard the rustling of leaves, he'd know where I was. I closed my eyes again and tried not to think about falling.

"Bianca, this isn't funny." His voice was hoarse, and I heard his footsteps moving closer to me. "Bianca, if you can hear me . . ." He paused, and his voice changed. "Please don't make this harder than it has to be. I'm not going to hurt you."

I heard a branch snap below me, and I knew he was close. All he had to do was look up. If he looked up, he'd be able to find me. This man who'd become my most intimate confidant was now my predator, and I was his prey. I opened my eyes and took a deep breath before looking down. An involuntary gasp escaped my mouth as I realized how high up I was. That was my first mistake.

"I've found you," his voice cracked as he looked up at me with dark eyes. "When will you learn? You can't escape me."

"Did you hurt him?" My fingers started trembling as I looked back down at him. "Tell me. Did you hurt him?"

"It depends on what you mean by *hurt*." He lifted his hands up, and I saw that his fingers were drenched in blood.

I closed my eyes; I had my answer.

"I did it for us," he said simply, and I felt my heart drop into my stomach. "Don't you trust me?" he asked me softly as he started to climb the tree. I saw the shiny glitter of the silver knife in his left hand before he placed it into his pocket, and my heart stopped beating for a second.

"I trust you." I nodded and waited for him to reach me.

That was my second mistake.

one

"Can I have this seat?" A deep voice interrupted my typing, and I stifled a sigh.

"Uh, sure," I replied, without looking up. I had to finish my latest movie review in the next ten minutes and e-mail it to my editor if I wanted to get paid for the article.

"Can I have some space on the table?" His voice was dry as he spoke again, and I pulled my laptop toward me quickly, my eyes never leaving my screen. "I don't mean to disturb you." He continued, and this time I ignored him completely. I didn't have time for chitchat. Not when I had to finish an article on Adam Sandler's latest movie and persuade viewers to go and watch it without completely lying about my feelings toward the acting and the poor jokes.

I typed away as quickly as I could, but I could feel that the man was staring at me. I bit down on my lower lip to stop myself from looking up at him and asking what his problem was. It wasn't his fault that I was on high alert and anxious. I knew that I couldn't have an expectation of privacy if I was working at a coffee shop, but I didn't normally have to worry about a stranger talking to me. People in New York never talked to strangers, not unless they were tourists.

I sighed and looked up. "Did you need help with something?" My breath caught as I stared at the man's face. He was handsome, or appeared to be under the Yankees cap that covered half of his forehead. His blue eyes looked into mine with a bright light, and I could see a hint of a smile on his full pink lips. I licked my lips unconsciously as I stared at the man across from me and attempted to brush my messy hair back. "I can move onto my back if you want. I mean, move back." I stuttered as he stared at me with his lips twitching slightly. "I don't mean I'll go on my back or anything, I mean I can move farther back, if you need more space." My face burned red as I tried to explain myself.

"No, you've done enough. Thank you." He nodded and looked down at his book in a dismissive fashion. Served me right, I suppose. I hadn't really given him the time of day, and it would be way too obvious if I tried to start up a conversation now. I looked at my watch and then back at my article; I had five minutes to sum up a lackluster review of a movie I'd thought was inane. If I didn't send it over, I wouldn't get paid. And now that this was my only form of income, I needed to get paid. I went back to typing, though my mind was partially on the man I was sharing the table with. His knee was rubbing against mine, and I couldn't help but laugh at myself for the slight thrill his touch was giving me.

"Loser," I whispered to myself under my breath as I wrapped up the article and attached it in an e-mail. I knew that I was sending the e-mail without rereading the article one more time so that I could try to chat with the man. Though, I really had no business trying to flirt with a strange man in a coffee shop. I was about to ask him what he was reading, when I got the strangest sensation that someone was watching me again. And this time I knew it wasn't the man sharing the table with me. I looked around the coffee shop and saw an older-looking man sipping his coffee and staring at me over a newspaper. As soon as our eyes made contact, he looked away and back down at his paper. I felt my heart racing as I stared at his coffee cup on the table. It wasn't from this coffee shop. I pressed Send on my e-mail and grabbed my bag up from the floor in a panic, spilling half of its contents on the ground.

"You need some help?" The man looked up from his book and then stared at the ground. He leaned down and picked up my lipstick and some mints and handed them to me. Our fingers brushed each other's as I took my belongings from him, and I felt a dart of electricity running through me at his touch.

"Thanks." I stared into his deep blue eyes and nodded quickly.

"Is everything okay?" His eyes crinkled in concern, and I was about to answer, when I felt the man in the corner staring at me again.

"I'm fine." I looked back down at my computer screen and stifled a groan. I'd received another message from Matt, a guy I'd spoken to a couple of times on the computer, yet had decided I didn't want to meet. I opened the e-mail slowly, not really wanting to read what he had to say. I'd much rather be talking to the hunk in front of me. I read the e-mail from Matt quickly and then deleted it without responding. He just wouldn't leave me alone. "Stalker," I muttered under my breath, and looked up again to see the hunk staring at me.

"Sorry, were you talking to me?" His lips were twitching again, and I shook my head.

"No, sorry. I just had an e-mail from this guy. If it was from you, I wouldn't be pressing Delete, trust me." I groaned out loud as I realized what I'd said. "I mean, because you seem like a really nice guy."

"I'm glad to hear that. Let me know if I can be of any help." He went back to his book, and I was about to ask him a question about what he was reading, when I felt the man in the corner staring at me again.

"Shit." I jumped up and grabbed my bag, hitting the hunk in the shoulder as I moved.

"You okay?"

"I think I'm being followed." I said as I shook my head and nodded toward the corner where the man watching me sat. "Sorry, I have to go." I grabbed my laptop and pushed it into my bag. "It was nice meeting you." I gave him a quick smile and ran out of the coffee shop. "This was our serendipity moment. I hope we meet again," I muttered as I gave the hunk one last look before darting down the street. I continued running down the street until I could no longer run anymore. I stopped outside a donut shop and leaned back against the wall, breathing deeply. I looked left and right to make sure I didn't see the man who I was pretty sure had been following me and then rubbed my forehead.

"You're going crazy, Bianca," I said to myself as I straightened up and started walking at a normal pace. I started laughing as I reached the subway station and went down to catch my train. Not one person had looked at me like I was crazy as I'd run down the street. Even though I'd been running like I was in the 100m sprint finals at the Olympics. That was part of the beauty of living in New York City. You could be who you wanted, and you weren't judged. The other side of the coin, the side of the equation that made me stop smiling, was the wonder of what would have happened if the man had been following me. Would anyone have come to my aid? I walked on to the subway and held on to the pole without looking at anyone. As I stood there I thought about both men in the coffee shop, one I'd wanted to get to know better, and the other, I hoped I never saw again. I shook my head as I realized how different I was now. My life had changed completely in the last year and so had I.

I never thought I was particularly brave until recently. I don't enjoy watching horror movies. I sleep with all my doors double-locked, and I go through and check that all my windows are closed tight every night before I go to bed— and I live on the eighth floor of my apartment building. No,

I'm not someone that anyone would call brave and definitely not an amateur sleuth. I've always been someone who likes to keep to herself. Some people would call me quiet, but those are the ones who don't know me well. Inside, I'm a dynamo of activity and fun.

I used to be the sort of person who froze when she heard a creak in the floorboards or heard a sudden scream. My father always used to call me his frightened little rabbit when I was growing up. I heard the term a lot, as there were always sudden and unexplainable noises in New York City. I don't think he realized that it was his overprotectiveness that led to my lack of trust of most people. However, my whole demeanor changed when my father died. The first twenty-five years of my life faded into obscurity when my father died.

My father died of a broken heart. Or rather I should say he died *with* a broken heart. I don't think he ever got over my mother's death. I'm not sure that I ever got over it either, even though I was a young girl when she was killed in a car accident. Her English ancestry was the reason I studied British history in college, and my love of her memory was the reason why when I was given my father's secret box, I knew I had to do something about its contents. My mother's death changed my father's life, and my father's death changed mine. The moment I read his letter to me was the moment I felt steel implanted in my backbone. It was the moment I knew that I wouldn't allow anything to frighten me until I found out what really had happened to my mother.

~♥

I wasn't surprised when the letter arrived. It was only after I read the note that I looked back at the envelope for clues. Only then did I realize there was no postage stamp. Whoever had left the note for me didn't want any clues leading back to them. I stared at the letter in my hands and shivered slightly. It read simply:

Beauty and Charm. One survives. One is destroyed. What are your odds?

I read it again, trying to make sense of the note. I wasn't sure what I was supposed to take from it. I picked up the envelope again to see if there was anything inside that I'd missed. While I hadn't been surprised to receive the letter, I had been surprised by its contents. I hadn't expected such a blatant threat, though it shouldn't have surprised me. My father had warned me, in the letter I'd found in his box, that there were people willing to do anything to keep their secrets safe. His letter had stated that he suspected that my mother's car accident hadn't really been an accident. However, his suspicions had come too late. It was only on his deathbed that he had started to remember conversations and actions that had happened prior to her death. His letter spoke of his sadness and regret at having shut down after my mother's death. He felt that if he'd not been in such a deep state of depression he would have made the connections earlier. His letter didn't directly ask me to find out the truth, but I could read between the lines. He wanted justice for my mother. It was the reason why he'd written the letter in the first place. The only problem was, my father didn't say whom he suspected. All he had left me was a one-page letter talking of his suspicions and two boxes full of paperwork from the corporation he'd used to work for, Bradley Inc.

After I'd read my father's letter and gone through the paperwork he'd left for me, I had started investigating. Well, I'd done my best to get on the inside of Bradley Inc. so I could find clues that might help me figure out what my father had found out and if my mother had been murdered. I hadn't been careful enough with my investigation, and so I wasn't surprised I had been contacted. But I was taken aback by the letter. Frankly, it wasn't what I'd expected to receive.

I stared at the letter in my hands again and frowned. There was a veiled threat and a challenge in the note: "One survives and one is destroyed." *Destroyed* was a pretty powerful word. *Destroyed* was sending a message. I could feel my fingers trembling as they held the letter. I knew that I was getting close to the truth, close to the answers that would prove my father's suspicions had been correct. I was about to take out a pen and paper and write down the words I thought were most telling in the note, when I heard a loud banging on the apartment door.

"Open up!" a masculine voice shouted as he banged. "Police."

Police? I walked to the door with a perplexed expression.

"I'm coming!" I called out as I opened the door. I immediately felt something was not right—someone had made it into the building without calling up. How had he gotten into the building without someone buzzing him in? I dismissed my thoughts as I realized the police must have master keys to every building in the city, though I still felt some discomfort as I looked at him.

"Are you okay?" The policeman had his hand on his gun in its holster, and I swallowed.

"I'm fine. What's going on?"

"There was a nine-one-one call from your apartment." He pushed past me. "And then a hang-up."

"I didn't make a nine-one-one call." I shook my head and pulled my cell phone out of my pocket. "Look, you can check my calls. There is no call to nine-one-one."

"It was made from your landline, ma'am."

"I don't have a landline." I frowned and followed him around my apartment. My voice rose as I wondered who had called nine-one-one on me. "There must have been a mistake. I can assure you that I didn't call nine-one-one and hang up."

"I'm still going to check through your apartment, if that's okay?" He didn't wait for an answer.

"I already told you that I didn't call the police, and I'm the only one who lives here." I called after him and watched as he walked down the hallways and into my bedroom. I stood still, unable to move as I thought back to the letter that had just arrived. Had the writer of the letter sent the police to my house? And if so, why? Why would the people who killed my mother want the police involved in the matter? It didn't make sense. I chewed on my lower lip, deep in thought, when I heard a slamming. "What's going on?" I walked to my bedroom quickly, my heart pounding. "What are you doing in my room?" My voice was jittery, and I tried not to look in the one place I was scared he would find.

"I was just making sure that no one was in your closets, ma'am. It doesn't hurt for me to make sure everything is okay." He walked out of my room with a slight frown. "All looks clear."

"I already told you that."

"You have any issues, you call us." His eyes searched mine as he spoke and then he handed me a card. "You can't be too careful these days."

"I'm very careful." I walked him to the door and wondered if I should tell him about the note I'd just received. I was about to, when I remembered what my father had always told me when I was growing up: "The pockets of the rich are deep. Bianca, only trust someone if they give you reason to trust them. Even the police aren't above being bribed." "Thank you for your concern, Officer." I nodded at him and waited for him to leave. My heart was pounding, and I needed to think.

"No worries. Stay safe, Ms. London." He nodded his head, and I closed the door. It was only after he left that I realized he knew my name. How did he know my name?

I leaned against the door and closed my eyes. What was going on here? Today was turning into one mysterious day.

First the note, and then the police showing up. I didn't know: who sent the note, why they sent the note, who called the police, how he had gotten into my building, and how he knew my name. I chewed my bottom lip as I tried to figure out what was going on. I stared around my apartment, and suddenly the coziness of the room felt claustrophobic. I'd always loved living in New York City, but today my small one-bedroom felt like a cell. That the building had seemed so safe when I moved in suddenly felt like a fallacy. I didn't know my neighbors, and I had no one to talk to about how the police-man had gotten into the building or the mysterious letter that had arrived.

The dirty peeling walls directly opposite seemed to be closing in on me as I stood there hoping for clarity to hit and questions to be answered miraculously. I walked to my tan leather couch and sat down, leaning back into the plushness of the cushions. It was the only nice piece of furniture I owned. And even then it had been a gift from my best friend, Rosie. I could barely afford the rent in my apartment as it was, and I wasn't living in Trump Tower either.

I picked up the bright red-and-orange-patterned cushions that my father had gotten me in India when I was a teenager and then froze as my cell phone rang. The noise was jarring in my eerily quiet living room. I normally always had the TV on or music playing; I didn't like being in quiet spaces for too long. It reminded me of how alone I was. I grabbed my cell phone and dropped it when I saw the screen. My father's phone number flashed on the screen. My *dead* father's phone number. I stared at it before reaching down and picking it up again.

"Hello?" I answered softly, my voice cracking as I wondered who was calling me from my dad's phone. I was pretty sure I still had it in a box in my bedroom. I took a deep breath to stop myself from freaking out and jumped off the couch. "Hello," I spoke into the phone again with my voice trembling, this time unable to hide how freaked out I was by the call.

"You should be more careful, Bianca," a deep male voice spoke into the phone. I couldn't make his voice out clearly, as the phone had a lot of static.

My voice rose. "Who is this?"

"You shouldn't let strangers into your apartment."

"I haven't let any strangers into my apartment."

"Anyone can be anyone. Haven't you figured that out yet?"

"What are you talking about?" My face started to feel hot as I sat there in fear.

"Be careful of those who seek to help you. They may do more harm than good." Then he hung up.

I stared at the phone in my hand and ran to my bedroom to find my dad's phone. The box of my father's things was on the bed, and the lid was off. I ran over to it and saw that the phone was gone. Who could have taken it? No one had been in my apartment in weeks. No one except the policeman, but why would a policeman go through my things? Unless he hadn't been there to help protect me from an intruder—perhaps he was there to find something to protect someone else.

I looked down at the business card he had given me and froze. It was blank. All he had given me was a piece of white card stock. It was then that I knew this was the next step in whatever was going on. I knew then that the policeman had been looking for my father's papers. The papers that he'd left me were full of clues. It didn't matter that I didn't fully understand them yet. Obviously someone else wanted them.

I walked to the window in my living room and looked down to the street. I stared at the homeless woman who'd settled into the block directly across the street a couple of weeks ago. The woman I gave a couple of dollars to once a week as I passed by her. The woman who quoted a different Bible verse to me every time she saw me. The woman who shivered even when the days were warm. The woman who wore a Cartier watch and had freshly dyed highlights. The woman who knew exactly when I left and entered the building. I didn't know who she was, friend or foe, but I knew that she was watching me.

I walked back to my bedroom and stared at my father's box for a few minutes before closing it carefully and placing it back in my closet. I was grateful that I had removed my father's papers from the box several weeks ago. I hadn't known why at the time, but I'm someone who always listens to her first instincts. I then went to my dirty-clothes basket, pulled out my clothes, and threw them onto the floor. I instinctively looked around the room again to make sure it was empty, even though I knew there was no one in there with me. I pulled out my mother's old cedar jewelry box that I'd hidden under the clothes and slowly opened it. I let out a huge sigh of relief when I saw the stack of papers hidden under the cheap costume necklaces I had bought at Goodwill. I carefully closed it again, carried it with me to the kitchen, and placed it in a plastic bag. Then I pulled my cell phone out again and made a call.

~

It had been four days since the note arrived. Four days that I'd been on tenterhooks wondering what was going to happen next. I'd never felt this anxious before. Or scared. However, I tried to continue living my life as I normally did. There was nothing I could do but wait and see what was going to happen next. I also knew what the next step of the plan was. I could do nothing but wait for my ex-boyfriend David to come through for me. He was my only access to more information. I hadn't wanted to trust him, but I knew that in a game of cat and mouse the one who got the cheese was the one who took the most risks. I just had to be patient. Though, it was hard. Even watching shows on the History Channel didn't capture my attention for long.

"I'm not dating online again," I muttered as I deleted another rude message from a man known as Matt, or as his profile said, KnightInShiningArmani.

Online dating was something I'd been doing since David and I had broken up. At first, it had taken my mind off everything that had gone down with David. Now, it helped me to occupy my thoughts when my mind drifted to dark areas. Generally, I enjoyed my online conversations, but there was something about Matt that had really turned me off. He just wasn't getting the hint. I'd made the mistake of talking to him twice on the phone before deciding that I wasn't interested in going on a date with him. He definitely looked handsome in his photos, but he'd been arrogant and demanding on the phone, and his e-mails had gotten creepier and creepier. I stifled a sigh as I saw another e-mail come through from Matt and picked up my phone to call my best friend, Rosie.

"This is Rosie speaking." Rosie's voice sounded tired as she answered the phone.

"Hey, it's Bianca," I said lightly, and walked over to my vanity. "What are you up to?"

"Just a little something called work," she responded with a sigh. I could tell she was tired from the lack of excitement in her tone. "What's up?"

"Want to grab a drink tonight?" I checked my reflection in the mirror and sighed. Months of facial exercises hadn't helped to define my cheekbones at all. "Not that I need any alcohol. My face looks puffy. However, I haven't seen you in over a month, and we need to catch up. There's some stuff I need to tell you about."

"I'm sure it doesn't look puffy, and yes, we need to catch up." Her tone changed. "I want to hear what you've been up to."

"Trust me, it does," I muttered, frowning at the bags under my eyes. "I'm going to make myself a face mask and put some cucumbers on my eyes."

"Must be nice to be self-employed," Rosie said jealously.

"Must be nice to have a steady income," I responded back tartly. I'd been freelancing, writing entertainment articles for a couple of online newspapers, for about a year, and I wasn't sure if I'd made the right decision. As much as I loved movies, my true love was for the kings and queens of England, and I really wanted to become a history professor. However, freelancing gave me the opportunity to play Sherlock Holmes, or, realistically, more like Stephanie Plum. I needed the flexibility in my schedule to allow me to investigate what had happened to my mother more freely.

"Touché." She giggled. "And yes. I'm down for a drink. It's been a long month and an even longer day."

"Boss back?" I made small talk even though I didn't want to. I really just wanted to tell her about the note and the fake policeman. I wanted to tell her about the woman who watched me from across the street and the feeling I had that someone was following me. I knew this wasn't the time though. I'd have time to tell her everything tonight.

"Yes, he's back from Shanghai, and he's acting like a bigger douche than ever," she moaned. "He's treating me like his assistant again. It's not like I've been running the department for the last month or anything."

"Drinks are on me, then," I offered. "Maybe he's treating

you like that because he knows you can take over his job and do a better one in a heartbeat."

"Bianca, you think very highly of me," she said appreciatively. "However, you can't afford to buy me all the drinks I'm going to need tonight." She laughed and then paused. "Ooh, you also have to tell me how your date went with that guy you met online."

"Oh, I told you about that?" I frowned into the phone, confused. I couldn't remember mentioning that I was going to meet Matt, but ever since I'd started doing detective work on the side, I couldn't really remember who I was telling what. I really needed to keep a journal of the information I was giving to different people. Rosie had been my best friend for years, but I knew that she wouldn't approve of my investigations, so I hadn't really told her much. But I was starting to think I needed to confide in her when I saw her later.

"Yeah, you told me you were going to meet that guy online, to help get over David, remember?"

"Oh, that was weeks ago, and I canceled it." I groaned. "I had a feeling that it wasn't going to work out." I stared into my eyes in the mirror as I spoke. I felt bad about keeping secrets from Rosie.

"Bianca, you can't cancel the date before you meet him. Plus, he looked hot in those photos you showed me online. All masculine and sexy."

"Yeah, he was hot." I nodded as I walked back to my computer. I shook my head as I sat down. I'd obviously told her about Matt if I'd shown her photos. "He just seemed like a bit of a creep."

"They're all creeps." She sounded annoyed. "Anyway, he looked cute."

"I don't want to date a guy who's creepy before we even meet."

"How was he being creepy?"

"Listen to this e-mail he sent me last night." I sat on the bed and put my laptop on my knees. "Hold on a sec. I'm going through my trash, since I deleted the e-mails."

"No worries." She paused. "Hey, I wanted to tell you that I saw David a couple of weeks ago."

"Oh?" My heart stopped for a second, and I took a deep breath. "How did he look?"

"Handsome as ever." She paused again. "Sorry."

"It's fine," I said stiffly as an image of David crossed my mind.

I didn't want to talk about David. Not over the phone. Not now. He was the most handsome guy I'd ever dated, with his dark brown locks and bright green eyes. He was tall and buff, and he looked like every woman's dream. Rosie had been shocked when he'd asked me out and we'd started dating. She hadn't known the lengths I'd gone through to get his attention. Though, to be honest, I'd never felt secure in the relationship, and when he'd cheated on me, I hadn't been that surprised. Our relationship had been complex, and no one else knew exactly how complex it still was.

"Have you spoken to him recently?"

"Not since we broke up." I bit my lower lip, hating to lie again. "I've started several e-mails though."

"Does he still call you?"

"He called me a few times, but nothing in over a month." I sighed. "Maybe he's moved on."

"He's a dick, and you know what he was thinking with." Rosie sounded hesitant. "I mean, I know guys have needs, but shit, he should have told you that he couldn't wait anymore."

"It wasn't that I didn't want to sleep with him." I sighed. "It just never felt right. I wanted it to be special." And it would never have been special with David, no matter how handsome I thought he was.

"I know. He's an asshole." Rosie went back to being supportive. "It's his loss."

"Exactly." I sighed as I thought back to David. "Did he say anything to you when you saw him?" I asked casually.

"He said hi." Rosie's voice sounded awkward. "And something else, but it didn't make sense."

"Oh?" My fingers froze on the keyboard. "What else did he say?"

"He said that there was more than one way to skin a cat."

"What?" I frowned. "What does that mean?"

"I don't know. I've been thinking about it a lot. I think he's trying to woo you." Rosie's voice became thoughtful. "I guess he figured out that just apologizing and calling wasn't going to cut it. I bet he's going to try to step it up a notch and really try harder to win you back."

"You think so?" I stared around my bedroom and thought for a second. This was the one room in my apartment that David and I had never really spent much time in. I lay back on my bed and sighed. "I was an idiot, wasn't I. I should have just had sex with him. I'm sure it would have been amazing. Maybe we'd still be together now." I felt odd saying the words, as if I were playing a part in a play. *You've been watching too many movies, Bianca*, I thought to myself.

"Don't blame yourself, Bianca. It's not your fault. Maybe this is what he needed, to see how much you mean to him. Maybe he'll be all romantic now. What if he takes you on a surprise trip to Paris or something? Wouldn't that be cool?"

"You think he'd really do that?"

"Who knows?" Rosie laughed. "Hey, hold on. I just got a package from a new and very cute delivery guy."

"Okay." I laughed and sat back up, still looking through my e-mails for the deleted messages from Matt. I wanted to get away from the conversation about David.

I should have known from his screen name that he was going to be an asshole. I mean, Knight in Shining Armani? Only a pompous asshole would choose such a name.

"Thank you, Billy." I heard Rosie speaking to the delivery guy and ripping open her new package.

I smiled to myself as I imagined her decimating the package so she could find out what was inside as quickly as possible. She'd always been impatient when opening packages and presents. I only hoped she treated any packages she received from me with more care. I stared at the plastic bag on my night desk and wondered if I was making the right decision to entrust my papers with her.

"Oh my God, are you there, Bianca?" Rosie's voice was jittery and excited.

"Yeah, why?"

"Someone just sent me a present."

"Ooh, what did they send?"

"A Tiffany's bracelet and a note." Her voice was growing louder with excitement.

"What does it say?" I asked casually as my stomach flip-flopped.

"It says 'My dearest Rosie, you don't know me yet, but I very much want to know you. Accept this gift as a token of my friendship.'" She paused. "And that's it."

"Who's it from?"

"I don't know." Her voice was low. "I wonder if it's Joe from accounting. I've seen him giving me a few rather obvious admiring stares recently, ever since I got those blond highlights."

"But you know Joe. Wouldn't it say 'You don't know my intentions yet' as opposed to 'You don't know *me* yet'?"

"Who knows? Maybe he's slow or didn't think it through properly." She laughed. "Who cares? I just got a bracelet from Tiffany's."

"I can't wait to see it tonight." I was slightly envious. No one was sending me gifts from Tiffany's. Not even David, who might or might not be trying to woo me back. I thought back to my own, more ominous note and wondered if there was a connection.

"I can't wait to show it off." Rosie's squeal interrupted my thoughts.

"Okay, I have the e-mails open. Are you ready to hear the craziness?"

"Yes, let me hear."

" 'Dear CreativeGirlNYC, Have you ever been to Rome? It's such a romantic city that I would love to fly you there in my private jet. I'd like to take you to the Trevi Fountain and Spanish Steps. Then we can share pasta and drink wine as we gaze into each other's eyes. KnightInShiningArmani.' "

"What's wrong with that?"

"It's weird. He knows my name is Bianca, and I know his name is Matt, so why doesn't he use our real names? And, well, we've never met. It's too much too soon."

"He's trying to sweep you off your feet." Rosie sounded matter-of-fact.

"Well, listen to the e-mail he sent me last night. 'Dear CreativeGirlNYC, I was very disappointed that you canceled our date and now won't accept my calls. I've been waiting for us to meet for a long time. In fact, I've been counting down the days until I can make you mine. I feel that you are playing games with me, and I don't appreciate it. If you are willing to meet me tonight, let me know.' "

"Wow, he's persistent."

"Then today, he just sent me another e-mail. 'Answer me,

Bianca. If you would like to meet for lunch we can still make it work. If not, it's your loss.'"

"Wow. He does sound like a winner, doesn't he?" Rosie exclaimed, and I nodded, though she couldn't see me.

"Now you know why I won't be dating online anymore." I closed my laptop.

"We'll find two hotties tonight and flirt the night away."

"Sounds good to me."

"You might finally get laid," she said, and then giggled.

"Rosie!"

"Hey, I'm just being honest. A vibrator can only do so much."

"I'll see you tonight," I groaned.

~⌒~

"Hey," Rosie whispered into the phone as I picked it up.

"Hey back at ya."

"Meet me at this new bar on the Upper West Side tonight. I've heard good things and want to check it out."

"What's it called?"

"Orange."

"Okay. I'll see you around six?"

"Yeah." She paused. "Six sounds good." Then she giggled; the noise sounded quite nervous, and I frowned into the phone.

"What's so funny? Is there a reason why you chose this bar, Rosie?" My brain started ticking, and I took a gulp of water.

"I'll tell you later," she said hurriedly, and then hung up.

$\sim$

I checked my watch for the tenth time. It was now six forty-five, and I was starting to get impatient. I looked at the menu again, and my stomach rumbled as I read the different entrée descriptions. I was so hungry, and I could already feel the glass of wine I was sipping going to my head.

I texted Rosie a photo of the cute bartender and then rubbed my temple softly. Hopefully the surreptitious photo I'd taken would make her hurry up.

"Hey." Rosie walked into the bar as if she owned it, oblivious to the stares of the men in the bar as she sauntered toward me. Her blond hair was perfectly coiffed and her Escada suit clung to her body perfectly.

"Hey!" I jumped up and gave her a quick hug and continental kiss—left cheek, right cheek, left cheek. "I just texted you, by the way!" I looked at her expensive suit enviously. "You're lucky I work from home, or I'd be borrowing your clothes." I laughed as we sat down. I instinctively grabbed to the right of me to make sure the plastic bag was still at my side. I was going to give Rosie a copy of my father's papers to hold for safekeeping. I'd taken the originals and put them in my safety deposit box at the bank, but I wanted to make sure that I had multiple copies out there just in case.

"How goes the writing? Seen any good movies lately?" She smiled at me briefly before turning to call the waiter over.

"Depends on what you mean by *good*." I shrugged. "I've been watching box office movies mainly, those are the reviews that get the hits. Not the art pieces we used to watch in college."

"Good old action movies, huh?"

"Action and cheesy romance." I smiled and picked up my glass of wine. "They all start to seem the same, but they pay well. I had an article on Channing Tatum get ten thousand views last week."

"Well, I'd pay to see him swinging those hips." Rosie frowned as she waited for someone to come over and take her order. "The service here sucks. I should have remembered from last time."

"Oh, you've been here before?" I asked her curiously. I was pretty sure she had said this was her first time.

"Yeah, once." She ran her hands through her hair and then leaned toward me and grinned. "I've missed you, Bianca. I feel like we haven't seen each other in ages."

"That's because we haven't."

"I bought you something the other day." She studied my face and grinned. "A book on Richard the Third and the lost princes or whatever."

"Oh awesome." I leaned back in my chair. "You know that some men at the Tower of London recently found . . ."

She interrupted me and said, "So you have to tell me all about that guy online." Then she paused and turned around. "Waiter!" she called out loudly. "Can you come over here when you have a chance? I'd like a drink sometime this year." She turned back to me with a glint in her eyes and a small smile. "Let's see how long he takes now."

"He's most probably busy, Rosie." I shook my head at her impatience. "You've only been here for a few minutes."

"Exactly, I've been here for a few minutes, and I'm still sober." She shuddered. "Something is wrong with this picture."

"You can have some of my wine if you want." I pointed to the bottle on the table, and she shook her head.

"No, I think I'm going to get a cocktail," she said quickly. "I need liquor tonight."

"So how's work?" I changed the subject and inquired about her job. I really wanted to talk about myself, but I didn't want to be rude.

"Challenging." She shrugged. "We're attempting to get the account of one of the top financial companies in the States. I can't tell you the name for legal reasons, but let's just say if we get it, we will be one of the top advisement companies in the world."

"Do you think you'll get it?"

"If I have anything to say about it, yes." She pursed her lips. "Of course, I'm not working on that deal. I'm helping James with the Bradley Inc. deal. If we get that, I think I'll get promoted. That's why I've been so busy."

"Oh." I looked down into my glass of wine; my heart was racing at her words. I hadn't known she was trying to do business with the Bradley Corporation. "That's David's dad's company," I said casually, pretending that that fact was unimportant.

"Oh yeah, that's where I saw him a couple of weeks ago. In the offices." She made a face, and I knew that she was worried that I was still upset that we had broken up. Rosie didn't know that I had never really had legitimate feelings for David, so his cheating hadn't really hurt me.

"I need to tell you something." I took a deep breath and lowered my voice. "It's about David and, well, the Bradley Company."

"Oh?" Her eyes narrowed, and she looked at me in interest. "What about them?"

"I think that the Bradley Company had something to do with what happened to my mother."

"What are you talking about?" She looked confused. "What happened to your mom? She died in a car crash, didn't she?"

"That's the thing." I took a deep breath, hoping Rosie wasn't going to think I was crazy. "I don't think she did."

"What?"

"Remember how my dad used to work as an inventor?" I rushed out. "Well, he used to work for the Bradley Company. In fact when the company was started it was called Bradley, London, and Maxwell. I think—"

"Hold on a second." She jumped up quickly. "I just need to go to the restroom, okay?"

I noticed someone in the corner of the bar staring at me. He looked vaguely familiar, but I couldn't place him. I nodded at Rosie slowly as my head started to feel heavy. I was being watched. I was certain of it. I took a deep breath and looked around me. Was I being listened to as well? Part of me was glad that Rosie had jumped up when she had. Then it hit me; it was the man who'd been staring at me from behind the newspaper at the coffee shop.

"That's fine." I mumbled back, the words tripping out of mouth in an existential fashion. I wanted to jump up and run, but I knew that wouldn't help. I'd ask Rosie for her advice when she came back from the restroom. I'd tell her everything that was going on and then hope she wasn't angry at me for keeping it all from her for so long.

"Watch my bag for me." She handed me her large black Balenciaga bag and walked away quickly. I put her bag in my lap and quickly unzipped it and placed the plastic bag with the copies of my father's papers in it and did it back up again.

"More wine, ma'am?" I heard the voice in front of me and I felt a prick in my arm as I looked up. I didn't see the face of the person as I looked up, because my vision became dotted. All of a sudden, I felt terribly drowsy, like I wanted to sleep. I closed my eyes for a second, and then the world went black.

The first time I regained consciousness, I could feel someone lifting me up. I tried to open my eyes to see what was going on, but my eyelids wouldn't open, because they were too weak. The second time I regained consciousness, I could hear two men frantically whispering something. It sounded like "The plan's changed. The plan's changed."

I opened my mouth to speak, but nothing came out. I allowed the dark void to suck me back in as my brain realized that the inevitable had happened. I knew that I'd rather be unconscious than frozen in fear while being blind and speechless. The void was good for now. The void would allow me to conserve my energy and stop the panic that was currently running through my body.

I drifted back into oblivion, and all I could think about were David's words the last time we'd spoken: *You're strong, Bianca. You can handle anything. I promise that you'll get over this.* I only hoped that I was as strong as he thought I was.

two

My head was pounding when I finally regained full consciousness. My body felt stiff, and there was an ache in my neck. I tensed as I realized that I was in a dark, cramped space I couldn't identify. The air around me was stuffy, and my brain still felt hazy.

I smelled him before I felt him. His scent was deep and musky, like an expensive cologne. It was then that I realized his arm was under my neck. I froze as my heart joined my pounding head, and he groaned as I rolled over and slowly crashed into his chest. My limbs felt numb, and my mind was fuzzy. I felt his fingers squeezing my neck, and I wondered if this was it. Was I going to die by strangulation? I reached my hands up to his fingers and sharply yanked them away, banging both of our hands into something hard above us.

"Careful," he muttered, and I froze as my eyes tried to focus in the dark. He was awake, and he didn't sound happy.

"Do I know you?" I whispered, trying to remember where I had been and what I'd been doing. My heart thudded as the faintest of memories came back to me. "Who are you?" My words sounded pained. What was going on?

"Who are *you*?" His voice was low, and he attempted to move away from me. "And where am I?"

"I don't know." I attempted to sit up but found it hard to move.

I could feel the panic welling up in me, and I tried not to scream. The last thing I could remember was drinking a glass of wine in a cute little bar on the Upper West Side while I waited for Rosie to get off work. I froze as I remembered two men frantically muttering something. I closed my eyes and tried to concentrate on the voices I'd heard. Was this man lying next to me one of the men who had kidnapped me? And if so, why was he trapped with me?

"You don't know who you are?" His tone sounded bemused, and I could tell from his voice that he was an arrogant asshole. "Or you don't want me to know?"

"No, I don't know where *we* are," I said slowly, trying not to show my fear and irritation. I knew that I couldn't show him my weakness or anger right now. I didn't know who he was. If he knew I was scared, that might encourage him to do something bad.

I lay there and tried to think what I had learned in my self-defense classes. *Don't panic, scream loudly, and kick them in the junk* is all I could remember my instructor saying.

"Damnit, Bianca," I whispered to myself. Now I wished

that I had paid more attention in the class instead of goofing around with Rosie.

"What did you say?" His voice was gruff, and I felt his hands gripping my waist as he shifted.

I remained silent and waited to see what he was going to do next. I could hear a loud throbbing sound, and the smell of fuel surrounded my nostrils. I rubbed my forehead, wishing that I could make sense of where I was. The man behind me shifted again, and I felt his hands higher on my waist this time.

"Get your hands off me." I pushed him away and hit my head against something hard. "Ow!" I shouted, and he groaned.

"Please tell me that you're not going to be like this all day and night."

"I hope not to be here with you all day and night," I retorted back, and then sighed. "Not that I even know where I am."

"We're in some sort of vehicle." He spoke matter-of-factly, and once again, I felt irritated.

"How do you know?"

"Feel the vibrations? We're moving, and whatever's beneath us isn't smooth."

"Okay, Einstein." I rolled my eyes, even though he couldn't see me. I lay there for a moment and paid attention to everything around me. He was right. "So you think we're in a car or something?"

"Who knows?" He sighed. "I've never been kidnapped before."

"Kidnapped?" I screeched, and I felt his hand move to my mouth.

"Be quiet," he whispered into my ear. "You're being too loud. We don't want them to realize that we're awake."

"Who is the 'we' you're talking about?" I whispered back, fear suddenly setting in. I wasn't sure what was going on here. Who was he? And why were we in the car together? Something had gone terribly wrong, and all I could think about was Rosie and if she was okay.

I was disoriented, tired, and extremely scared. I took a couple of quick breaths and then started panicking again. What if the oxygen ran out? Was I about to die? Who would kidnap me? I had no money. I wasn't a spy. There was nothing to be gained from kidnapping me. Then I remembered the plan. I knew that I had to expect the unexpected. This was the unexpected. I took a deep breath and tried to calm my nerves. At least I wasn't alone. I froze for a second. Why wasn't I alone?

"I don't know who." He sighed. "I don't know why anyone would want to kidnap me." His voice sounded tired and sincere, like he really didn't know why he was here. He also didn't sound familiar.

My breath came a little easier then. I didn't know who he was, but I was pretty certain that he wasn't one of the men I'd heard earlier. I tried to remember what my father had told me when I was younger and feeling uncomfortable.

Talk out your worries, Bianca. No one can make you uncomfortable unless you give them the power. That was just one of many pieces of advice he'd given me. He'd been scatter-brained and focused only on his work most of the time, but he'd always had a wise word to lend me when I'd needed it. I missed him every day.

"I really want to scream right now." I tried to move away from him, still uncomfortable.

"Don't scream." His hand flew to my mouth again. "If they realize we're awake, they might do something drastic." His fingers pressed against my mouth, and my body stilled as I wondered if he was trying to cut off my oxygen supply.

"Drastic like what?" I mumbled against his palm as he pulled it back.

My tongue accidentally tasted his skin, and I swallowed hard as I realized just how close together we were. His skin was salty and sweet and reminded me of honey-roasted peanuts. I wanted to laugh at the absurdity of my thoughts. I shifted as his smell overwhelmed my senses again. I felt a slight chill run down my spine as I waited for his response. Goose bumps were popping up on my arms and chest, and my whole body was awakened in the most instinctual sense possible.

"What do you think?" He sounded annoyed, and I felt an urge to slap him. "Lean into me," he whispered into my ear.

"What?" My eyes widened at his words. My body jerked back at the breath of air that filled my eardrum. I felt tense and aware of every inch of his body next to mine as my skin tingled from the contact. I was mad that I was oddly turned on by this crazy situation. I didn't even know who this man was or what he was going to do to me.

"Lean into me. My body will provide warmth and will help to calm you down," he repeated slowly, as if speaking to a fifth grader. "You'll go into a panic if you don't."

"You don't know me." I glared at him. My eyes had adjusted slightly to the dark, and I could make out the outline of his face. He was definitely not anyone I remembered seeing before.

"Listen, lady, I'm trying to help you so your body doesn't go into shock."

"What are you? A doctor?"

"Just shut up for a minute." He pulled me toward him and pushed my face into his shoulder.

At first, I panicked and tried to pull away, but then I realized that he was right. It was oddly comforting to be held in his arms. His body was warm and hard, and I felt protected. I closed my eyes as I snuggled next to him and tried to pretend that he was someone I cared about. Someone I actually knew. For a moment, he was actually someone I wanted to be snuggled next to.

It had been so long since I'd actually been intimate with someone. All the guys I'd been talking to recently had seemed obnoxious and annoying, aside from David, who hadn't been someone I'd had thoughts of being with for a long time. Though, of course, he hadn't known that in the beginning. We had broken up because he hadn't been a fan of my making him wait for sex. And as a result, he hadn't been a fan of mine. We'd argued so much toward the end of our six-month relationship that I had just ended it to be done with him. I'd been happy that I didn't have to pretend anymore, yet I'd been scared to trust him with part of the truth. Sometimes I wondered if that hadn't been a mistake. Maybe telling him part of the truth and asking for his help in getting to the bottom of my mother's death hadn't been the right way to go. I'd gone with my gut, but I had wondered many times if he could be trusted. Especially in moments like these when I was scared and lonely in the back of a truck. Being kidnapped with a strange man made me doubt that I'd made the right decision.

"I'm not going to hurt you," he whispered softly. "We're in the same position here. We need to support each other." His tone had changed, and I felt my body relax slightly. His tone was soothing, as opposed to sinister. I didn't feel like this man was going to harm me. At least not now.

"What's your name?" I whispered against the man's shoulder. "I feel like we should at least know each other's names, now that we're being intimate." I attempted a joke and groaned inwardly as I heard how stupid I sounded.

"Intimate?" He sounded surprised.

"Intimate doesn't mean sex, you know." I was irritated again. "We are crowded together in a small space. Your arms are around me. My body is pressed against yours. We're being intimate." I bit my lower lip after I spoke. *Shut up, Bianca.*

"Trust me. I know." He groaned and shifted, and I could feel something hard pressing against my stomach. *Oh boy.*

I stilled as I realized what it was. I swallowed quickly as my body reacted swiftly, my skin heating up and my stomach churning. Part of me was delighted that he was excited by me. The other part was disgusted and made me want to slap myself and him. Rationally, I knew that his member was reacting to our being in such close quarters in the only way it knew how.

"Jakob," he said gruffly, and I turned my face up to his.

"What?" I whispered, then pulled back quickly as my lips lightly grazed his. "I didn't realize we were so close." My heart was beating fast now, and my tongue darted out and gently licked my lips.

"My name is Jakob," he whispered again, and I could hear a hint of humor in his tone.

"I'm Bianca."

"Nice to meet you, Bianca. It's a pity it had to be in such circumstances." He tried to shift again, and in doing so, my head slipped from his arm, bumping into the floor.

"Ow!" I cried out loudly and instinctively.

"Shh." His hand flew to my mouth, but it was too late. The vehicle stopped abruptly, and I heard doors slamming. He kept his fingers pressed against my lips, and his skin felt slightly rough against my lips. My body stilled as I lay there, and I resisted the urge to reach out and bite his fingers.

The waiting was the hardest part. It felt like hours went by as we lay there in the silence, only the sounds of our breathing letting us know we were both still alive. Then I heard the sound of footsteps and wished that I were still in that unknown void. My body tensed up and then started shaking in fear.

"It's okay, Bianca. It's okay." Jakob's voice sounded worried, and in that moment I decided to give him the benefit of the doubt. I found myself wanting to trust him, even though my brain was screaming at me to trust no one.

There was a loud banging above us, and I looked upward, wanting to see what was going to happen next, even if that meant coming face-to-face with death. I swallowed hard with fear but kept my eyes peeled upward.

"So you're awake?" a deep, menacing voice yelled at us as the trunk opened. A stocky man stood there, his deep blue eyes cold as they stared directly into mine. He had on a ski mask, and all I could think was that his lips looked odd.

I'd always thought that lips were the most sensuous and sexy part of the face, but now I realized that they were sexy only when seen with other parts. Lips by themselves were not sexy at all. I started giggling hysterically as I stared at his mouth.

"What the fuck?" The man glared at me as if I were crazy. "You think that's funny?"

"No . . ." I swallowed again, wanting to throw up. My hand moved to my face to stifle my laughter as fear overtook me. It was then that I felt Jakob move behind me.

"Let us out." His voice was demanding as he tried to get out of the trunk.

"Stay still." The man pushed Jakob back into the trunk with such force that I heard him hit the back of the trunk hard. His hand fell down on my hip as he fell back, and I jumped slightly.

"Sorry," he whispered as he fell back.

I nodded my understanding. I was too scared to talk or even turn to see if he was okay.

"Let us out," Jakob demanded again, this time less forcefully.

"We sure will." The man grimaced. "Hey, Billy. Hurry up."

"I'm coming!" another voice called back to him. "I'm just getting the shots ready."

"What shots?" I screeched, and attempted to straighten my legs.

"Don't move, lady." The man pulled out a gun and pointed it at me. "Make one more move, and you're dead."

Jakob spoke up. "Is that really necessary?"

"Is that necessary?" the man echoed mockingly, then laughed evilly. "What do you think?"

"I think you're enjoying this too much," Jakob continued, his voice harsh. "Have some humanity. You've got a scared woman in front of you."

"Be quiet." The man stood there and stared at us for a second before continuing. "When my boss gave me this job, I was delighted. I don't get enough fun in my life."

"You're sick." Jakob's arms circled my waist to calm me as we lay there. "You're very sick."

"I listen to my boss's orders. If anyone's sick, it's him." The man shrugged.

I stared at his fingers on the gun. They were short and grubby, and his nails were full of dark grease. I wondered if I should attempt to knock the gun out of his grasp, but I knew it was unlikely that I'd succeed.

"Okay, where are they?" The other man approached the man with the gun. He looked young—younger than I imagined. And he didn't have on a mask.

I tried to take a mental photograph of his young, handsome face. He had light brown hair and brown eyes. He was dressed nicely in khaki pants and a white shirt. He looked to be the complete antithesis to the scruffy man in front of us.

"Billy, go put your mask on!" the first guy shouted.

"Oh, yeah." The other guy looked at me for a second, and I could see fear and concern in his eyes. I had a feeling he knew now that I'd be able to identify him if I ever got the chance.

"What an idiot," Jakob whispered in my ear, and I nodded in agreement. "Should we try to make a run for it?" His fingers gripped my waist tightly.

His body tensed behind mine, and I knew that he was just as anxious as I was. For some reason, it made me feel more connected to him. He was no longer just the strange man I'd been sharing the back of a car trunk with. He was no longer someone I believed to be involved in the kidnapping. I could tell from the fear in his voice and the slight trembling of his muscular body that this man, this Jakob, was a fellow kidnapping victim. He was someone like me, who was worried for his life. I could hear it in his voice. He was anxious but also angry.

I shook my head slightly, still unable to look at him. My face just wouldn't turn, even though I was really curious to see what he looked like. "I don't think we should risk it," I mumbled under my breath. I was pretty sure he couldn't hear me, but the talk was for me as much as it was for him.

"What did you say?" The guy in front of me took a step toward me, and pushed the gun closer to my face. My heart stopped. This was it, then. I was going to die.

I shook my head quickly and furiously. "Nothing." I squeaked out. "I didn't say anything."

"That's what I thought," he growled, and reached in and grabbed my arm. "Get out." He pulled me out of the car, and I stumbled to the ground, feeling disoriented.

I thought about making a run for it, but then I remembered Jakob. I didn't want to leave him by himself. I had to make sure that he was all right as well. I stood there and peered into the trunk. My breath caught as I finally got a glimpse of Jakob in proper light. I swallowed hard and tried not to stare. "You." I gasped as I stared at him. It was the man who had been sitting at my table at the coffee shop.

He was incredibly handsome. He had a very low crop of dark brown hair, big, serious blue eyes, and a sexy scrawl of stubble around his chin and jawbone. He looked back at me, and I saw his eyes narrow as he took in my appearance. I wanted to smoothe my hair and wipe the grime from my cheeks. I wished I had some lipstick. I felt like an idiot for worrying about what I looked like when I was in such a scary situation. A small, hysterical laugh wanted to burst out of me again, but this time I was able to control it. I wanted to ask him if he recognized me, but I knew this was not the right time.

"Get out." The man grabbed Jakob and pulled him out. "And don't try no funny business, or I'll shoot you." He pushed Jakob next to me and pointed the gun at both of us. "Hurry up, Billy!" he shouted to his cohort, sounding stressed.

I looked around me then. I had no idea where we were, but I knew we were no longer in New York. At least, not in the city. We appeared to be in an old empty warehouse of some sort.

I looked to my right and tried not to gaze at Jakob. He was taller than he'd seemed in the car. And more muscular. His body looked very fit and very strong. Part of me thought he'd be able to take out the guy in front of us easily, but then I remembered the gun. The gun changed the whole equation.

"What you looking for, lady?" the man hissed.

"Nothing," I whispered as I stared into his menacing eyes.

"Good." He seemed to sigh in relief when Billy walked back to us with his mask on. He had rope in his hands—and two needles. I grabbed Jakob's arm as they approached. I was starting to feel light-headed.

"What do you want?" Jakob's voice was commanding, and he looked down at me briefly as I held on to him. "If it's money you're after, I can—"

"Shut up." The man pointed the gun at him, and I screamed. The man froze for a second and gave me another look. "Be quiet."

"Sorry," I whispered.

"Billy, tie them up." Billy paused for a second, and the other man pushed him toward us. "Tie them up."

"How?" Billy asked, and I wondered if he was new to the kidnapping business.

"With the rope." The other guy sounded really annoyed.

"But facing each other or away from each other?" Billy muttered.

"I don't know, and I don't care."

"Imbeciles," Jakob muttered, and I looked up at him. I could see anger in his eyes.

"Don't make a run for it," I whispered. "I don't want them to shoot you."

He looked down at me and there was a glint of surprise in his expression.

"Are you talking again, bitch?" The guy pointed the gun at me, and I shuddered.

"Hey, watch your mouth!" Jakob shouted, and I saw the man flinch.

"Please don't shoot him," I pleaded. "I'll be quiet."

"Put your backs to each other," the guy commanded, and then nodded at Billy. "Tie them up like this. Wrap the rope around their stomachs and then tie up their wrists."

"I won't run." I looked at him. "You don't have to do this."

"Shut up!" he shouted. "Inject them, Billy."

"Inject us with what?" My eyes widened, and before I knew what was happening, I felt a needle in my arm. My eyes immediately felt drowsy, and I felt myself falling into oblivion. I could hear Jakob shouting at them as everything went black, but I passed out before I could comprehend what he'd said.

three

"Wake up."

A voice in my dreams was getting louder and louder. I groaned as I tried to block it out. My head was aching, and I didn't want to open my eyes. My whole body felt stiff, and all I wanted to do was sleep off all the pains in my body.

"Wake up, Bianca." The voice was more insistent this time, and I froze as I realized that I wasn't dreaming.

My eyes flew open, and my body stilled as I stared at a large expanse of turquoise water in front of me. Then I remembered what had happened before I'd blacked out.

"Jakob?" I whispered hurriedly, feeling panicked.

"That's me," he answered me quickly, and I made a face at the water at his slightly snide tone. All my worries and concerns for him quickly fled.

"What's your problem?" I asked him softly, feeling out of it and sweaty.

"Besides from being kidnapped and tied up?" he responded back to me snappily, and I wondered what had happened to the caring man in the back of the car.

"Hey, don't take it out on me." I knew he could hear the confusion in my voice. "I didn't kidnap you."

"I know." His voice was less stressed sounding. "Sorry, I'm just being irritable."

"I understand." I nodded slightly. And I did. This situation would infuriate anyone. "It's so hot," I moaned as I felt the hot sun beating down on me. Sweat was trickling down my face and making me even more uncomfortable. "I'm sure that's not helping to make you feel better."

"We're not in New York anymore."

"You don't say." I shifted and fell back against him slightly. The ropes were chafing my wrists, and I was starting to feel claustrophobic, tied to him. I blinked a couple of times, trying to adjust my eyes to the bright sunlight and trying to forget that we were constrained so close together. "Where do you think we are?"

"No idea."

"Do you remember me?" I asked inquisitively.

"Remember you?" He sounded confused.

"From the coffee shop?" I continued. "We were sitting at the same table and I dropped my bag." I wanted to tell him that I'd been a bitch only because I'd been in the middle of a deadline, but kept my mouth shut.

"Oh, yeah. You're the girl that thought someone was watching you." He spoke slowly. "I guess you were right."

"I guess so." I sighed. "Though, that wouldn't explain why you are here as well."

"A man came up to me when you left the coffee shop." His voice was stiff. "He asked me what we'd been talking about and how I knew you."

"He did?" I gasped.

"I told him to mind his own business." He sounded irritated. "Perhaps that wasn't the smartest thing to do. I should have told him I had no idea who you were. Maybe I'd be at work now instead of tied up with you."

"I'd much rather be in my small apartment with the window fan that barely works than tied up here with you," I retorted, feeling irrationally hurt by his words.

"Aren't you a pleasant one to be around." Jakob's tone was smooth behind me, and I was irritated that I had allowed him to make me lose my cool already.

"I'm just saying how I feel," I retorted again, and we were both silent. I wasn't sure what it was about him, but he rattled me. Especially now that I had seen him properly. I swallowed hard as I thought about the salty taste of his skin against my tongue. He'd tasted good, but he looked even better. His eyes had been so vividly blue and discerning. We'd made eye contact for only a few seconds, but I'd felt like he was looking into my soul. Something about him had me off-kilter. I knew it was because I was attracted to him, but I wanted to ignore the fact that my body already had designs on him.

"I know." His back stiffened against mine. "Let's try not

to take this out on each other. We're going to have to work together to get out of this mess."

"How long do you think we've been here?" I felt a drop of sweat running down my face, tickling my cheek, and I tried to ignore it.

"I'm not sure." He sighed. "I just woke up a few minutes ago myself."

"I can't believe they injected us." My voice rose in panic. "I didn't expect this." I looked around at the desolate beach and shuddered. I hadn't expected this at all.

"I didn't have any expectations when I realized I'd been kidnapped." His voice was dry.

"What do you think they're going to do to us?" I whispered. "Do you think those two men are still here?"

"I don't know." He sighed again. "I don't remember much after they injected us."

"What are we going to do?" I deliberately kept my tone calm. "And where do you think we are?"

"I have no idea where we are," he replied. "I smell the ocean though. We have sand beneath us and I'm hearing the sound of trees in the wind."

"Yeah, I can see the ocean." I shook my head in an attempt to shake off the drops from my face. "I don't know what ocean though." I sighed as I stared at the large expanse of water in front of me. "Or what beach we're on. For some reason I don't think we're in South Beach." I attempted a joke and heard Jakob chuckle.

"I guess all the spring-breakers decided to leave when they

saw us," he responded, and I smiled. At least he had a sense of humor. That was something. I shifted on the ground and tried to move forward, but I didn't get far. I'd almost forgotten that we were still tied together.

"The sand feels harder than I remember it feeling when I've gone sunbathing." I spoke again as I wiggled my ass, trying to get more comfortable.

"Yeah, this isn't the most comfortable position I've ever been in." He sighed. "Maybe we should try to stand up and figure out a way to get out of these ropes."

"That sounds like a good idea." I agreed and then froze. "Hold on." I gasped as I saw something white out of the corner of my eye. "I think someone left us a note." I moved my head as far right as I could, but I still couldn't read it. There was a small white shell holding the piece of paper down, and it was obstructing my view of the words.

"What does it say?"

"We need to shift slightly so I can read it." I tried to shuffle in the sand, but my body and his together were too heavy for me move. "Please try to move with me."

"Okay."

"Okay. One, two, three—move right!" I shouted out, and we scooted our butts to the right about an inch, bumping back against each other as we moved. I twisted my head as far right as I could and still couldn't read it. "One more time!" I called out again, and we moved together in sync.

"I need to try to brush the shell off of the paper." I spoke determinedly. "Try to relax your body as I attempt to move forward and shift it, okay?"

"Okay," he answered quickly, and I leaned forward, moving my arms to the right, attempting to shift the shell.

A part of me was pleased that we seemed to be working so well together. I almost yelled out loud in happiness as the shell rolled off the paper, but then I read the note. I read it silently at first and then aloud, my ears alert to hear how he responded.

" 'Without the truth, there is no answer,' " I said softly.

"That's it?" He sounded as perplexed as I felt.

"No." My voice was low. "There's another line."

"What does it say?"

" 'In pain, there is darkness. In light, there is nothing.' "

The words seemed to carry in the wind, and we sat there in silence. I watched as the wind picked up the piece of paper and carried it down the shore. I closed my eyes as I thought about what the third line had said—the line I had been too scared to read aloud. My body felt tense, and I no longer trusted Jakob as much as I had earlier. The line flashed again in my mind. *Your bodies are now one, but not as united as they will be by the time I'm done.*

"I don't really know what that means. What do you think?"

"I don't know." I chewed on my lower lip. "I can't figure it out. Obviously, it's some sort of clue, but I have no idea what it means. Maybe something will happen in the dark?" Maybe Jakob was going to try to do something to me? I tried not to panic.

"I guess, though that doesn't make sense. *In pain, there is darkness* isn't the same as if the note had read *In darkness, there is pain*." His tone was odd. "Though, the day is still young."

"What do you mean by that?" I asked quietly, but he didn't answer.

"We're going to have to work together to get untied." He spoke up suddenly and then paused. When he spoke again, his voice was lower, almost seductive. "Unless you want to stay tied together, of course."

"Why would I want to be tied with my back to a man?" I retorted, and shivered with suspicion.

"I agree. If I'm going to be tied to someone, I very much want us to be facing each other, or preferably, I'd like to be tied on top of her." He chuckled slightly as I gasped, and I was glad he couldn't see my red face. "Come on, Bianca. Look around and see if you see anything sharp."

"Sharp?"

"Like scissors?"

"Oh, you think those two bozos dumped us here and left us with scissors?" I retorted, and looked around, suddenly wishing I were here by myself after all.

"Look for anything sharp, like a rock or a tree stump—anything that might help us saw through the rope."

"All I can see is the ocean." I paused. "Or the sea. Or whatever this body of water is that I'm facing." I could hear the shrill of terror emanating from my voice as I stumbled over my words.

"Calm down, Bianca."

"How am I supposed to keep calm?" I shouted, and tried to move.

I could feel my body starting to shake. I wanted to be away from him. His body pressed against mine was no longer comforting. It was ominous and foreboding, and I needed my space.

"Stop." His voice was strong. "You need to look for something sharp."

"Why don't you look?"

"I can't see right now."

"What?" I stilled. "What do you mean?"

"I mean, I can't see."

"Oh my God, did they do something to your eyes? Are you blind?" My heart started racing as I realized that things would be a lot harder if Jakob couldn't see. I felt guilty for feeling slightly relieved as well. If he couldn't see, it would be a lot harder for him to do something to me.

"They blindfolded me," he said patiently, and I felt like a bit of a fool for jumping to conclusions.

"Oh, okay." I turned my head as much as I could. "We're going to have to try to stand up."

"We'll have to lean back into each other and use each other as support," he agreed, and I felt him push his back into mine. He felt hot against me, and I yelped as I felt a slight shock at the added pressure of his body against mine.

"Are you going to act like this all day?"

"Are you going to annoy me all day?"

"Bianca, what do you want me to do?"

"Have you tried wiggling your nose and forehead?" I asked softly, slightly embarrassed at my tip.

"Sorry, what?"

"Wiggle your nose around. It might shift the blindfold on your face."

"And you know this how?"

"Just do it!"

"I knew you were a closet freak." He laughed, and his body moved up and down against mine.

"What are you doing?" I snapped, way too aware of how close we were.

My mind ran back to the third line in the note. What had the writer meant by saying our bodies were now one? Had they known how annoying and exhilarating it would be to be tied to someone? Or were they trying to warn me about Jakob? My thoughts were running through my mind a million miles a minute, and I knew that the note on the beach was related to the letter that I'd received. They were both too cryptic to not have been related. My mind flashed to the note I'd received in my apartment and the man who had been looking through my father's box. For a brief second, I wondered if Jakob had been the same man, but then I remembered they looked nothing alike.

"Jakob." My voice was light. "What's going on?" I spoke again, trying to ignore my thoughts as he bounced around behind me.

"I'm wiggling my nose like you said."

"And you need to move your whole body to do that?" I snapped, unable to hide my tension any more.

"My God, you are a bitch, aren't you?"

"You're not exactly Prince Charming."

"It seems to me that you'd be happier with the Marquis de Sade," he snapped back, but then he laughed and confused me.

"What's so funny?"

"I was just laughing because really I should be flattered."

"Flattered about what? Being kidnapped?" My voice rose, and I was incredulous about his words. Was he a psycho? I had dismissed that thought earlier, but now I wasn't quite sure. Maybe this was part of the plan. Maybe I had trusted the wrong person.

"No, silly. I'm flattered that I turn you on."

"Excuse me?" I squeaked out as he continued to wiggle against me.

"That's the only reason I can think of for you acting so tense and irritable."

"Really? That's the only reason you can think of?" I banged back against him hard, hoping to wind him but really only hurting myself. I could feel anger building up in my stomach, joined by a certain and sudden irrepressible thrill. "Just wiggle your nose, your eyebrows, and your cheeks, and try to get that thing off." I sighed in exasperation. My body was on high alert, and my mind was already working overtime.

There had to be a reason why we were here together. We couldn't have been randomly kidnapped. Maybe the man that had been following me thought Jakob was some sort of contact of mine. Maybe my kidnappers thought he knew something about my investigations. Or maybe not. Maybe he had his own story. If I could figure out his story and background, maybe I could figure out why we were both here. There was, of course, the possibility that he had more sinister aspirations, but I couldn't allow my mind to focus on that.

"Yes, ma'am," he responded, and continued his erratic body movements against me for the next few minutes.

"So, can I ask you a few questions?" I said, and then took a deep breath and waited for him to respond.

"Yes, my name is Jakob; yes, I'm single; yes, I like sex; no, I'm not a freak; and no, I don't do drugs; though I do like a drink every now and then." He spoke matter-of-factly, and I giggled.

"Well, I'm glad we got that out of the way," I said, and I smiled to myself at his goofiness. "However, those aren't the answers to any of the questions I was going to ask you."

"Yes, okay, I admit it. I have smoked weed. Once, or twenty times," he responded again, and I shook my head.

"I guess you experimented in college, huh?" I got into his banter easily and then frowned at myself for getting distracted. "That's not my question either though. I'm trying to figure out why we're here. We have to have something in common. I can't believe that we were randomly kidnapped together."

"Aside from the fact that the man you said was following you came up to me and asked me what we'd been talking about? Aside from the fact that I told him to mind his own business, and he told me to be very careful what I said and to who? I thought I was being punked in the coffee shop. Now, I realize I wasn't. But, hey, yeah, we can see if we have anything else in common. Feel free to ask me anything you want."

"Okay, I'm thinking." I stared at the ocean, hoping it would give me insightful questions to ask, but all I could keep thinking about was the fact that he was single.

We sat there in silence as he attempted to get the blindfold off and I thought about questions to ask him that wouldn't give too much of my own story away. I tried to take in my scenery more thoroughly so that I could ignore him as much as possible. We were on a beach—that I was sure of. The sand beneath me was a light white-yellow, with few shells. It was the kind of beach I'd want to vacation on if I'd been given the opportunity. The water was a gorgeous transparent blue, with calm waves. The sky was a soft light blue, with luscious, fluffy white clouds, and I could see the sun in the horizon, mocking me.

Even though our section of beach was partially shaded, it was still frighteningly hot. My whole body felt like it was on fire, and I was thirsty. I closed my eyes for a few seconds and took a couple of deep breaths.

"Where were you when you were kidnapped?" I asked him, the first question that came to mind.

"I was leaving work, walking to my car, when two men approached me." His answer sounded logical enough. "They asked me for directions, I responded, then I felt a prick in my arm. The next thing I knew I was waking up in the back of a car."

"With me?"

"No." His tone changed. "They picked you up after I was already in the car."

"So that means that there were other people in on it." I bit down on my lower lip, gnawing hard as I thought. "I think that guy from the coffee shop was watching me that night. I think that he must have been in on it with Billy and the other guy."

"I suppose that makes sense. I doubt those two numb-skulls could have put this together by themselves. They didn't seem very bright."

"I agree." Something suddenly occurred to me, and I gasped out loud. "It makes me wonder why our kidnapper chose them to do the job—it's almost as if it wasn't very well planned out."

"Maybe they figured the gun was enough?"

"Yeah, that's true." I shivered as I remembered the gun. I could feel that I was about to start panicking again as my brain was five steps ahead of my body. My only consolation lay in the fact that if our kidnappers had wanted us dead, they could have just shot us. Unless they thought that was too easy. Maybe they were testing us to see how deeply into despair we'd go. Maybe this was a test to see how depraved human beings could be? *Get it together, Bianca.* I knew that this was not the time for my overactive imagination to kick into high gear.

All of a sudden my stomach growled, and I felt hunger gnawing at me from inside. I tried to ignore the pangs and cravings that had suddenly emerged inside me. How were we going to eat and drink? I thought back to a movie I'd watched as a teenager called *Alive*. It had been about a plane crashing in the Andes, and one of the men had eaten the flesh of his dead friend to survive. The movie had been based on a true story, and I could still remember the documentary I'd seen about the man who'd eaten his friend's flesh as he was interviewed. His eyes had a haunted look as he spoke about what he'd done, but he'd had to do it for survival. My eyes popped open, and I shuddered as I thought about the possibilities of what could happen. What would Jakob and I have to do to survive?

"Take a chill pill, Bianca," I muttered to myself as my brain ran away with all the craziest scenarios it could think of.

"Sorry, what did you say?" Jakob asked as he continued moving.

"Nothing," I whispered back, feeling tears coming to my eyes.

"Oh no, are you okay?" His voice changed, and he sounded concerned. "Don't cry. They didn't shoot us. We're okay. I think I nearly have the blindfold off. Once I do, we can work on getting these ropes off and figuring out what's going on."

"No, I'm not okay." I gulped. A seagull flew past then and dove into the ocean. I scowled as it ascended with a fish in its mouth. "Go ahead and mock me, why don't you," I shouted at the bird, jealousy in my stomach as I thought longingly of the fish in its mouth, and Jakob's body stilled.

"Are you losing it?"

"No, I'm not."

"Just remain calm, Bianca."

"Whatever."

"I'm surprised my charm hasn't won you over yet," he said softly.

"What are you talking about?" I frowned at his words. Something he'd said had made bells go off in my head, but I wasn't sure what.

"I'm just trying to make small talk."

"Well, don't," I snapped. "Just work on the blindfold."

"I'm trying," he snapped back, and fell silent again.

I moved my head to the left and the right as much as I could, but all I could see was sand and ocean and some trees in the distance. I tried not to think about who or what was lying in wait for us while we struggled with the ropes.

"I think it's moving!" he gasped excitedly, and he started moving more and more energetically. His back rubbed against mine, and I kept my mouth shut, even though I wanted to tell him that moving his whole body around wasn't going to help shift the blindfold on his face. "So, Bianca, are you in the habit of wearing blindfolds?"

"Are you asking about my sexual proclivities, Jakob?" I answered him, my body on high alert as he rubbed back against me.

"I wasn't asking what you ate last night, that's for sure."

"You're an ass."

"I know. You told me that already." He laughed. "But yes, go ahead and continue talking about what you can remember from last night, and we can try to figure out why we're here."

"Last night, I was waiting for my friend at a bar. I hadn't seen her in a while. I wanted to tell her about some stuff that was going on." I bit my lower lip as I thought about Rosie. "I remember looking at the menu. I was going to have the steak." I sighed and thought back to the previous evening. Or what I thought was the previous evening. I had no idea how much time had passed. "I was waiting to order until Rosie got there. I wanted us to have a nice evening." I paused, not wanting to get into everything I'd wanted to tell Rosie about. "I ordered a glass of Moscato."

"You like sweet wine?" He spoke softly, even though he was still bobbing around.

"Yeah, I do." I froze as I remembered something. "I didn't drink Moscato though."

"Oh?"

"The bartender sent me a bottle of something else." I closed my eyes and tried to remember. "It was a bottle of pinot noir. He said it was on the house." I opened my eyes again. "Some new vineyard from Upstate New York had asked local bars to serve the wine."

"Interesting."

"Anyways, the waiter brought over a bottle of wine and poured me a glass while I waited for Rosie. I texted her asking where she was, and she arrived a few minutes later." I paused as I tried to remember every detail that I could. "She hurried toward me and apologized. I remember she was angry because the waiter didn't take her drink order fast enough. She was telling me about her job and then . . ." I frowned. "I can't remember exactly. She needed to go to the restroom, and I saw a guy. The guy I think was following me."

"Why do you think he was following you? What did he look like?"

"I can't remember." I sighed loudly. "I can picture him standing in the corner, watching me, but all I can see is his shadow. I can't remember his face."

"What happened next?"

"Someone came up to the table." I shook my head, as if that would help me to remember more details. "I can't remember who. All I remember next is waking up in the car trunk."

"What happened to your friend Rosie?"

"I don't know." I froze and my eyes popped open. "I left something in her bag. I hope she's okay."

"I think she's okay. I think she'd be here with us, if they were worried about her. They obviously just wanted to kidnap us."

"Yeah. I wish I knew why." Though, that wasn't completely accurate. I was pretty sure I knew why I had been kidnapped, I just didn't know why he had been kidnapped as well. I was pretty sure I'd been kidnapped because of my investigating the Bradley Corporation, but what, if any, connection did Jakob have?

"Do you know the Bradley Corporation?" I spoke slowly, as if the answer to his question was of no more importance than the color of his eyes.

"I've heard of it." He responded to me without pause. "I can't say I know it well. Why?"

"No reason." I licked my lips. I was started to feel dehydrated. "Now I wish I hadn't drunk that wine last night. I bet I wouldn't be feeling so parched if I'd just stuck to water."

"It is odd that you received a free bottle of wine, and not just a glass." He spoke thoughtfully.

"Do you think that has anything to do with me being kidnapped?" I bit my lower lip. "I can't remember much after that."

"I don't know." He sighed. "I didn't have wine last night. I'm more of a beer man."

"Surprising."

"Why's that?"

"You seem more like a whiskey guy," I responded swiftly. "I can picture you in a study with a crystal decanter." I groaned inwardly. I had a tendency to speak before I thought. I didn't want him to think I was interested in him.

"I do like whiskey—Yes!" he exclaimed.

"Wow, you really like whiskey."

"No, no, I can see." He was excited. "Shit."

"Yeah." I sighed. I knew exactly what the 'shit' was about.

"Where the fuck are we?" He sounded worried, and I knew he was thinking what I was thinking. How the hell were we going to get off this island?

"So about that whiskey . . . ?" I tried to crack a joke as we sat there in silence. Come to think of it, as much as I didn't like Jakob, I was glad I wasn't here by myself. If I were alone, I'd be sobbing already. "Do you think this is like that movie?"

"What movie?" he finally asked. *"Swiss Family Robinson?"*

"No, that crazy movie where that guy is pretending he's dead, but really he's waiting to see what happens."

"I have no idea what movie you're talking about."

"*Saw*. That's the name of the movie."

"Weren't they in a locked room?" He sounded confused.

"Yeah." I nodded. "So?"

"In case it escaped you, we're not in a room."

"I *know* that," I huffed. "I just meant, do you think that someone put us here so they can watch us, like some sort of experiment?"

"You mean, like *It's a Mad, Mad, Mad, Mad World*?"

"What?" I was surprised at his response. I didn't know many people who'd watched that movie. In fact I didn't know many men that enjoyed movies that didn't have explosions and sex.

"They made a remake. Um, I think it's called *Rat Race*."

"The movie with Whoopi Goldberg?"

"Yeah. These rich men send a bunch of idiots on a quest around the country and place bets on what they think will happen."

"I know. I saw it." I grinned to myself. I bet I'd seen every movie he could think of.

"So, you think we're being watched? Do you think there are cameras watching our every move?"

"Shit, that sounds a bit like *The Truman Show*!" I exclaimed. "Or *Hostel*." I shivered. "Shit, if it's *Hostel*, we're so dead. That movie was so scary. I thought I was going to—"

"Bianca, as impressed as I am by your knowledge of movies, I'm afraid I have more pressing concerns on my mind." His voice sounded superior as he cut me off, and I stuck my tongue out at the sea. "For the record, I don't think there are cameras watching us."

"For the record, neither do I. And yes, I do know a lot about movies. I know a lot because I'm a movie critic." Okay, so maybe I wasn't exactly a critic. All I really did was watch a lot of free movies and write synopses, but I wasn't about to admit that.

"Oh?" He sounded impressed for a second. "For the *New York Times*?"

"No." I muttered. "They aren't the only newspaper that reviews movies."

"Okay," I could tell that he was trying to be patient with me. "Let's try to focus on the matter at hand right now and we can talk about movies once we're out of these ropes." I could feel my face burning at his words. He was such an arrogant jerk. "Let's try to stand up." He continued.

"And go where?"

"We need to walk and see if we can find a rock."

"I already told you that all I can see is sand and water."

"And?"

"And so that means I'm not seeing any rocks."

"Well, if we keep sitting on our fat asses, we're not going to see anything."

"Are you calling me fat?"

"Oh my God, you're not going to be *that* girl."

"What girl?"

"Lean back against me and let's slowly try to stand up."

"What girl?"

"Bianca," he groaned. "Please, let's just try to stand up."

"You're not all that yourself, you know," I blurted out, and he laughed.

"One, two, three." He leaned back into me and struggled to stand up. "You have to attempt to stand as well."

"You didn't say 'go.'"

"What?"

"You didn't say 'one, two, three, go.'"

"Are you joking?" He sounded exasperated, and I grinned. *Take that, Jakob. You're not the only one who can be difficult.*

"Do it like this: One, two, three, go." I leaned back into him and tried to stand up. At first, I thought we weren't going to make it, but then he pressed his back against mine, hard and still.

"Lean back into me. Let me act as your support. Trust me, Bianca. You need to trust me." His voice was gentle. "That's it. Press your weight against me. Don't try to balance on your own two feet."

"If I wasn't a klutz, I'd take offense to that statement," I responded as I pressed against him again and shimmied up.

There was a point where I thought I was going to fall right back down, but Jakob seemed to sense it, because he shifted his position to support more of my weight.

"I did it!" I was exuberant as I stood on my two feet. For a couple of minutes, I forgot that I was suspicious of him.

"Yes, *we* did." His voice was full of humor, and I smiled reluctantly. "Good job."

"Thanks," I said. "Yes, *we* did."

"It's okay. It's amazing how much help I can be in a pinch." Then he started moving. "Come on. Let's see what we can find."

I was silent as we hobbled down the beach. I turned slightly so that I could see what was on the other side, and my stomach dropped. There was nothing but jungle behind us.

"So do you think this is a deserted island, or are we at the edge of some primitive country?" I asked softly as I took in the lushness behind me.

It was beautiful, really scenic, and I knew that if I'd been looking at a photo of the setting, I would have been impressed. I might even have made a comment about wishing I could visit. Now that I was here, though, there was no place I'd rather *not* be.

"I have no idea." He shook his head, and his ass rubbed against my back. "Sorry about that."

"It's fine."

"So we have two options," he said, and stopped walking. "We can venture into the bush and see what we find there, or we can go into the ocean."

"You think we should drown ourselves?" My voice was loud with shock."No." He paused. "There may be rocks on the ocean floor."

"Oh." I stared at the ocean and nodded. "That's true. I didn't think about that. I should have though. The last time I went to the beach, I cut my big toe on a rock. I was so scared, because it started bleeding, and I was scared that a shark would smell the blood and come after me . . ." My voice trailed off as I realized that I was babbling. It was another negative trait of mine—oversharing when nervous. I felt my lips twitching in fear as I thought about how little I really knew about Jakob. This was not the time to let down my guard.

"So, Jakob," I asked hesitantly. "You seem like you have a lot of knowledge on how to get out of ropes."

"Yeah, I play with them a lot."

"You play with ropes?"

"It can be fun." His voice dropped. "Sexy even. The texture makes for a good way to—"

"I'm not asking about your sex life."

"We learned a lot about ropes when I was in the Scouts and when I took sailing lessons." He continued as if I hadn't just embarrassed myself by bringing up sex. "Though, I'd be down to experiment with them in the bedroom."

My body reacted involuntarily to his comment. I think the combination of the sun, dehydration, hunger, and closeness was getting to me. My legs trembled as we stood there pressed against each other. I didn't bother responding to him.

I had nothing to say, and I was scared that I'd say something too flirty. I didn't want to flirt with this man. I didn't even know who he was. I didn't know why we were here together. I knew that while my guard was partially down, I couldn't let it down all the way, not until I'd gotten to the bottom of why we were both here.

"So, yeah," he continued. "We can either try the ocean or we can see what awaits us in the bush. I'm pretty sure I'm seeing some coconut trees. They have sharp husks that fall off all the time. We can try cutting the rope that way."

"I don't know." I shivered as I stared at the deep, dark trees. "What if there's something in there?"

"Something like what?"

"I don't know." I bit my lower lip, and my mind flew to the TV show *Lost*. Growing up with a father who was an inventor and becoming an avid movie watcher had helped me to have a very active imagination.

"Bianca, you can tell me what you're thinking."

"How do you know I'm thinking anything?" I burst out.

"I can tell." His voice changed. "Now tell me."

"I don't want you to laugh or tell me I watch too much TV."

"Fine." His voice was sharp.

"Have you ever seen *Lost*?"

"Don't tell me you're worried that polar bears or smoke monsters are in there?" He sounded incredulous.

"Well, you never know."

"So you want to try the ocean?"

"Well, I don't know." I stared at the calm water and sighed. "What if the current gets rough, or what if a shark comes?"

"We're going to have to take that chance."

"Let's try the ocean," I decided after looking at the mysterious jungle behind us. "I can kick a polar bear, but I don't know what to do with smoke monsters."

"Or hyenas, or wild boar, or monkeys, I assume."

"Thanks for that," I hissed, and shivered. He laughed then, and I felt my insides softening at the sound of his voice. "I'm glad I'm not alone," I said softly as we walked to the ocean.

I was being only slightly honest. The other part of me was being calculating. I wanted him to think that I trusted him. I wanted him to think I was glad he was there. Once he thought my walls were down, he might lower his walls as well.

"I'm glad you're not alone as well. Solitude is overrated," he agreed, though, I couldn't tell if he felt any closer to me. We continued shuffling along the sand and then stopped as we reached the water. "Okay, are you ready?"

"I guess so." I nodded and then paused. "Oh, shit. I just realized we're going to get wet."

"And?"

"We can catch a cold if we keep wet clothes on. And we'll be really uncomfortable in wet clothes—they'll feel so heavy on our bodies."

"It's like one hundred degrees out, Bianca. I'm pretty sure

our clothes will dry out quickly. And if they don't, we can just take them off and let them dry."

"What? I can't take my clothes off." I trembled at the thought of disrobing in front of him. He was a stranger to me. He couldn't see me almost naked. No matter how handsome he was.

I took a deep breath as I thought of the note. Was this a part of the master plan? I thought about David then. Handsome and not-really-with-it David. He'd be so angry if he knew that I was about to get almost naked with a guy I'd just met. I'd been with him for six months and he hadn't even gotten that far. Though he knew that I wanted information about his family business, he didn't know that our entire meeting and relationship had been orchestrated by me.

"Let's do this. Okay, Bianca?"

"Okay." We waded into the water and walked around, trying to find a rock with our feet.

"So tell me about yourself," he said after a few minutes of splashing around. The ocean floor was soft and sandy, and I felt frustrated. Where were the rocks when I needed them?

"What do you want to know?"

"Describe yourself to me."

"You've already seen me." I was hesitant and too embarrassed to say more. "Twice now."

"I barely saw you." His voice was casual. "I can't really remember what you look like."

"I'm pretty average." I shrugged.

"Tell me."

"Well, you can already tell I'm about five six, not as skinny as a model." I paused and waited for him to say something in response, but he didn't. "I've got really dark brown hair and greenish eyes."

"Greenish?"

"Well, they're a brown-green."

"Hazel?"

"No." I stopped and dragged my big toe through the sand. "Hold on. I think I felt something," I muttered, and held my breath. "False alarm." I sighed. "Anyway, my eyes sometimes look green and sometimes look light brown."

"Is that possible?"

"Yes." I laughed. "It's your turn."

"My turn?"

"Tell me about you."

"You saw me though. And the fact that you recognized me from the coffee shop means you do remember what I look like."

"Barely. I can't really remember what you look like," I lied as an image of his handsome face flashed through my mind. "I just recognized your blue eyes, that's all."

"Well, as you can tell, I'm tall, dark, and handsome. The doctor would probably say I'm six two. I weigh in at a respectable two hundred pounds. Most of it is pure muscle."

I rolled my eyes at his comment. He certainly wasn't on the modest side.

"I've got dark brown hair, that's almost black and blue eyes that twinkle in the sunlight."

"Are you joking?" I groaned.

"Well, you asked." He laughed.

"I wasn't asking you to give me your online dating profile."

"I don't date online."

"Of course you don't." I made a face and looked down at the water.

"Do you?"

"Do I what?"

"Date online?"

"I have in the past." I cringed. "There are too many psychos online though."

"Yeah, but I'm sure there are some nice guys as well. My brother dates online."

"Good for him."

"He doesn't seem to have any problems."

"Well, I think it's easier for men. They have all the pickings. It's us women who have to scramble."

"You have to be careful online. You never know who you're going to meet." His words seemed casual, but I heard a hidden meaning behind them.

"You never know who you're going to meet in real life either."

"True," he agreed. "You never really know what someone's intentions are, do you?"

"No," I responded. "No, you don't."

I thought back to Matt and how my life had taken a disturbing twist after talking to him. I had no proof that he was related to any of the crazy events that had happened, but I had my suspicions. I really hoped that Rosie had paid attention when I'd read her the e-mails I'd received. If she was okay, that could be vital information for her to give the police, now that I'd been kidnapped.

"I'm sure you do fine." Jakob interrupted my thoughts. "A beautiful girl like you must have all the men lining up."

"Thanks."

"I mean, what with your winning personality, love of all movies and monster TV shows, and your green-brown eyes, well, I don't know how any guy could turn you away."

"Very funny." I laughed slightly. "You forgot to add that I'm so captivating that someone chose to kidnap me."

"It must be because you're an heiress."

"Trust me. I'm not an heiress." I sighed. "So either they kidnapped the wrong person or they took me for another reason."

"Yeah, who knows." His voice was curious. "Why do you think you were being followed?"

"I'm not really sure." I lied, not willing to tell him everything. "I think it has something to do with a research project I was involved with."

"Ooh, political investigation? That sort of stuff? Is the mayor taking bribes or something?"

"No, nothing like that." I chuckled slightly. It seemed like Jakob had an even greater imagination than I did. "Why do you think they took you?"

"You mean, aside from my good looks?" He sighed. "Or aside from them thinking I know you?"

"Yeah, aside from your good looks, Don Juan."

"I don't know." He sighed. "I really don't. Unless you orchestrated it so you could have your wicked way with me."

"Uh-huh." I laughed. "That's it."

"You didn't have to kidnap me," he continued. "I would have said yes without this elaborate plot."

"Yes to what?"

"Your seducing me."

"You wish," I gasped, and my face went red.

"I'm joking." His voice turned serious. "I'm rich. Very rich. If I wasn't kidnapped because of you, then I'm pretty sure I was kidnapped because I have money."

"I knew you were rich!" I exclaimed, and then I remembered what had made me pause earlier. He'd called himself charming. It reminded me of the letter I'd received back in my apartment that night. What had it said again? *Beauty and Charm. One survives. One is destroyed. What are your odds?* It flashed through my mind, and I wondered if that had been a warning. "Do you have a private jet?" I asked him softly, my mind wandering quickly, trying to make connections.

"Why do you ask?" His voice was very monotone, and I felt his back tense.

"I was just curious," I replied nonchalantly.

"How did you know I was rich?"

"You're wearing a Rolex, right?" I frowned, and reminded myself to be more cautious when voicing my thoughts. I didn't want to make him suspicious of me and I didn't want to give anything away, in case this was a setup. I was worried that I was asking the wrong questions. I suspected he either thought I was a gold digger or feared my questions were revealing too much.

"I didn't realize you noticed."

"Sorry. I just remembered seeing it as you got out of the car." I thought back to that moment. It seemed so long ago now. "I remember it gleaming," I explained. "I noticed the face, though I guess I'm just now processing it. My ex had a Rolex as well."

"Oh, was he rich?"

"I guess." I sighed. "It didn't matter to me."

"It just surprised me that you noticed my watch was a Rolex." He sighed. "It wasn't personal."

"I didn't mean to snap. It's just a sensitive subject."

An uncomfortable silence fell between us then. I wondered if it was going to be like this the whole time we were here. Would we laugh one moment and be on tiptoes around each other the next? What if we were stuck here forever? What if he tried to kill me? I shook my head to clear my thoughts. Jakob wouldn't have been so concerned about my feeling safe and not going into shock if he had plans to kill me.

"He was obviously an idiot." Jakob's voice broke the silence and I listened to him curiously.

"Who?"

"Your ex." His voice sounded gruff. "He's an idiot if he let someone like you go."

"Oh." My heart fluttered at his words and a pleased smile

crossed my face. "I guess he just wasn't lucky enough to be with me."

"Even the shining Rolex couldn't keep you with him." He laughed to himself, and this time I wasn't worried that he was being suggestive or malicious.

"It takes more than a Rolex to keep me."

"As it should."

We continued walking along the sand, and all I could think about was the feel of his muscles against me. They were so hard and strong. His body, though hot and sweaty, felt delicious against mine. It was comforting and sensual in a way that I'd never experience before. His warmth heated me up inside and I knew that we were both playing with fire.

"Ouch!" I cried out as my toe stubbed something sharp. "Oh my God, Jakob." I squealed. "I just stubbed my toe. There's a rock! Oh, but it's too big to lift."

"I see it. Okay." His voice was deep and commanding again, and I shivered. There was something about a man who took charge that made me take notice. "We're going to have to get lower."

"Oh no. Really?" Just thinking about trying to shift down lower was making my limbs feel even more tired.

"Do you see another way for us to cut the rope?"

"I guess not."

"I'll try to get my hands free first. Then I can try to break the rope around our waists and then get your hands."

"Why are my hands last?"

"Do you want to be first, then?" He sighed.

"No, it's fine."

"Okay. One, two, three, drop!" he shouted, and we splashed down into the water, keeping our heads just above the surface.

I gasped slightly as I tried to stop myself from swallowing the salt water. "Thank God the water's warm."

"Okay, I'm going under."

"Okay," I mumbled, and my body stilled as I realized that this meant I was going under as well.

I closed my mouth quickly and tried to hold my breath as my head was submerged beneath the water. My eyes nearly popped out of my head as I realized that we were surrounded by a bunch of small fish. I was just about to run out of air, when I felt myself being lifted out of the water again.

"I didn't get it." He sounded angry with himself.

"Next time, give me some warning when you're taking me under with you." I spat the salt water from my mouth. "I nearly drowned just now."

"Yes, Bianca."

"When we went under, a whole heap of—"

"Okay, we're going under in one, two, three." He cut me off, and before I knew what was happening, we were going under again.

This time, I made sure my mouth was closed as I went under, and I concentrated on trying to keep as still as possible as I bounced against Jakob's back. I knew the exact moment he found the rock, because his body moved back and forth maniacally, bobbing me around in the water like some sort of buoy.

I kept my eyes shut and mouth closed as we bobbed around under the water. I was scared that I was going to pass out. A part of me wondered if this was how it was going to end for me. Why had I been so trusting as to go into the ocean with him? He weighed more than me and was stronger than me. If he wanted to keep me underwater and drown me, he could. My life flashed before my eyes as I stared at the fish as they swam around inches from my face. Just as I was about to try to elbow him, he jumped back out of the water. I took a large gulp of air and said a quick and thankful prayer.

"You stayed down too long just now!" I called out angrily. "I nearly ran out of oxygen!"

"I'm sorry." His voice sounded contrite. "I nearly got the rope off," he gasped excitedly. "I should have come up earlier. I just wanted to get it off so badly."

"It's fine," I said weakly, suddenly feeling exhausted.

"You okay?" His excited tone changed, and he sounded genuinely concerned.

"Yeah, I'm fine. It's just been a long day, and I don't want to end it by drowning."

"I know. It'll be okay. You'll see." I felt his back muscles tense against me, and our shoulders and asses rubbed against each other for a few seconds without our attempting to move away.

"From your mouth to God's ears, please."

"Yes, ma'am. Are you ready for us to go under again?"

I sighed. "Let me take some big breaths first." I sucked in oxygen like I didn't know when I'd have it again. I tried to concentrate on staying calm, but my mind was distracted by the feel of his legs pressed against mine. He was strong. I could feel that in his movements. He was strong and power-ful. I wondered what he'd be like in bed. If he'd be a gentle giant or totally dominating. I felt my fear and worry being re-placed by wonder and lust. He shifted back against me, and I felt his ass brushing mine again. Part of me wondered if he wasn't deliberately rubbing back against me. I was just about to ask him, when he jerked slightly.

"Okay. One, two, three, under!" he shouted, and down we went again.

This time, it was easier. I was accustomed to being tossed around against his back. I stared at the fish now, not feeling apprehensive or scared. They were so small yet so beautiful. I was amazed at the different colors and shapes.

There was one that seemed as fascinated with me as I was with it, and it just seemed to swim in place, staring at me. It had an odd shape, with a bright yellow tail and yellow fins. I noticed that the rims of the fish were yellow as well. It also had dark navy lips and spots on its scales. I'd never seen any-thing like it before. I was so captivated by the fish that I was taken aback when Jakob jumped out of the water again.

"I got it!" he exclaimed, and I felt his shoulders move as he stretched his arms up.

"Lucky you." I felt envious of his freedom as my wrists chafed together in the water.

"I'm going to try to break the rope around our waist now." He paused. "I'm going to try to tear it at the front of me."

"Sure. Take care of yourself first."

"It will be easier."

"Whatever," I mumbled. "One, two, three, go!" I shouted, and took a deep gulp of air, waiting for him to go down into the water.

This time, I was lying down on his back, trying not to sputter as the water moved over my face. It was weird staring up at the sky through the water as I waited for him to cut the rope. Being attached to him felt constricting but somehow comforting as well. I knew as soon as he had cut through the rope, because my body immediately started drifting away from his. I tried to stop myself from moving, but I found it hard to get my feet on the ground. I started panicking slightly, but then I felt Jakob's strong hands grab my waist and pull me to the surface.

"Hey, it's okay." He looked down at me and held me close to him. "I'm not going to let you float away." His hands were firm on my waist, his fingertips digging into me. He pulled me toward him and gently and I felt his body pressed against mine as I moved my arms to the side.

"I'm glad to hear that," I sputtered gratefully.

"I'm going to help you get the rope off your hands now." His eyes gazed down into mine, and I nodded slowly, caught up in his bright blue irises—irises that rivaled the beautiful aquamarine of the water surrounding us. His lips were so close to mine, luscious and pink, and I suddenly wondered what they tasted like. Would they be salty and sweet like his skin?

"I can do it." I attempted to move away from him, but he held on to me tightly.

"I'll help you." He sighed. "Let me help you." His fingers lingered on my waist for a few seconds and then along my arms to my wrists. He grabbed my hands and played with the rope for a few seconds and then looked back up, into my eyes. "I have you in the palm of my hands," he whispered softly and leaned toward me.

"What do you mean by that?" I whispered back at him, my stomach jumping as his fingers brushed my wet hair away from my face.

"Nothing." He shook his head. "I'm just saying, I could do what I wanted to you right now, but all I'm doing is saving you. I hope you'll trust me after this."

"Untie me and I'll trust you." I nodded, unblinking.

"Can I get a kiss as well?" His eyes sparkled as his lips came dangerously close to mine.

"What?" I closed my eyes and waited to feel his lips on mine.

"Open your eyes, Bianca." He whispered against my lips. I could feel his breath gliding over my skin as I opened my eyes slowly. I swallowed hard as I stared up at him. "We're going to go down again now." He looked toward the water and then back up at me.

"Fine." I tried not to feel disappointed.

"Okay, I'm going to pull you down by your arms. Try not to move around too much."

"I can't really stop that."

"Just try." His voice was stern, and I rolled my eyes. It was then that I noticed the red on the sides of his wrists.

"My God, what happened to your arms?" I exclaimed, my eyes widening as I realized that he had scraped his skin off.

"I bumped into a sharp rock." He grinned. "Several times."

"Shit." I bit my lower lip. "That must have hurt."

"It's fine, but now you know why I'm offering to help you."

"Yeah, don't scratch up my wrists, please." I gave him a weak smile and tried not to stare at his bloody wrists.

If he had been able to scrape that much skin off his wrists in order to get free, he had to be pretty pain resistant. That meant if push came to shove, I'd have to think of a better way to escape from him than just kicking him in the nuts.

"I'll do what I can. Now hold on. Take a big gulp of air." He winked at me, and before I knew what was happening, we were going underwater again.

This time, Jakob held on to my arms as we went under. He gripped my wrists, and I felt him moving my hands back and forth carefully and quickly against the rock. I closed my eyes as the rock grated against the inside of my wrist. I was not going to cry. I was not going to feel queasy. I felt oddly bereft not having the warmth of Jakob behind me.

I tried to think of other things as Jakob worked on getting

the rope away from my wrists. I thought back to the previous day. I'd been so excited to finally tell Rosie about the box I'd found in my dad's apartment after he'd died. It had been a year since my father had passed away, and I'd found his letter. I wished now that I had told her what I'd found back in the beginning. I also wished more than anything that I had told her on the phone about the papers I was giving her for safe-keeping. I could only hope she noticed the plastic bag full of papers in her bag and was curious enough to read them. If she read them, she would know that there was more to Brad-ley Corporation then meets the eye. She'd know that it was my father's inventions that had made the company billions of dollars. She'd know that my father had been about to leave the company and take his patents with him and then my mother had died. I knew that couldn't have been a coinci-dence as soon as I saw the dates. I hadn't wanted to say any-thing to Rosie over the phone, because I'd been scared my phone was being tapped. It was irrational, but after the inci-dent with the police officer, I'd no longer felt safe in my own home. I knew the Bradleys were onto me. I knew because I'd told David part of the reason I wanted to know more about his company. I wanted the Bradleys to know that I knew something. I wanted them to know because that was part of my plan. In war, the winner wasn't the army that attacked without the other side knowing, it was the army that attacked and leaked only the information they wanted the other side to know. David knew that I wanted more information on my fa-ther's patents because I had some questions after his death.

He didn't know that I thought his father had something to do with my mother's death. And he didn't know that if my father's papers were correct, and my research was valid, I was actually a majority shareholder in the corporation. The only problem I had was that I was playing a game of cat and mouse with the kitten. David was not the kingpin at Bradley Corporation; his brother, Mattias, was. Mattias was the one I suspected of sending the notes and of orchestrating this kidnapping. He wanted to send me a message to stop investigating. He wanted to scare me. The only question now revolved around Jakob. I had no idea who he was and what role he played in this puzzle.

As Jakob moved my hands back and forth, I thought about how easy it would be for him to drown me. If he worked for Mattias, it would be easy for him to keep me quiet, though I had to believe that this wasn't the case, I tried to turn my mind to more positive thoughts, as I didn't want sadness and paranoia to permeate my mind. There was one fact that I knew to be true. Whoever Jakob was, he wasn't anyone's henchman. He was too commanding, too direct, too strong. He was a man that gave orders. He didn't take them.

Jakob was the sort of man I thought my father must have been like before my mother died. As Jakob moved my hands back and forth, I tried to ignore the small jabs of pain. They didn't even match up to the heartache I felt every day. I'd grown up with my single father since I was five years old. My dad had never remarried. It was as if a part of him had died with my mother. He never spoke of the pain, but the light came on in his eyes only when he spoke of her. When I had read my father's letter, I'd been in disbelief, and then anger. I'd wanted to seek vengeance for my father, but that quickly changed to my wanting to seek out the truth. I wanted to find out what really happened to my mother the day that she died. That accident hadn't just killed my mother, it had killed my father inside as well. I had no idea what I was going to do once I found out the truth. I figured that I would deal with that once I knew what the truth actually was.

"Are you okay?" Jakob questioned as we burst out of the water. He turned me around to face him, and I could see the concern in his eyes.

"Yes." I panted for air. I didn't tell him that my wrists were aching and stung where they'd been scratched.

"I think I'll have it off in the next go-around."

"Okay." I nodded feebly.

"I'll try not to bang your wrists up too much this time." He winked at me and smiled. "Okay. One, two, three, and lift off!" he shouted, and down we went again.

I was as still as I could be as he moved my arms back and forth. I could feel the tension in the rope starting to feel weaker, and my excitement started building. I was nearly free. As soon as the rope broke, I pulled away from Jakob and jumped up to take a deep breath and stretch my arms. Jakob surfaced right behind me, and we grinned at each other like fools.

"Thank you." I smiled at him gratefully as I stretched my arms out. "This feels wonderful."

Then I dove into the water and swam. It felt amazing to be able to move my hands and arms freely. Though the water was warm, it was still refreshing.

"I've never felt so free!" Jakob yelped, and I turned onto my back and started floating so that I could watch him.

He gave me a huge grin, and I watched as he quickly unbuttoned his shirt and tossed it on the shore. My heart started racing as I stared at his naked, smooth chest. His pecs were pronounced, and he had a taut six-pack beckoning to me. I could almost feel his skin beneath my fingers. It would be soft and silky to the touch—I just knew it.

"Do you go to a tanning salon?" I thought out loud as I stared at his sun-kissed skin.

"No." He laughed. "I'm naturally tan. My mom was Italian."

"Oh, really?" I looked at his golden hair and bright blue eyes.

"You sound surprised." He laughed again. "My mom's family was from northern Italy. There are a lot of fair-haired people there."

"I guess I didn't know that." I rested my head back and let my ears submerge in the water as I stared at the sky.

It was so quiet, and everything was so calm. I didn't even see any birds. I felt like I was at the edge of the world somewhere, and Jakob and I were the last people on Earth. We were like Adam and Eve, only we didn't appear at the beginning—we appeared at the end. I shivered as my thoughts went morbid. That was one thing I hated about myself. My mind always went running a hundred miles a minute. I stopped swimming and started to tread water, pushing my head back so that I could feel the sunlight on my face.

Suddenly I felt Jakob grab me around the waist. "What are you doing?" I gasped as I pushed him away. The second my fingers connected with his bare shoulder, I felt a small jolt of lust run through me.

"I was calling you." He smiled down at me. His eyelashes were wet, and his blue eyes seemed to be glowing.

"I didn't hear you." I stared at him as he reached out and pulled me toward him. This time I didn't push him away. His right hand gripped my waist and his bare chest felt hard against me.

"That's why I came to get you." He wiped some water off his forehead. "We should explore and see what we're going to do tonight."

"What do you mean?"

"We need to see if we can find food, a clean natural water source, shelter, somewhere to sleep."

"That sounds smart." I sighed. "How long do you think we're going to be here?"

"As long as they want us to be, I suppose." His eyes bored into mine, and his expression turned blank.

"But how will we know how long that is?"

"I have no idea." He shook his head. "I have absolutely no idea."

"I wish we had some answers." My hand pressed against his chest, and we stared at each other silently for a few seconds. I could feel his heart beating beneath my fingers, and I tried to ignore how warm and silky his chest felt. "Or at least some clues."

"We do have a clue though." His left hand moved down my back, and I swallowed as it stopped on my lower back. "We have that note that you read earlier, and we know that you were being followed. Let's swim back to shore and see if we have anything else in common. We're obviously both here for a reason." His mouth moved closer to mine, and I was positive that he was going to kiss me. I tilted my face up and waited to feel his lips on mine, but instead he let go of me and floated on his back. I watched him for a few seconds, staring at his magnificent body as he moved through the water like Michael Phelps. An image of the note I'd seen on the beach flashed in my mind as I watched him swimming away from me. The last line read *your bodies are now one, but they're not as united as they will be when I'm done.* I needed to figure out what that line meant. Did the note refer to our bodies being one because we were tied together? Or did it refer to something more intimate? The man in the coffee shop had been staring at me for quite a while. Maybe he'd seen the look of lust and appreciation when I'd glanced at Jakob at the table. Maybe Jakob really had been at the wrong place at the wrong time. I started swimming back to shore as I continued to think about why Jakob was here. Maybe it wasn't a coincidence that he was here. And maybe it wasn't a coincidence that he'd been at the coffee shop either.

~⁀

We swam back to the shore and walked out slowly, suddenly deflated. We'd solved our first problem, but now everything else seemed insurmountable.

"So." I stood there awkwardly and ran my hands through my drenched hair. My clothes clung to me like weights, and I had a feeling that I looked like the second coming of the Loch Ness Monster. "What now?"

"I think we should take our clothes off and let them dry." He spoke matter-of-factly and undid the top of his pants. "We'll only get sick if we keep them on. We can lay them out on the sand. The sun should dry them fairly quickly."

"I guess." I hesitated as my fingers gripped the bottom of my shirt. "Maybe they'll dry with us wearing them?"

"I doubt it." He undid his zipper and pulled his pants down. "And I don't want to be walking around feeling uncomfortable either."

"Yeah," I mumbled as I stared at him, mesmerized, as he stood there in just his boxer briefs. His soaked, leaving-nothing-to-the-imagination boxers. I made myself avert my gaze and looked farther down his body. His legs were hairy, stocky, and tan. Shit, he was just getting hotter and hotter. I swallowed hard as my eyes worked their way back up and saw his package sitting there in his white boxer briefs.

"I suggest you take your clothes off as well." He gave me a look as if it were the most natural thing in the world for him to tell me to get naked.

"Don't look." I blushed as I started removing my top.

"You do realize you're not changing, right?" His eyes twinkled at me. "I'm going to see you in your underwear in a minute. Do you really need me to close my eyes now?"

"I guess not." I wrinkled my nose and quickly pulled my shirt off. I looked down at my chest self-consciously, thanking God I hadn't worn my see-through white lace bra. The bra I had on had pretty full coverage, albeit with some sexy black lace that I thought was cute.

"Your bra looks wet." He frowned. "You should take that off as well."

"There is no way in hell I'm taking my bra off." I glared at him.

"Hey, I had to try." He grinned, and I shook my head.

"You're a pervert." I narrowed my eyes at him and ignored the rapid beating of my heart as I went to take my pants off.

"Aren't we all?"

I tried to remember what sort of panties I had on. At least they weren't a thong. I wore those only when I was going on a date, to make me feel sexy. They were way too uncomfortable to wear on an everyday basis. I unzipped my pants and let out a sigh of relief as I realized that I had on a pair of plain white briefs and not my Hanes granny panties with the green and yellow flowers.

His eyes narrowed as he watched me pull my pants down quickly. I stared at the ground as I stood there in my bra and panties. "Nice." His voice was soft.

I looked up at him. He wasn't smiling as he stared at me in silence. There was a very primal feel about everything. All of a sudden we weren't just two strangers kidnapped on an island. We were the last two people on earth. My stomach roared as I stared at his almost naked body. This time my hunger wasn't for food, it was for him. He took a step toward me and his fingers brushed water off of my shoulder. My skin felt like it had been branded by his touch. His eyes narrowed as he stared at my body, giving me the once-over, leaving every inch of me tingling at his glance. The water was starting to dry on his skin and I could see the faint remnants of dried salt on his arms and chest. I wanted to lean forward and lick him to see just how salty he tasted.

"You're beautiful." His voice was husky as his fingers ran down my stomach. I knew that I should breathe, but the moment felt so surreal that I didn't want to do anything to stop it. We both stood there for a few minutes looking at each other and then around at our surroundings. The sun was starting to set, and the silence around us reinforced how alone we were, how cut off we were from civilization.

"We're going to be okay, Bianca." He reached down and took my hand. "If anyone tries to harm you, they'll have to go through me first."

"I'm scared." My voice shook as I looked up at him. "We don't know what's going to happen."

"We don't know what's going to happen, but I'm willing to bet that no monsters are going to attack us." He reached down and rubbed his hand against my back. I jumped slightly at the feel of him against my bare skin.

"Yeah," I whispered. "That's something."

"I think we should wait until tomorrow to locate food and water if you think you'll be okay. It's going to be night soon, I think, and I don't know what time the sun sets here. I'd rather we not go exploring and find ourselves stuck somewhere in the dark." He sighed. "I can go and get some coconuts for now. We should be good for tonight with the jelly and water."

"I guess so." I sighed. "We won't dehydrate already, will we?"

"I think we'll be okay." His expression was serious. "The coconuts will tide us over for the night. Hopefully I'll find some with soft jelly."

"How will you crack them open?" I frowned at him.

"I didn't think about that." He sighed, and I could see a flash of anger in his eyes.

"You'd think those assholes would have left us with some food and water," I muttered.

"Yeah." He looked toward the ocean, his face obstinate and his fists clenched. "If I had an opportunity to speak to those two bumbling fools, I'd kick their asses."

"Yeah." I sighed. "And then we wouldn't be here, but I don't blame you for not trying, Jakob. They had a gun. A gun is mightier than the fist."

"I would never knowingly put your life at risk, Bianca. I hope you know that. I know we don't really know each other, but you have to know that I would never want anything to happen to you."

"Thank you, Jakob. I appreciate it." I nodded at him and smiled briefly. There was something about the look in his eyes that made me want to trust him, but there were too many unanswered questions. I needed to figure out why we were both here before I could fully trust him. "I'm glad I'm not here alone." I said the words to be nice, but I knew that they were true as soon as I uttered them. Being on this island all by myself would have been a nightmare.

"I'm glad I'm not here alone as well." He smiled at me weakly. "Now let's go find some coconuts and then get some sleep so that we can get up early and explore by sunlight."

"Sounds good to me." I yawned and gave him a quick smile.

"I just hope I can fall asleep." His eyes darkened when he looked down at my body. My body trembled at his gaze, and I tried to ignore his innuendo.

"Let's worry about sleep after we find some coconuts." I mumbled and walked away from him and toward the trees. I heard him behind me as we walked away from the ocean. "So what book were you reading?" I stopped and looked back at him curiously.

"Huh?" He looked back at me in confusion and I smiled at him gently.

"In the coffee shop you were reading a book. What was it?"

"Oh yeah," He nodded. "I was reading *A Tale of Two Cities.*"

"Oh, interesting." I wasn't sure why I was surprised by his answer. "You interested in the French Revolution or just a Dickens fan?"

"Both, I suppose. I've always been interested in fiction and nonfiction that talks about revolt. Or more specifically humans going to any extremes to right wrongs or seek answers." He spoke causally, but a part of me froze inside. Did he know more than he was letting on? "What do you think?" He touched my shoulder, and I jumped. He gave me a concerned look, yet I didn't know what to say.

"What do I think about what?" I looked him dead in the eyes, ready to find out what he knew.

"The book? Have you read it? When you mentioned the French Revolution, I assumed you'd read the book. I've always been fascinated with social structures and the power balance between the aristocracy and plebeians, if I may call them that."

"Oh, yeah." I ran my hand over my forehead, trying to calm my overworking brain down. "I've read it. I studied history in college."

"Interesting, you'll have to tell me more about that later." His eyes widened and he pointed at something eagerly. "Look, there are some coconuts on the ground." He ran ahead of me, and I watched him pick up the coconuts and shake them. "They're soft inside." He shouted back at me and grinned. "I can hear the liquid inside of them."

"That's great!" I shouted back.

"At least we know we'll survive one night at least." He ran back toward me and I nodded in agreement. He stopped in front of me, his azure eyes sparkling with genuine excitement, and I knew at that moment that whatever the reason Jakob was here, it wasn't to kill me. I also knew that I was going to find it very hard to resist him, if he continued giving me looks that turned my limbs to jelly.

four

"So tonight we're just going to sleep on the beach?" I looked at Jakob with horrified eyes.

"Sorry, princess. There won't be any eight-hundred-thread-count Egyptian cotton sheets."

"I don't care about luxurious sheets. I don't even have luxurious sheets at home." I ignored his surprised expression and continued. "What if a wild hog comes and tries to attack us?"

"Wild boar."

"What?" I looked around.

"A wild boar might attack us. Not a wild hog."

"Do you think I really care about the semantics of the situation?!" My voice rose, and he laughed gently. I watched as his face transformed from its more natural mature look into a lighter, more boyish expression. I couldn't stop myself from smiling back at him. "It's really not that funny," I continued softly.

"Don't worry, Bianca. I'll protect you."

"Uh-huh." I stared at his bare chest and bulging biceps and then looked away. "How do you intend to do that?"

"I'll watch out for you"—he shrugged—"in case anything tries to attack."

"Thanks," I muttered softly, then sat down on the sand, lay back, and closed my eyes. I heard Jakob lie down as well, and we drifted off to our own thoughts.

～9

The sound of silence is deafening, especially to someone like me, who'd grown up with the constant buzz of traffic and sirens in New York City. The sand was coarse and hard, and I was incredibly aware of how close Jakob and I were to each other. I shifted in the sand a few times and sighed.

"You can't sleep either?" he whispered, and I considered pretending I was asleep. He didn't wait for me to respond but continued talking. "When I was younger, all I wanted was silence. Now I wonder why."

"I used to want silence as well. Silence made me feel safe. I mean, yes, sometimes, the silence makes you feel all alone," I responded, and stared at the clear, dark sky. "But sometimes you want that quiet space to just be with your thoughts. Other times—times like this—well, you don't really want to be alone with your thoughts, do you?" I paused and then attempted to change the direction the conversation had taken. "I've never seen so many stars before."

"Neither have I." His voice was gruff. "The sky is beautiful tonight."

"I feel like we're in a whole new world." I nodded as I stared up. "A whole new beautiful but completely desolate world."

"Why didn't you read to me everything that was in the note?" His tone changed, and I froze.

"What note?" My breath caught.

"The note you read earlier."

"I don't understand," I mumbled, as he sat up and looked down at me with questioning eyes. How could he know there was another line? I'd watched as the note had blown down the beach.

"You didn't read all of it, did you."

"How did you know?"

"I didn't until just now." He leaned back. "I had a feeling that there was more to what you read. It was the way you read it and then paused and said that was it. I was pretty sure that that wasn't all there was."

"Yeah." I made a face. "Sorry."

"So what did it say?"

"Something about our two bodies being one, but we might not always be so united."

"You didn't have to hide that from me." He shifted closer to me and ran a finger down my cheek. "I want you to trust me, Bianca."

"I want to trust you, too." I stilled as his fingers brushed my lips gently, and then he withdrew his hand and ran his fingers through his hair. I wanted to reach over and touch his lips and see if they were as soft as they looked.

"You have a thing about intimacy, don't you." He changed his line of questioning, and I looked away from him and frowned. "Humans are such funny creatures." His voice was soft.

I looked back toward him. His face was illuminated by the moon, and there was something inscrutable about his expression.

"I'm not sure what you mean." I shivered.

"In the trunk, you made a comment about us being intimate. Then you were so agitated by us being tied together."

"Who wouldn't be agitated?"

"I'm just saying that I noticed. You have intimacy issues."

"I don't have any issues." My voice dropped, and my hands lay like wooden blocks at my side.

All of a sudden, I became aware of just how little I had on—and how little he did. I wanted to cover myself but didn't want to prove his point any further. I knew that part of this game we were playing was mental as well as physical. He was trying to test me and push me, to see if he could break me by making me uncomfortable. He wasn't sure if he could trust me either. I wasn't going to let him see any weakness. I couldn't. Not when I didn't know what his agenda was. I was attracted to him in a way that I'd never been attracted to another man. The animal magnetism I felt toward him made me want to push him down on the sand and kiss him. I had to keep reminding myself that I didn't know why he had been put on the island with me. If the reasons were nefarious, I was going to have to be on high alert. I couldn't allow my body to fool me into trusting him too much. Not yet.

"You look naked." His voice grew husky as he gazed down at me. "If I didn't know better, I'd think you were a siren trying to seduce me." His voice drifted as he looked out to the water. "Or a nymph. You could be a water nymph."

"I'm not trying to seduce you."

"I know." He scratched his chest. "What would you say if I touched you right now?"

"I wouldn't say anything." I moved away from him slightly. "I would slap your hand away." I took a deep breath, trying to calm my nerves.

"There's no need to be scared." His voice dropped. "I only touch women who want me to."

"That's good."

"Do you find me attractive, Bianca?"

"I haven't thought about it."

"They say the devil dresses in leather and his mistresses dress in satin. . . ." His voice trailed off. "It's a strange thing, the two of us being here."

"It is indeed." I sighed, my head spinning and my eyes drowsy. I wanted to sleep so badly, but I didn't want to let my guard down around him. Not now that he was acting all funny.

Silence befell us again, and he stood and stretched. His stomach muscles rippled as he flexed, and I watched him carefully. I felt an odd thrill as I stared at him. Part of me was scared by his obvious strength, and another part of me was turned on by how hot he was. I was disappointed in myself for my base attraction to him. He was sexy, and my body was taking notice even though my brain was screaming out that it didn't trust him. I wanted to feel the strength of his body holding me down as he kissed me all over. I wanted to feel the touch of his tongue on my already ultra-sensitive skin. My head felt hot with fever, at the memory of his body pressed against mine in the water. All he had to do was reach down and grab my arms, and I would be like putty in his hands.

"How limber are you, Bianca?" His voice was suddenly above me, and I blinked up at him and swallowed hard.

"Why?"

"I have an idea."

"What's your idea?"

"Do you trust me?" He kneeled down and looked me in the eyes. "It won't work unless you trust me."

"I don't know." I stared into his clear, open eyes, and I could feel a part of me weakening. "What's the idea?"

"I need to know that you trust me first." He spoke lightly, but his stare was intense.

"I trust you," I whispered back, lying, and then yawned.

"You're tired. You should sleep. We'll talk again in the morning."

"I'm okay." I shook my head. "Tell me."

"Your safety is my concern, Bianca. I want the truth as much as you do."

My body stilled at his words. What did he know about the truth? What truth was he talking about? The truth of why we were on the island, or the truth of my mother's death? I knew all my thoughts were rambling together incoherently and that

I had no real reason to believe he knew anything about my mother. I closed my eyes for a second and tried to calm down. I didn't want to say anything that would arouse any suspicion in him, if he was here for nefarious reasons. I had to remember that I was the only one who knew what my father suspected. Not even David knew the full truth. I had to be very careful with what I said.

"I want us both to remain safe," I said as I opened my eyes and sat up. I attempted to brush my hair back as I looked at him,

"So you're very rich, aren't you?"

"I have money, yes." He nodded, his eyes watching me like a hawk. "Why?"

"Just curious. I'm trying to figure out if you were kidnapped because of me or because they wanted you for another reason."

"That would be helpful to know. At first, before I saw you and you reminded me of who you were, I assumed it was because I had money."

"Yeah, it would make more sense for you to be kidnapped for money. I just don't know why the same kidnapper would take both of us. I don't have any money."

"Unless it's some sort of Kidnappers-R-Us sort of scenario. *We'll kidnap whoever you like, for a fee*," he said jokingly, and then gave me a wry smile. "Sorry, that wasn't funny, was it."

"Not really." I gave him a short smile and then spoke again. "How important is your money to you?"

"Not as important as the truth."

"What about life?"

"Do I think money is more important than life? Is that what you're asking me?" He cocked his head and surveyed my face.

"Yes. What would you give up for money?"

"I wouldn't give up my chance at true happiness." His tone was tight. "I wouldn't give up my life."

"Would you give up love?"

"Would I give up love for money?" His face distorted. "What sort of questions are these?"

"I was just curious." I shrugged. "I was just wondering how important money is to someone who's rich."

"I see. Isn't money important to everyone? To me, it's not more important than life. And I don't know about love. Is it more important than love? I don't think so. But then, what is the cost of love?" His tone changed. "How much is a broken heart worth?"

"I don't know." I shrugged.

"Is it worth a life?"

"I don't think—"

"How far would you go for revenge? Do you think we should be responsible for the sins of our fathers?" His voice held a hint of anger.

"I do." I nodded, my voice earnest. "At this point in my life, I do."

"I agree. Though, I don't know that it's really a black-and-white matter, is it?"

"I don't know." I swallowed hard as I realized that Jakob's eyes had glazed over. Suddenly the night air felt very cool against my skin.

"But I'm getting too serious, aren't I." He gave me a short smile. "I should let you sleep."

"It's fine. I'm just confused. You were going to tell me something and then you just changed the subject. Why did you ask me if I trusted you?"

"I think you're holding something back, and I'm confused myself. I don't understand why someone was following you. I don't understand why a man came up to me and questioned me after I sat at a table with you for a few seconds, and I don't understand why we're both here. I was asking you if you trusted me because I think that's going to be the only way we figure this out."

"I don't know what to think." I replied honestly. His words made sense logically. And maybe it would be helpful in other ways for me to tell him what was going on. I just didn't know what to do. How could I tell him that I suspected my mother had been murdered by my father's former business partner? How could I tell him that a billion-dollar business was possibly mine? How could I tell him that my ex-boyfriend was the son of the man I thought had murdered my mother? How could I tell him that I'd been investigating one of the top corporations in the world for fraud and murder? How could I tell him, when nobody else knew? I thought about the patents and incorporation papers I'd put in Rosie's bag the night I'd been kidnapped. I knew that whoever was after me wanted those papers. They wanted to know what information I had. I'd made a mistake telling David that my father had worked for Bradley Corporation. I'd wanted more access into the company. I'd wanted a meeting with his brother, the elusive CEO, Mattias Bradley. All I'd gotten in return was a series of warnings to stay away. I'd been lucky and surprised when David had called me and told me Mattias's plan. I'd gone along with it because I had no choice. I had to trust in David. However, I hadn't expected this. I hadn't expected Jakob.

"I just think that it'll be better if we try to talk things out," he said, and I stared at him trying to figure out who this man was and what role he played in everything. "But let's leave it for the morning. We can talk more then. Let's try to get some sleep."

"It's hard to sleep here," I said, trying to talk my way out of my discomfort and confusion. "I thought New York was humid, but this air is so thick."

"Yes, it is." He nodded his agreement and sat back down next to me. "Tell me, Bianca. Do you think you could kill someone if you had to?"

"What?" I swallowed as my body froze. "What do you mean?"

He stared at me for a few seconds with hard, glittering eyes, and then he laughed.

"Nothing. I'm being too solemn." He shook his head. "Let's get some sleep."

I lay back down on the sand and closed my eyes. Even

though my body was exhausted, my brain refused to let me sleep. Every hair on my body was on high alert as I lay there waiting to see what would happen. My skin tingled from awareness as I felt Jakob staring at me. I wanted to roll over or run away and hide.

I wasn't sure what had happened to the easy camaraderie of the day, but as I lay there waiting for daylight, I knew that I was more confused than ever. My gut told me to trust him. My body told me to touch him. However, my brain told me to be wary. Some of his comments had seemed a bit off, and I wasn't sure if my instinct to trust in him was influenced by my attraction to him.

I shivered as I thought about his last comment. *Do you think you could kill someone if you had to?* What sort of question was that? Was it a warning? I wished I had asked him "Could you?" I'd wanted to but was scared of his answer. His face had looked so serious, so different from earlier. I pictured his face as it had been when we'd swum in the ocean earlier and how careful he'd been with me as he'd cut the rope from my wrists. His blue eyes had shown concern for me. His lips had been pleasant. His arms had been strong and muscular, and his chest was perfect. An absolutely perfect specimen.

I flushed as I realized that my thoughts were starting to go down a different road again. I was sexually attracted to him in a way that I couldn't control, and it scared me. I didn't want my attraction to him to make me let my guard down. I'd already done that a little bit. I knew my mask was slipping, and I was letting him in, little by little. I had to remember to focus on why I was here. I needed to find out the truth about my mother's death. It suddenly struck me that if it wasn't a coincidence that he was here then he might know more information. Maybe he knew more than he was letting on. Maybe if I divulged some information, he'd trust me a bit more as well. I didn't know if he knew anything, but it was worth a shot. Unless, of course, he was here for another reason altogether.

My breathing stopped for a second as I realized that the truth might be staring me in the face. What if I wasn't going to get off the island? What if Jakob had no plans of helping me figure out the truth? What if Jakob was here to kill me?

The sun beating down on my face woke me up, and I jumped to my feet feeling anxious and disoriented. I looked around the beach, but Jakob was nowhere to be seen. I went to the ocean to wash my face and wet my hair. My stomach grumbled as I splashed the cool water on my skin, and my throat felt parched. If I didn't get food and water soon, I would be close to collapsing. The hot sun had already begun to sap my energy, and black and white spots danced before my eyes. I knew I was close to fainting, and I was scared. When David had warned me that I was going to be disappearing for a while, I hadn't imagined it was going be like this. Being kidnapped and taken to a deserted island wasn't how I'd expected everything to go down.

I walked out of the ocean and back to the beach, slowing, not wanting to expend too much energy. I stood upright for five minutes, drying in the sun before pulling my top back on. Staring at my pants, I knew that, even in my modest state, I wasn't going to put them back on. My top fell just below my waist, and I ignored the slight self-conscious feeling of walking around in my panties. The new day had brought with it renewed and even more complex feelings of fear, confusion, and self-awareness.

I stared at Jakob's large white shirt and had an idea. I quickly pulled off my top and put his shirt on, laying my top on the sand to sit on top of it. His shirt was so large that it covered my ass and made me feel more comfortable walking around. I sat there for a few moments trying to decide what to do. I wasn't sure if I wanted to go look for Jakob or if I should go look for food. I knew better than to drink the salt water, but my thirst was absolutely killing me.

"It suits you," Jakob's voice called out from behind me, and I felt my body relaxing. He was still alive, then.

"Hey, I hope you don't mind." I jumped up and smiled weakly as he walked toward me. He looked even more magnificent in the light of a new day.

"What's mine is yours." He shrugged. "It's just the two of us."

"Thank you." It was then that I noticed the bananas in his hand. "You found food?"

"I saw some banana trees in the jungle." He nodded over to the trees. "I figured you might be hungry."

"I am." I nodded. "Thank you," I said again, as he handed me a bunch of bananas.

"I couldn't find any more green coconuts on the ground." He frowned. "Or any natural water sources."

"Oh." I peeled a banana and ate it eagerly.

"So we have nothing to drink." He ran his hands over the top of his shimmering unruly dark hair and frowned.

"What are we going to do?" I knew that at this point it was going to be better for us to work together. I was just going to have to watch his every move.

"We'll have to go look for natural water or hope it rains."

"Rains?" I frowned. "What are we going to do? Stick our tongues out?"

"Something like that." He grinned. "The rainwater here will be safe to drink. It'll be pure. We should find something to act as a container."

"Um, don't you think that's a waste of time?" I looked up at the clear sky. "I don't think it's about to rain anytime soon."

"The weather can change in an instant, Bianca. Weather is like people. Things change when you least expect it."

"So you're saying that appearances can be deceiving?"

"That's exactly what I'm saying." His eyes narrowed as he stared at me, and his expression changed. "All that glitters is not gold."

I looked away then and concentrated on eating my banana. I gobbled it down greedily, eager to have some food in my stomach. I quickly peeled a second banana and starting eating it just as voraciously.

"Don't eat a third one." Jakob grabbed the rest of the bananas from my hand. "You've had enough for sustenance. If you have any more, you'll become thirstier."

"I'm still hungry." I stared at the bananas in his hand.

"No more. Not now." He shook his head, and I wondered if I had enough energy to push him down and grab the bananas back from him. "Don't even think about it." His eyes narrowed, and he took a step toward me. "I'd have you pinned to the ground in five seconds flat, and I wouldn't care if I winded you."

"I don't know what you're talking about." I took a step back from him, my face flushing at the thought of him holding me down.

"I'm very strong, Bianca." His lips curled up as he leaned forward to whisper in my ear. "And I wouldn't be averse to getting you underneath me."

"Well, *I'd* be very averse to that."

"Are you ready to go looking for water?"

He took a step back, and I noticed that his hands were clenched into fists. That wasn't a good sign. His body language had me off-kilter. I couldn't figure him out at all. Was he friend or foe?

"Shh." He turned around, his eyes wide and his nostrils flaring. His hands reached out to me, and his fingers gripped my shoulders. "Do you hear that?"

"Hear what?" I whispered, and tried to listen carefully. All I could hear was the sound of the waves in the ocean and a few distant birds. Jakob's body was tense as he stood next to me, and he closed his eyes.

"There's someone else here." His eyes opened again, and I could see anger and an emotion close to fear in his irises.

"What do you mean?"

"There's someone else on the island with us." He let go of my shoulders and looked around hurriedly. "There shouldn't be anyone else here." He shook his head as he paced up and down.

"Are you sure?" I walked over to him, my heart beating fast. "I don't hear anything."

"I'm sure." He nodded. "Close your eyes and listen carefully."

I closed my eyes and listened. At first, all I could hear was the sound of my own heart beating rapidly. Then I could hear Jakob breathing next to me. Then I smelled him. Masculine, virile, sweaty. I ignored the smell and tried to focus. It was then that I heard the sound of an insect I'd never heard before. It sounded like a very low buzzing. I tried to concentrate harder. I could hear the birds whistling and chirping. Wait. I froze. The birds were chirping, but someone else was whistling. That wasn't a bird. My eyes flew open and darted to Jakob's.

He was staring directly at me, his nose a mere couple of inches from mine. "We're not alone."

I swallowed hard then. My fingers reached for him of their own volition and I held on to his arms. He moved in closer to me, took me into his arms, and rubbed my back. His chest was warm and comforting. All of a sudden, he didn't seem like the enemy. I'd seen the look in his eyes. He'd been as taken aback as I had. There was someone else on the island with us. And neither of us knew who—or why.

~

"What are you doing?" I reached for his arm as he pulled away from me.

"We need to go see who's here with us."

"Shouldn't we hide and wait to see who comes to us?"

"Cowards wait to defend. The brave know the fight is won on the offensive."

"Huh?" I stared at him blankly. "Were you in the military?"

"No." he shook his head. "Have you heard of *The Art of War*?"

I shook my head. "No, what's that?"

"It's a book. It was written by Sun Tzu. He was a military general and a Chinese philosopher. A great philosopher. Sun Tzu said, 'If ignorant of both your enemy and yourself, you are certain to be in peril.'"

"We don't know if the person is our enemy."

"We don't know that they aren't."

"What shall we do?"

"Come." He grabbed my hand and then stopped me still. "You have to trust me, Bianca. We're going to have to pretend that we know each other, do you hear me? We can't let anyone know that we are strangers as well. That will make us weak and easier to take down."

"But we don't know each other." My eyes widened at the urgency in his voice. "I don't know you," I whispered.

"We cannot show any division." His fingers squeezed me tighter. "It will be easier to take down two enemies than two friends."

"Sun Tzu again?"

"No, that's just me." He grinned weakly, and I watched his face transform as his eyes lit up for a brief second. He looked like a completely different man when he wasn't all intense.

"I see."

"And my answer is yes, by the way," he whispered as he let go of me.

"Your answer to what?"

"Your unspoken question last night." He stretched and stood tall, his shoulders back and strong. "I could kill someone if I had to." He looked at me, his eyes dark again. "There are many things I could do if my life and the truth depended on it. I need you to promise me one thing, Bianca."

"What's that?"

"We need to talk later. You need to tell me everything that you know about why we're here." He leaned forward and whispered in my ear. "It might be the only chance we have at survival."

And then he walked away toward the jungle.

I didn't know what to do. I wasn't sure that I wanted to follow him. Part of me wondered if I was following him to my death. How did I really know that there was someone else in the jungle? All I'd heard were a few whistles. Maybe it was a bird after all. Maybe it was a parrot? Parrots were supposed to be able to mimic human sounds. I stood there frozen, not sure what to do. However, time doesn't always wait for us to make a decision. My decision was made for me when I saw Jakob freeze. I looked at his hands and watched as they tightened into fists. I took a couple of steps back in fear. This was it, then. We were about to find out who was on the island with us.

"Hello," another male voice called out smoothly. "Lost as well?"

"Something like that," Jakob replied, and I looked past him to see who he was talking to.

My eyes widened as I stared at the other man. He looked unassuming and pale. He was only slightly taller than I was, and he had dark brown hair. I couldn't see the color of his eyes from where he was standing, but I could see a pleasant smile on his face. He looked like a regular guy. I wondered how he had gotten on the island and why he hadn't called out to us earlier. I hadn't seen a boat or aircraft anywhere, so there was no way that he could have been dropped off after us. I hurried toward Jakob, and the man's face turned into a huge smile as he looked at me.

"Why, hello there." He smiled as he walked toward me. "It's nice to meet you both." He had a slight accent, and I noticed that he was limping slightly.

"Are you okay?" I moved toward him, but Jakob grabbed my arm. I looked back at him, and he shook his head acutely, but I ignored him. There was nothing to be frightened of with this new man. I was strong enough to take down a man with a limp, if it came to a fight.

"I hurt my leg." The man continued to smile at me. His eyes were bright and blue. He was more handsome than he'd appeared from far away. "Am I glad that I happened upon you both. I thought I was going to be stuck here by myself."

"We're glad you found us as well." Jakob walked up and put his arm around my shoulder. The possessiveness of his action annoyed me, and I tried to move away from him, but his grip on my shoulder was tight. "It must be scary to be on the island by yourself. What's your name?"

"I'm Steve." He offered his hand to me, and I shook it. I was surprised at how strong his grip was. I'd assumed he'd have a limp handshake, like most unassuming men. His firm grasp didn't match his appearance. And the light in his blue eyes seemed artificial somehow. I knew immediately that I didn't trust him.

"Bianca." I smiled at him, trying to show him that I was friendly and not sizing him up. My father had always told me to never let a person see that I was evaluating them. If a stranger knew or sensed that you were studying them, they'd retreat and become resentful. I didn't want Steve to have any ill feelings toward me. If he thought I trusted him, he might be more willing to give me information. I was almost positive that this wasn't a chance encounter.

"A beautiful name for a beautiful woman." His eyes flirted with me, and my smile wavered, slightly uncomfortable at his boldness considering Jakob's arm was around me and his whole stance was extremely possessive.

"I'm Jakob." Jakob's voice was light as he ignored Steve's outstretched hand. "How did you get here?"

"I'm not sure." Steve frowned. "I fell asleep on the beach at the resort and woke up in the jungle."

"The resort?" Jakob smiled. "There's a resort on the island?" His smile didn't reach his eyes, and he pushed me behind him slightly. "I think you must be mistaken."

"There must be a resort, right?" Steve smiled back. "How else did I get here?"

"Good question." Jakob looked at me for a second and then turned back to Steve. "Forgive me if I'm not as convinced by your story as you may have hoped, but I'm having a hard time accepting the fact that you think you're still on the same island as your resort."

"I don't really know where I am." Steve's eyes grew worried as he rubbed his head. "I'm hot, and I'm thirsty, and I'm slightly disoriented. All I can remember is having a drink and then falling asleep. I feel like shit now, might have a bit of a hangover."

"It sounds like you've had a rough time of it."

"How did you two get here?"

"Bianca and I were kidnapped, so we're not really sure how we got here, and for that matter, we don't even know where we are."

"You were kidnapped? Together?" Steve sounded surprised, and his smile weakened a little. His reaction was strange. It wasn't how I expected someone to react to the news that someone had been kidnapped.

"Yes," Jakob answered at the same time I said "No."

"Which one is it?" Steve looked back and forth at us.

"They kidnapped us both at separate times." Jakob's voice was firm. "Neither of us knows why, but we're so glad that we're here together."

"So you know each other?" Steve's gaze was on me, and I could see that he was searching for answers in my eyes. I wanted to be honest with him, but I didn't want Jakob to be mad.

"Yes." Jakob nodded. "We're lovers."

"Oh!" I gasped, and blushed. I felt my face growing red at Jakob's words, but I tried to ignore the butterflies in my stomach at the thought of him touching me, of his lips trailing down my neck. His fingers pressed into my back and trailed down to my ass suggestively. I wasn't sure if this was part of his game, but I knew that I didn't want him to stop. I wanted to feel his hands all over me. I wanted to touch him and feel his hardness, between my legs. I wanted to . . .

"You'll have to excuse her." Jakob chuckled and pulled me into his arms, suddenly making my thoughts turn into reality as my breasts crushed against his chest. "Bianca gets a bit shy when I discuss our intimacy in public."

"Jakob." I tried to push him away, and his hand fell to my ass once again and squeezed it firmly. I struggled against him, but his hold became tighter, and I couldn't move.

"Later, my dear." He smiled down at me gently, his eyes issuing me a warning as he pulled me closer toward him. I could feel his hardness pressing against my stomach, and I knew his little charade was turning him on as well.

"I guess I'm the third wheel." Steve's smile was completely gone, and I was cautious of how quickly his demeanor had changed. He'd gone from friendly to surly in moments, and I began to realize that his casual and friendly demeanor was definitely a pretense.

"We're happy for the company," Jakob spoke, sounding anything but happy. "Maybe between the three of us we can figure out exactly what's going here. I for one don't want to spend the rest of my days on this island."

"Yes, I'll be happy to stay with you both here." Steve nodded. "I really want to figure out a way to get off the island. And of course I want to know why I'm here. Why we're all here. Having that knowledge would be good. That would be really good." He looked at me then, his eyes slightly narrowed and his lips thin. There was something about the way that he'd spoken that discomforted me. He didn't sound scared. Or afraid. He was acting way too calm for someone that had supposedly been on a beach and woken up on a deserted island.

"I agree." I shivered next to Jakob. I was still in his arms, and I was suddenly glad for more than one reason that he had laid his claim on me.

As much as I wasn't sure about Jakob's intentions, I knew that Steve was bad news. I couldn't ignore the feeling that he was definitely here for a more sinister reason.

"Should we go take a seat?" Jakob nodded back toward our pants. "Get to know one another?"

"Sounds good. I need a bit of a rest." Steve nodded, and we all walked back to the sand.

"I don't trust him," I whispered into Jakob's ear as we walked back, and the look in his eyes told me that he agreed with me.

"Let's not let him know that." Jakob's breath tickled my ear as he whispered back at me. I wasn't sure if I agreed with him. Part of me thought it would be a better idea to let Steve know that we didn't trust him from the get-go.

"I guess I'm really not at Sandals anymore." Steve gave me a look. "Serves me right for sitting on the beach and drinking all day."

There was something off with Steve's story. He'd said that he had been relaxing on the beach when he had fallen asleep. And then he'd woken up in the jungle. I looked at him again and gave him a weak smile before looking down at the sand and thinking. He was wearing pants and a blue shirt. Why would he have been wearing pants and a shirt on the beach?

The other thought that struck me was how calm and collected he seemed. He was so calm that he'd been whistling casually. If I'd woken up in the middle of a jungle after falling asleep on the beach, I wouldn't be whistling as if I had no cares in the world. I'd be frantic as hell. Something didn't add up. And all of us knew it. The only sounds around us were those of the waves crashing in the ocean and some birds chirping.

I stared at Steve and then at Jakob. They were sizing each other up, and I could feel the sudden tension in the air. Steve looked back at me and ran his hands down the front of his

shirt. "I'm glad I'm here, Bianca. I can help to protect you."
He then looked at Jakob pointedly.

"She doesn't need your help. She's got me." Jakob responded in a menacing tone and I wondered just how true
that was.

Both of them turned to look at me then. I stared back at
them and offered a small awkward smile while my insides
churned. I felt like Little Red Riding Hood, but I had no idea
which of my supposed saviors was actually the wolf.

five

"There's something off about that guy Steve," I whispered to Jakob as we sat down on the sand. "I don't know if I trust him."

"I could have told you that as soon as I saw him."

"What are we going to do?" I bit my lower lip and tried to stop my body from shaking.

"We'll sleep together tonight," Jakob whispered in my ear as we watched Steve hobble over to the ocean.

"What?" My voice rose, and my stomach flipped over.

"We'll sleep together." He pulled me toward him. "We have to act the part."

"I don't know if I want to act any part." I swallowed hard as our legs grazed each other's. I felt a small spark of electricity run through me.

"I don't trust him." His voice was low. "We have to show a united front."

"We don't know him." *And I don't know if I trust you either.*

"His story doesn't add up." His eyes narrowed as we watched Steve splashing his face with water. "He didn't just fall asleep at a resort."

"I was thinking the same thing, but why is he here, then?" I lay down on the sand. I wasn't sure why I was arguing with him, when he was bringing up the same points I had just been making internally. "Why are you here? Why am I here? Maybe he was drugged like we were?"

"He wasn't a part of the plan." He shook. "I'm positive of that. Whoever wanted us here didn't intend for this man to be here as well."

"You don't think so?" I shivered.

"Whoever orchestrated our kidnapping had everything planned to the most finite detail. They had your drink laced with something, for heaven's sake. They wouldn't just have a third person show up. Not like this. It doesn't make sense."

"So then why is he here?"

"That's what I intend to find out." His eyes narrowed as he looked toward the ocean. I could see his muscles flexing as he stretched his arms out. I swallowed hard as I stared at his toned body. If it came down to a fight, Jakob could definitely take Steve down.

"You don't think he's the one who put this all together, do you?" I whispered as Steve limped back to us. I knew that I didn't think that, but I was curious to hear what Jakob had to say. Mentally I was starting to feel confused. Really confused.

"I don't know." He looked down at me and paused. "None of us really knows anything."

"I need to tell you why I think I'm here." I spoke quickly as I decided suddenly to trust him. "I need you to know what I've been up to."

"Tell me later." He nodded. "Let's wait to talk until he's gone to sleep. He's walking back now." He looked toward the beach and I saw Steve hobbling back toward us.

～

We spent the rest of the day sitting on the beach chatting idly about why we thought we were on the island. I was pretty sure that none of us was being honest or up front about our pasts. I knew I wasn't. I mumbled on about life in the city being dangerous and how the rise of human trafficking made women like me a target. Both men nodded in understanding, but I knew they had to be thinking that had nothing to do with all three of us being on the island together.

Jakob didn't bring up going to explore in the jungle, and I didn't ask him either. I wasn't sure that either one of us was willing to go explore now that Steve was a part of our pack. There was something about him that reminded me of a serial killer. Maybe it was the way his eyes followed my every movement. Or maybe it was the way he stared at my breasts and licked his lips. His fingers also looked too manicured. I could tell from his fingernails that he wasn't a man of labor. Then there was the fact that his accent kept changing. It ranged from British to Australian, and I wasn't sure if he was putting it on or not.

"I'm a man of leisure." Steve lay back on the sand. "I come and go as I want."

"That must be nice," I answered politely, as Jakob just stared at him.

"It's not a bad life to lead." He grinned at me and then looked at Jakob. "I sometimes feel like a nomad, taking an odd job here and there, but it's a great way to see the world."

"I'd love to travel the world one day."

"That's a nice dream," he replied to me, and I frowned, not knowing how to take his comments. *That's a nice dream?* Did he think that I wasn't going to make it anywhere?

Steve seemed to sense my annoyance, because a couple of seconds later he pulled a flask of something out of his pocket and took a long swig.

I reached for it eagerly as he handed it over to me.

"What is it?" Jakob frowned at me and shook his head as I was about to take a swig.

"Gin." Steve grinned. "I always carry a flask around with me."

"Give it back, Bianca." He grabbed the flask from my hand and handed it back to Steve.

"Hey, I was thirsty." I glared at him. He was fast getting on my nerves. I knew we were trying to work together, but I didn't need him acting like he was in charge of me. I could take care of myself.

"Alcohol won't help you." He shook his head and looked up at the sky. "I don't think it's going to rain today."

I resisted saying *I told you so.* "So what are we going to do?"

"We need to find water." He looked down, and I could see him thinking. "We need to go to the ocean."

"What? We can't drink the salt water. Even I know that will kill us."

"No, we're not going to drink the water." He jumped up. "We need to collect the rocks."

"The rocks?" I froze. "Why?" I had images of him pummeling Steve—and maybe myself—to the ground. I could almost see the pools of bright red blood in the sand. I shivered at my morbid thoughts and shook my head.

"I think I know how we can get some water." Jakob's eyes looked at me searchingly, and I knew that he had witnessed my shoulders shaking.

"From the rocks?" I frowned. How were we going to get water from the rocks? "You've heard the saying that you can't squeeze blood from a stone, right? I'm pretty sure you can't squeeze mineral water from it either."

"Bianca." He gave me a wry smile. "Please, just start collecting rocks from the ocean."

"What are you going to do?" I huffed. "I'm not your slave." *You can tell me what the plan is; I'm not too dumb to understand,* I thought.

"I'm going to show Steve what he needs to do." He gave me a smile and then looked down at Steve, who was watching us with a curious expression on his face. "You do agree that it wouldn't be fair if we asked Steve to shuttle rocks back and forth, what with his bad leg and all."

"I'll do whatever I can to help." Steve frowned, and I could tell that he was annoyed that Jakob had pointed out his inferiority. "I may have a slight impediment, but I assure you that I can still get the job done." His tone was snide as he spoke to Jakob. Then he looked at me and smiled. "I can assure you, Bianca, that I'm very capable of getting the job completely done."

"Come with me," Jakob said, grabbing Steve's hand and pulling him up hard. "I'm going to need you to dig a hole."

"A hole?" I exclaimed, my mind once again drifting to thoughts of someone getting their head smashed in by a giant rock.

"Bianca, why aren't you going to get the rocks?" Jakob snapped, and I ran toward the water.

My heart skipped a beat as I reached the water and looked back. I saw Jakob and Steve walking farther away from the water toward the sand dunes. I reached into the water and pawed at the ocean bed. Why did he want me to find rocks? And why was Jakob having Steve dig a hole? Was he planning on killing one of us and then burying the body? I looked out at the empty horizon and shuddered. What I wouldn't have done to have seen a yacht sailing along the smooth waters in that moment, or even a young guy on a Jet Ski. I'd feel bad about leaving Steve and Jakob behind, but I'd make sure to get help.

"Have you found any rocks yet?" Jakob's smooth voice made me jump as he entered the ocean behind me.

"Not yet." I shook my head and went back to running my hands along the seabed. "How many do we need?"

"We're going to need quite a few. The larger the better."

"What for?"

"Survival." He walked away from me. There he was with that word again. I wished he wouldn't keep saying it. The word *survival* made me think of death, and the last thing I wanted to be preoccupied with was my own mortality right now.

I stared at his back for a few seconds before turning around.

"So did your parents have a happy marriage?" Jakob called out to me as we looked for rocks.

"I think so," I answered, not knowing how to respond. "My dad really loved my mother. He was devastated when she died." I felt a pang of pain in my chest as I recalled my father sitting on the couch staring at a photograph of my mother. "He never loved anyone after her."

"So it was true love, then?"

"Yes, I believe it was."

"It's ironic what love can do, isn't it?" He came closer to me.

I could see a fairly large rock in his hands, and I stilled. "What do you mean?"

"Love can make you feel like you're on top of the world, but it can also crush you. It can crush you so that you feel like you don't want to live."

"I think love is what people make of it." I bit my lower lip. "It only controls you if you let it."

"What if external forces are making those decisions?"

"I would hope that adults could make their own decisions

when it comes to love." I shrugged. "And if they can't, maybe it isn't really love."

"It's easy to be philosophical about love, isn't it?" His tone changed, and he looked away from me.

"I guess so." I stared at the rock in his hand, contemplating telling him about my father and how he'd let the loss of my mother take over the rest of his life. I loved my father more than anything, but I was still so angry at him for letting her death dictate the rest of our lives. Especially if there were signs related to her death that he'd missed because all he could think about was her grief. "So what are you going to do with that?" I asked softly, and took a step away from him. I knew that now wasn't the time to tell him about my father's letter. I saw his eyes narrow as I moved back, and a small smile curved on his face.

"Are you scared, Bianca?" His voice dropped, and his eyes glittered into mine as he took a step toward me.

"No," I lied, staring at his face, trying hard not to show him that I was unsure as to how I felt about him.

"That's a pity. You should be." His eyes fell to my legs and then back up to my eyes. He shifted the rock into his right hand, and his left hand reached up to my face. His fingers ran down my cheek, and he sighed. "I think there's a lot to be scared of on this island." His thumb moved to my trembling lips, and then his arm dropped back to his side. "You shouldn't be so trusting, Bianca."

"I'm not." My lips trembled as I stared at him. My eyes wouldn't leave his face or chest, and I could feel the blood in my veins heating up.

"Keep looking for rocks. I'll be right back." He took a step back, and I watched as he walked back up the sand to where he had left Steve.

I shook my head as my fingers ran to my lips. I closed my eyes for a second, remembering the feel of his fingers on my lips. I groaned as I realized that I was in trouble. My tongue flicked out of my mouth, and I licked the faintest taste of him off my lips. I turned around and groaned again. I was in really big trouble. I continued looking for rocks and tried to distract my mind from my attraction to Jakob.

There had been something odd in his questioning. Why had he been so concerned about my parents' marriage? Did he know what I was investigating? I closed my eyes and prayed that when I opened them I would be back home in my apartment. Everything was getting so confusing. At first, when I'd read through the papers I'd found in my dad's box, I'd been bored. Then I'd read through them again, and my curious nature kicked in. There had to have been a reason why my father had thought they were important. There had been some papers related to a corporation my father had been part owner and founder of, some patents for a bunch of different inventions, and some paperwork that called for a dissolution of the company and a request for all three founders to exit the company with what they had brought to it originally. My father had wanted his patents back, Bradley was to take his money, and the third party—someone called Maxwell—was to receive only a percentage of the profits from the previous year. The dissolution had never been signed, but it was drafted a week before my mother's death, if the time stamp was anything to go by. There had also been a report from a private detective about my mother's car crash. A report that suggested my mother hadn't died in an accident, but the report had ultimately resulted in an inconclusive answer.

I thought back to the corporation my father had been a part of: Bradley, London, and Maxwell. I was pretty sure that this was the corporation that was now called Bradley Inc. I'd found the Bradleys, but I'd had no luck finding the Maxwells. Running into David and catching his eye had been the best thing I'd done thus far in the investigation, but I'd soon realized that he knew nothing about the family business. It was his brother, Mattias, that now ran the company. It was his brother who had access to all the secrets of the company. It was his brother who I had yet to see. I could find no public information on him anywhere, not even Google. This had been the reason why I'd divulged some information to David about who I was. I wanted—no I needed—to gain access to Mattias. But it hadn't worked out that way. I was starting to wonder if fate had changed its plan for me and was handing me something on a silver platter. I took a deep breath and tried to stop my shaking fingers. In that moment, I wished that I could talk to David more than ever. No matter what had happened in the past, he would know exactly what to say to calm me down.

～

"Okay, I found another two." Jakob walked up to me with two more rocks in his hands. "You take this one and follow me back to Steve."

"What are we going to do with them?" I asked him again, feeling annoyed and curious.

"All will be revealed soon enough," he replied, and handed me a fairly large rock. "Let's go."

"I'm coming." I rolled my eyes and followed him back to the sand.

We walked back to Steve, whose face was shining a bright red. I could tell that he was going to have a terrible sunburn on his face and grimaced as I realized that I was probably as burned as he was. My skin wasn't used to such direct sunlight.

"How's that hole looking?" Jakob dropped the rock on the ground a couple of feet away from where Steve was frantically digging.

"Not that great." Steve looked surly and tired.

"We'll help. Come on, Bianca." Jakob dropped to his knees and looked up at me. "Start digging."

"Digging?" I sighed and dropped down next to him. "Why are we digging?"

"You'll see."

"I'm tired," I groaned and wiped a mass of sweat off my forehead.

"We need this hole to be about three to five feet, so let's get to work." He immediately started throwing sand behind, and I joined him. The sand grains felt cool next to my fingertips, and I dug quickly.

"The sand is getting colder and colder," I commented out loud.

"That's because we're getting closer to the water," Jakob answered and gave me a small smile.

"What water?" Steve asked, and I pointed to the ocean. He looked like he wanted to ask another question, but he didn't. I looked up and saw Jakob giving me another small smile.

I smiled back at him and continued digging.

"Pass me the rocks," Jakob commanded after about ten minutes of us frantically digging in silence.

"Okay." I stood up and handed them to him with a question in my eyes. I watched as he placed the rocks at the bottom of the hole we'd dug. "What are you doing?"

"We're creating a natural filter." He smiled at me. "We need some driftwood."

"Where can we get that?" I stood up. "Should I go look?"

"I'll come with you." Steve jumped up and gave me a wide smile.

"No." Jakob shook his head. "Bianca will go by herself. You'll help me pat the sides of the wall down while we wait for the wood. We don't want the sand to fall into our water hole."

"Water hole?" I gasped and looked into the hole we'd dug.

"If it works properly, the salt water will rise up in that hole." Jakob grinned. "The rocks will act as a filter and should remove most of the salt."

"Wow." My jaw dropped. "That's cool. I had no idea."

"I took a survival course once." He shrugged. "I thought the information was useless at the time. Now I'm glad I did it."

"Of course you did." Steve's eyes narrowed.

"Pat down the sides of the hole." Jakob gave him a derisive look and stood up. "You sure you're okay to go by yourself, Bianca? I can come with you."

"I'll be okay." I nodded.

"Go farther up there." He pointed to the left. "You don't have to go into the jungle by yourself."

"I don't mind."

"I do. You're not going in by yourself." His expression grew serious. "I'll stay here with Steve and keep the sides solid."

"Okay." I stared up at him.

"Good luck." He leaned down and gave me a light peck on the lips. His eyes were laughing at me as I pulled back in shock.

I walked away quickly, with my heart beating. His lips had tasted salty but also warm and tender. I hadn't been prepared for his kiss. I hadn't been prepared for how good it would feel. My whole body tingled as I walked toward the tree line in search of wood.

～

Jakob's plan had worked, and we had water to drink. It was still slightly salty, but we had filtered it enough that it wasn't unbearable, and it quenched our thirst.

"Another banana?" He handed one to me as we watched the sunset.

"Thanks." I took it from him gratefully.

"Would you like one, Steve?"

"I'd like a big, fat, juicy steak with scalloped potatoes and mixed veggies." Steve smiled at me. "And for dessert, a big slice of cherry cheesecake."

"Don't," I groaned. "That sounds so good."

"Doesn't it though?" He grinned at me and took the banana from Jakob. "This doesn't quite match up, does it?"

"No, it doesn't." I chewed on my banana and sat back. "But it's so pretty here. Whoever kidnapped us all really chose a beautiful spot."

"We should really talk and see what we can figure out." Steve's expression changed, and he looked at Jakob and me carefully. "I'd like to know if we have any connections."

"I'd like to know that as well." I nodded and thought back to Jakob's earlier comments.

"Tomorrow." Jakob stood up. "We're all tired right now. We might miss something. Let's talk tomorrow morning when we're all fresh."

"I'd rather talk—" I started, but Jakob grabbed my arms and pulled me up into his arms. I fell against him, and he grinned before his lips crushed down on mine. I melted against him, and my hands flew to his face as he kissed me hard.

"I'd rather make love," he whispered against my lips as he pulled away slightly.

"Jakob!" I gasped, and looked down at Steve, who was staring at us with narrow eyes.

"Don't worry, Steve. Bianca and I won't shock you tonight. Though it will be hard for me to keep my hands off her. I won't lie."

"I don't blame you." Steve stood up. "I'm not sure I'd be able to resist, myself." He looked to the ocean. "I'll go farther down the beach and sleep there, give you both some privacy."

"Oh, you don't have to do that," I called out after him as he started walking, but he didn't stop.

"Let him go." Jakob's hand rubbed my back. "We have things to do tonight."

"I don't do casual sex," I muttered, and tried not to stare at the front of his boxer briefs. Of course, my eyes couldn't turn away as I stared at the huge bulge. I shifted my position and looked up to see him staring at me with an intense expression.

"I wasn't talking about sex," he said slowly and seductively, as his eyes dropped to my breasts.

It took everything in me not to place my hands over my skimpy bra. I'd almost forgotten that I was standing here in my underwear. I'd taken his shirt off after it had gotten wet in the ocean. Now I was once again fully aware of how close to naked I was and how close to naked he was as well. I swallowed hard as I felt an imperceptible change in the mood. It was no longer light but filled with sexual tension.

"I see." I spoke, wanting to fill the air with something other than anticipation.

"What do you see?" He leaned back, and I watched as he stretched his arms out. The muscles in his chest rippled, and I swallowed hard, praising myself for not reaching over and running my fingers down his chest.

"Um, what?" I mumbled as he adjusted himself.

"Bianca, I think we should sleep side by side so that we can keep each other warm, and we need Steve to believe that we are together. Our clothes are still damp, so we can't really put them back on tonight."

"Yeah, I guess."

I shivered at the thought of him pressed against me. It would feel different from when we had been in the back of the trunk and lying next to each other last night. In the trunk, I'd been scared and worried. I also hadn't known yet how hot he was. And we'd been dressed. Last night, I'd been fearful for my life. I hadn't trusted him, and we hadn't been touching as we slept. Now, well . . . now it was a different story. I already felt slightly turned on.

I wanted to groan. How could I be in this situation? If David knew how turned on I was right now, he'd be furious. He'd always called me frigid and a prude, but that hadn't been it. I'd just never really been that sexually attracted to him, even though he'd been very handsome. I shook my head slightly as I thought about David. It was over, and I was glad it was over. I didn't want to waste any more time thinking about him.

"I can tell you're cold." He grinned, and I cocked my head to the side.

"How?"

"Your nipples look as hard as pebbles."

"Oh!" I gasped, in shock at his words.

"Or are you just happy to see me?" His eyes fell to my

heaving breasts again, and he licked his lips slowly. "I won't be upset if you say that's why."

"You're disgusting." I glared at him.

"And you're wet." He spoke softly and took a step toward me.

"I'm not wet." I shook my hair and felt drops of water cascade down my back.

"Liar," he whispered.

"What?" I gasped as he placed a hand on my stomach and allowed his fingers to slide down. "What are you doing?"

"I just wanted to show you how wet you were." His fingers left my stomach and he wiggled them in my face. I could see drops of moisture on the tips. "See?" He grinned, and I watched as he licked the drops off his fingers.

～

We picked up our clothes and laid them out on the sand a bit farther away from the water, moving in silence. I was still slightly turned on from our interaction, yet I was also annoyed with myself and with him. I wasn't sure why I hadn't slapped him for being so fresh. I so wanted to put him in his place, but a part of me really enjoyed the innuendos. When he flirted with me, it was easier for me to forget where we were and the circumstances we were in. I was still completely puzzled as to why we were here. It made absolutely no sense to me. And while it made no sense, I was going to go along with his facade that we were together.

"We should talk before Steve gets back." Jakob's voice was low. "I think we need to make sure that we only talk about personal stuff when he's not around."

"Makes sense. At least the police must be looking for us," I muttered as we sat down on the sand.

"You think so?" He gave me a deep look.

"Of course." I nodded. "Rosie's probably freaking out right now. She knows I'm not the sort to just disappear. Plus, I left her some stuff in her bag. When she sees it, I hope she figures out that I was onto something."

"Onto what?" He asked curiously. "Or are you not going to tell me?"

"I want to tell you." I could feel my head pounding as I stared at him. "It's just hard. You'd be the first person I tell. I haven't even told Rosie yet, though, I wanted to tell her that night." I froze as I remembered something. "Oh my God, I might have taken a photo of the guy that was following me as well."

"Huh?" His eyes narrowed.

"I sent Rosie a photo of the bartender that night to get her to hurry up, as she was running late. I thought a handsome man might make her move faster." I thought back to the night I was in the bar and tried to remember if anyone else had been in the frame of the picture.

"I see." He frowned. "You seem a bit man-crazy."

"What?" My voice rose, and I glared at him. "What does that mean?"

"Just that you seem to date around a lot." He shrugged.

"You get that because I took a photo of a guy in a bar?" I cocked my head to the side as my annoyance showed through my rigid voice. "That's how you respond to the fact that I might have sent a photo of someone who was involved in our kidnapping to my best friend."

"I was just stating a fact, based on my observation of you. You dated that rich guy, and then you were online looking for someone, and now you're picking up guys in bars."

My jaw dropped as he spoke. He had a better memory than I did, but he was really twisting things. "I never said I was picking up any guys in the bar." I shook my head. "You really like to jump to conclusions, don't you."

"I know I don't let my women get around." His eyes bored into mine. "When a woman is with me, she's with me alone."

"I don't cheat on guys." I stared back into his eyes. "If that's what you're implying."

"When a woman is with me, she doesn't even think of another man," he continued, and sat back. I tried to ignore his muscles as they flexed.

"Good for you. I'm sure that's hard for them."

"I don't do back talk either."

"You sound like a real prince to date." I rolled my eyes. "Are you a boyfriend or a teacher?"

"I'm both." He grinned. "But, we digress. If you have a photo of that man it would be great. However, right now that doesn't really help us, does it?"

"No, I guess it doesn't." I stared at his face for a few seconds, studying his eyes and then looking at his body language. I knew that I either was going to have to trust him or not, but I had to make a decision. I could feel the nerves in my stomach as I tried to make a decision; each one was more wound up than the other. "My father left me a letter when he died." I said finally, the words sounding stilted as they came out of my mouth.

"Okay . . ."

"I think I was being followed because of the letter." I gazed out at the ocean. "Actually, that's not exactly right. I was being followed because of what I did after I read the letter."

"What did the letter say, and what did you do?"

"You've got to understand that this isn't me." I looked back at him with a frown. "If you would have told me five years ago that I'd be acting like some older version of Nancy Drew, I would have told you you were lying."

"Nancy Drew, huh?" He raised an eyebrow. "That must have been some letter."

"It was." I chewed on my lower lip for a few seconds before continuing. I needed to make sure I was making the right decision, but I knew that there was no way for me to be certain of that fact. I knew that between Jakob and Steve, I trusted Jakob the most.

"So, are you going to tell me anything else?"

"My father was poor when he died. He didn't leave a will, he didn't have anything to leave in his will. He had no money.

Though, he should have had millions. He invented the self-painting machine, the thirty-minute cooker, and the first prototype for the mini car."

"Really?" He looked back at me with a blank expression that surprised me. Most people were shocked and amazed to find out my father had created so many products that had changed the way millions lived their lives.

"Yes, really." I snapped, annoyed by his lack of reaction, not knowing why I felt so upset. I knew a part of it had to do with the fact that I was trusting him with something I'd never told anyone before, and he wasn't reacting in the way I'd hoped he would. "So when he died, he basically left me a letter that told me that he didn't trust his old business partners. He left me some papers that led me to believe that he should own the rights and be receiving the royalties for those products."

"I see." He pursed his lips. "So you're trying to get the money you think is yours, is that it?"

"Yeah." I nodded and looked away from him again. I wasn't sure why I didn't tell him about my mother's car accident and the fact that my father had believed that she'd been killed. I didn't tell him that the real reason I was investigating was to get justice for my mother. I wasn't sure that he'd understand. I thought back to the letter my father had left me; the letter that had led to my kidnapping and being stuck on this island.

My Dearest Bianca,

My darling daughter, as I lie here writing this letter, there are so many things I wish I could go back and change.

First, let me apologize to you. I spent too many years carrying around my grief at your mother's death that there are many times I didn't fully appreciate how alive we both still were.

Your mother meant the world to me and I see her living on in you. She would be so proud of the historian you've become. Stay inquisitive and beautiful, my darling. I'm so sorry that I wasn't able to leave you anything in my will. I wasted my life away and there are many things I wish I had told you before today.

There's one thing I think you should know. One thing I've agonized over telling you. I don't think your mother's car crash was an accident. As I've gone through my papers and recalled various conversations from the days before her death, it has occurred to me that there may have been people that wanted to see me incapacitated. People that knew that your mother's death would change everything in my life.

My darling, I may not be able to leave you riches in the bank, but go through the papers in the box and you might find the truth. The truth will provide for your children and bring justice for your mother's death. Writing this letter and knowing how strong you are is giving me great solace in the sadness of my last days. All I ask is that you be careful

of who you trust. Friends can be foes and foes can be friends.
Remember that I love you and I'm sorry.
Fight on like your beloved Mary, Queen of Scots.

All my love,
Papa

"Are you okay, Bianca?" Jakob moved closer to me. I could see the concern in his eyes. "You just spaced out for a long time."

"I was just thinking of my dad." My body trembled as his fingers ran down my arm.

"Thinking about the money?" His mouth twisted and I sighed. Jakob was really preoccupied with money. It seemed like he became irritated every time the subject was brought up. I was going to have to remember that.

"No, I was just wondering if we were kidnapped because the Bradleys think I'm about to take over their company." I chewed on my lower lip. "A police officer, or someone posing as a police officer, came to my house recently. I'm pretty sure he was look-ing for some papers my father left me. Some papers that might entitle me to a majority share in Bradley Inc. Ever since I told my ex that I wanted to do some research on the company and meet his brother, Mattias, strange things have been happening."

"Your ex, David?"

"Yes."

"So you told your ex that you think you're the rightful owner of his family company?"

"No, not exactly. I told him that my father used to work there and I was doing research on his inventions. The self-painter has revolutionized the way people get their home painted. It costs less than fifty dollars, and a room is primed and painted in an hour. The paint he created to work with the self-painter is only sold by Bradley Inc., and it made their company tens of billions of dollars last year. Even contractors are using it for their businesses."

"I know what the self-painter does." His voice was dry. "Let me get this straight. You told your ex-boyfriend that your father created the product, actually multiple products, that made his family company one of the largest corporations in the world. And then you told him you were doing research on said company, and you expected that he'd be cool with that?"

"I just wanted to talk to his brother, Mattias, the CEO. I know he has access to the files. I know his father had to have told him where the private files are kept." My words tripped out of my mouth in a hurry as I sought to explain to him, why I'd tried to incorporate David's help. "I just needed David to introduce me to Mattias."

"That was pretty convenient that you ended up dating the heir to the company you were researching." His eyes bored into mine and I didn't even flinch at his question.

"Yes, it was." I smiled widely at him. There was no way I was going to tell him how hard I had to work to get into a relationship with David. I was embarrassed by some of the things I'd done. Not even David knew the truth about our meeting.

"So did you meet Mattias then?" He leaned back and rested on his elbows as he stared at me.

"No." My face paled as I remembered the phone call from David that told me his brother had no interest in meeting me. His voice had sounded odd, as if he'd been coached. "I never got to meet him. In fact, I don't even know what he looks like."

"How can that be?"

"I don't know. The only information online about him is a brief blurb on the company website saying he is the CEO. He has no web footprint whatsoever."

"Weird. I wish I knew how he did that. There are things I'd love to get erased from online."

"So that's basically it. A couple of days after David's call, I started feeling like I was being watched. And then the letters came. And the police incident." I stopped then and looked around me. "And here I am. Or I guess here we are." I looked at the dark sky and stared at the stars glittering down at me. I felt as if they were communicating with me, telling me to keep some things to myself.

"That's all of it?" I could hear the question in his voice. It was almost as if he knew that I was holding back part of the story. It was almost as if he knew that there were other things that David had told me. Things that I definitely was not going to share.

"Yeah, that's it." I said, and ran my hands down my

matted hair and attempted to comb the knots out with my fingertips. I grimaced at the frizzy mess that met my touch and cried out as I yanked a few hairs too roughly. "Ouch."

"Hey, be careful with yourself." Jakob reached over and touched my hand and pulled it away from my hair. "Leave it alone. It looks fine."

"Sure it does." I smiled at him. "No need to lie to me."

"It's natural." He smiled, his eyes lightening as the conversation changed. "I like women who are more natural." His fingers touched the top of my head and then ran down the arch of my nose. "Your cheeks look rosy red and I know that's not from blusher or bronzer." He leaned forward and lightly licked my cheek. "Yup, no taste of makeup."

"Obviously." I stared back at him in shock, I could still feel the tip of his tongue on me and my body was on high alert, waiting to see what he was going to do next. "So do you have a girlfriend?" I asked softly, pretending like I didn't care about his answer.

"No." He laughed heartily. "I don't do girlfriends."

"Oh, okay." I wasn't sure if I was happy or sad at his response.

"Though I don't expect my woman to mess around."

"What do you mean?"

"I'm just saying, when a woman is with me, there is no one else in her life. When I take a lover, she knows I own her body."

"I see." I bit my lower lip and squirmed in the sand, imagining him as a lover.

"But that's neither here nor there." He looked away and lay back. "Shall we try to sleep now? We should get up early and explore part of the jungle. I think we should try to wake up before Steve gets up. I want us to explore the jungle without him. See if we see anything suspicious."

"Suspicious like what?"

"I don't know." His eyes darkened. "A gun maybe?"

"What?" My eyes stared into his. "You think he has a gun?"

"I don't know." He shook his head. "But I think we need to figure out how he ended up on the island with us. And he's been on his walk for an awfully long time. It makes me wonder where he's gone. Why would a man with a limp be venturing on a long walk in the evening by himself on an island with two strangers?" His eyes pierced into mine. "It doesn't make sense. We need to figure out why he's on the island."

"But we don't even know why *we're* on the island." I stared at him and then at the darkened figure of Steve farther down the beach as he walked back toward us. "He's on the way back."

"Let's change the subject now." He looked toward Steve and then leaned toward me. "I trust you." His voice was soft. "Though you could be a wolf in sheep's clothing." He paused. "Anyway, tomorrow we should go explore in the jungle. I also think that's going to be our best bet for finding fresh water."

"Okay."

I lay back on the sand and stared at the sky. Our shoulders

rubbed together, and I closed my eyes, wondering if he was going to suggest that we snuggle up. He didn't say anything, but I felt him reach out for me and pull me toward him. I lay there on my side with my back to his chest, and I closed my eyes as my body started trembling slightly at being so close to him.

"You're too close." I shifted slightly away from him. I was uncomfortable being so close together—or rather, I was uncomfortable feeling his practically naked body pushed up against mine. And when I say uncomfortable, I mean I loved it. I was most uncomfortable because I wasn't sure if I was going to be able to prevent myself from turning over and running my fingers across his chest.

"That's the point, isn't it?" he whispered against the back of my head. "That's how we'll stay warm."

"I'm plenty warm already, thanks." I turned around abruptly as I felt his manhood push up against my ass. "I think it's better if we face each other," I continued weakly, not wanting him to see how he was affecting me.

"I don't mind that at all." He grinned and pulled me toward him. "Not at all."

I groaned inwardly when I felt his hardness press against my stomach and my breasts press against his chest. This position was even worse, even more intimate, and I shifted again. Only this time, my legs grazed his and we both froze for a moment as a small spark of electricity passed through us.

"So tell me more about you." He spoke softly as his finger

idly trailed down my arm. "The you that's not connected to getting the money you think you're owed."

"There's not much to tell," I mumbled, and then paused. What the hell did his comment about money mean? I was about to ask him, but I knew Steve was getting closer. I couldn't risk getting into an argument with Jakob with Steve so close.

I was also finding it hard to think straight. My body felt like it was starting to catch fire, and all I could think about was how raw and masculine he smelled. I so badly wanted to run my fingertips down his chest and then across the stubble on his face, but I managed to stop myself.

"The more we know about each other, the easier it will be for us to figure out why we're here."

"I guess." I sighed and looked into his eyes. "Though, I can't see why anyone would kidnap the two of us. I'm really a nobody, asides from the investigation. I can't think of a reason why anyone else would want to kidnap me."

"Nobody's a nobody," he said, and then we both laughed.

"Well, I don't have any money. My father was pretty lower-middle class. He was an inventor like I said, though he didn't get credit for any of his inventions that became a big hit. My mother died when I was just a kid. My dad never re-married. I went to college, studied history, got a job working as a researcher for a well-known historian, he helped get me into the master's program at Columbia. I was going to go on for my PhD, but my father died, and things changed." I was silent for a few seconds. "I found his letter and decided to focus my energies on finding out the truth, and so I took a leave of absence from the program and my job. Now I'm self-employed." I smiled then. "And I make less than forty grand a year, so if anyone is trying to make money off me, they're in for a surprise."

"Your dad didn't leave you any money?" He frowned.

"Did you not just hear me when I said he didn't make much money?" I laughed.

"I suppose that's why you like dating rich men, then, huh?"

"Excuse me?" I pulled away from him then and jumped up. "What's that supposed to mean?"

"I'm just saying most women in your position would be happy to date and marry a rich guy, right? And it's obvious you've got an eye for the finer things in life."

"What are you talking about?" I glared at him as he jumped up and stood next to me.

"Isn't that ultimately what this is all about? You trying to get access to the money that a large corporation made off your father's inventions?"

"No," I hissed at him angrily. Did he really have that little respect for me? I knew that he didn't know me well, but I was still hurt by his assumptions, even if that was what I'd led him to believe.

"Shh." He grabbed me and pulled me into his arms. "Steve is looking over at us." He kissed the side of my neck gently as his fingers ran down my back and cupped my ass. I felt my anger subsiding at his touch and I felt strangely bereft when he pulled away from me.

I tried to ignore how glorious his body looked in the moonlight. He was so virile and strong. If he wanted to take me, all he would have to do is pin me to the ground and kiss me. His strength would be a big turn-on, especially if he just ripped my panties off. I could feel myself growing wet at the thought. If he wanted me, he could have me.

"It's not anything bad to be impressed by wealth, Bianca. Plenty of women and men have been blindsided by the allure of money. I'm not saying this as disrespect to your character, but it's something I've noticed. I mean just earlier, look how quickly you recognized my Rolex." He continued talking about money as if he had no idea at the inner sexual turmoil running through my mind.

"Only because my ex had one."

"Exactly my point." He smirked.

"How is that your point?"

"You dated a man rich enough to own a Rolex."

"Are you kidding me? David's money didn't matter to me. I didn't even know David was rich when I first met him." I shook my head at him. Though, only part of that was true. I did know that David was rich, but his money had been the last thing on my mind when I met him.

"Really? How's that possible? Girls like you seek out rich men."

"Girls like me?" I gaped at him.

"Women who try to use their looks and body to trap a man."

"Are you joking? This isn't a real-life remake of *How to Marry a Millionaire.*"

"What?" He looked confused.

"It was a movie with Marilyn Monroe and—"

"I don't need the details." He cut me off. "Why did you bring it up?"

"Because you insinuated that I'm trying to use my looks to catch rich men, as if I can't provide for myself. I've never tried to date a guy because he has money."

"My apologies," he shrugged. "I guess I've been around too many beautiful women that have tried to use me and then tried to trap me for my money."

I stared at him in shock for a few moments. I'm embarrassed to admit that a part of me was flattered by what he'd said. I didn't consider myself any great beauty, and I knew I didn't have the skinniest or hottest body out there. I was pretty sure that, even if I'd wanted to, I wouldn't have been able to trap a rich man.

"You're an asshole," I finally muttered. "I didn't trap anyone."

"So you don't want a man with money?"

"No." I walked to the water's edge and stared at the illuminated ripples of water as they ebbed and flowed.

"I'm sorry if I offended you." Jakob walked up next to me, reached out, and touched my shoulder. "Like I said, I'm accustomed to many women in the city approaching me because I have money. I didn't mean to displace that onto you."

"It's fine." I shrugged but didn't look at him. I was so angry that he would associate me with a gold digger, when I was anything but one. I felt so hurt inside. I'd trusted him enough to tell him part of my story. The fact that I was attracted to him made me feel like I'd made a mistake in telling him anything. Maybe I was letting my physical attraction to him override my gut instincts.

"Stand still," he whispered. "Steve is watching us. I don't want him to think we're arguing."

I nodded and remained still.

"It's a gorgeous night, isn't it?" he asked softly, and I just nodded again in response. "I love the water."

"So do I."

"This is exactly the sort of place I'd choose to be lost in if I had a choice," he continued, and I looked at him for a second. There was a strange tone in his voice, and I realized that he looked sad.

"You okay?" It was my turn to touch his shoulder, and he looked at me with dark eyes.

"That's the ultimate question, isn't it?" He gave me a wry smile. "How do we ever really know if we are okay? I'm physically okay. I'm mentally okay. I'm emotionally okay. Yet I'm stuck on an island with someone I don't know and I have no idea what's going to happen. That should scare me. That should have me freaking out."

"And it doesn't?"

"I don't know." He shrugged. "I really don't know."

"I just don't understand why we're here. Why us? Why you? Why me?" I cried out. "Why him?" I whispered and nodded toward Steve.

"And why bring us to this island?" His eyes narrowed. "There has to be a reason."

"Do you think we're going to die?"

"Not if I have anything to do with it." He pulled me toward him, and I rested my head on his shoulder, enjoying the feel of his body against mine.

He was warm and hard. He felt solid, and that's what I needed. His hands slid around my waist, and I felt them on my ass, softly stroking and pulling me toward him. I looked up at him, and he was already gazing down at me with open, questioning eyes.

"I see what you were talking about with your eyes before." He spoke lightly. "They seem to be changing from green to brown right before me."

"It's the moonlight and refraction." I smiled up at him weakly. "The way the light bounces off my irises makes them appear different colors."

"They're beautiful." He leaned down and stared into them more intensely.

I could feel my heart beating rapidly as his hands moved up and caressed my back. His lips moved closer to mine, and within seconds, they were pressed down on mine.

At first, his kiss was soft and sweet, and I kissed him back gently, wanting to enjoy the moment. All too soon, his lips moved more urgently, crushing into mine as his tongue demanded entry into my mouth. His tongue was salty and rough as it entered my mouth. He was all-consuming, and I was immediately overwhelmed as he sucked on my tongue and ran his hands through my tangled hair.

I pressed against him and ran my hands down his back. It felt as magnificent as I had imagined, and I moaned as I pushed into him harder. A guttural groan escaped his lips as he pulled back from me slightly. I didn't know if this was real or part of the act.

"I'm so hard right now. I want to fuck you very badly, Bianca." His eyes bored into mine, unsmiling.

"Don't look so happy about it," I quipped back with my heart racing.

"This is no time to be making jokes." He pulled me toward him, hard.

"I wasn't joking," I whispered, and shifted against him slightly.

He gasped as my hand accidentally brushed against his cock, and he grabbed it. "Don't tease me." He held my hand in his, and I swallowed hard.

"I'm not teasing you." I shook my head at him, not sure what he was talking about.

"You feel this?" He brought my hand to his briefs and pressed it against his cock. "I'm rock hard right now," he muttered. "I want to push you down onto the ground and fuck you so hard that you'll forget that you met me only two days ago."

I swallowed hard as my palm pressed against him. I could tell that he wasn't lying. He was hard and thick against my hands, and it took everything in me to not grab him and squeeze him between my fingers.

"So what are you going to do?" I finally spoke, and he sighed.

"We're just going to go to sleep." He dropped my hand. "Though that's going to be hard for me. Ignore the unintended pun." He winked down at me.

"So this isn't awkward or anything." I took a step back and gently rubbed my bruised lips.

"You look so sexy." He sighed as he stared at me. "I want to push you down on all fours and take you from behind. I'll pull your hair as I enter you, and you'll scream out my name." He cleared his throat then. "Come on. Let's just get some sleep."

"Are you sure you don't need to take care of business first?" I stared at his crotch meaningfully as he laughed.

"Do *you* need to take care of business?" He looked down at my crotch, and I crossed my legs. There was no way I was going to let him know how heavy and wet my panties felt.

"I'm fine," I lied, and walked back to where our clothes were. "I'm going to sleep now."

"I'll join you." He walked besides me. "Hopefully tomorrow we can figure out some answers."

"Yeah." I nodded. "I sure hope so." I sat back down and stretched out on the sand.

Jakob lay behind me and spooned me. I felt his cock press into me as his arms slid around my waist, but I didn't complain this time. I didn't even think about how right it felt to be wrapped in his arms when I had only just met him.

I wished that I could call Rosie then to figure out what she thought. She was probably panicking right now. She'd left me at the table to go to the washroom and when she'd come back, I was gone. Whoever had kidnapped me had to have dosed the wine I'd been given. That meant it had been premeditated, which meant it wasn't a mistake that I was here, as I'd partly hoped. Someone had wanted me, Bianca London, on this island for a reason. A reason I thought I knew. Until I realized that I wasn't alone. I thought I knew why I was here, but why were Jakob and Steve with me. I had nothing guiding me as to why.

I shivered slightly as I realized the severity of the situation. Jakob's hands wrapped around my body tightly, and I snuggled back into his arms and closed my eyes. I didn't know if I liked Jakob all that much, though, I was wildly attracted to him. But I was definitely glad that I was here with him and not alone. I would never admit it to him but being wrapped in his arms made me feel safe—well, as safe as I could feel in this situation. My mind drifted to Rosie and the package. I was praying that she'd found it in her handbag and had gone to the police. She might not understand what all the papers meant, but someone in the police department should. Hopefully it would at least lead them in the direction of the Bradleys.

I fell asleep quickly. I guess the day had exhausted me, and even though I wanted to enjoy being cuddled next to Jakob, I

couldn't keep my eyes open. My dreams were sweet and delicious, and I didn't want them to end. However, a hand fond-
ling my right breast stirred me out of my slumber. My eyes
opened slowly, and I realized that I couldn't have slept for
very long. The sun hadn't risen yet. I lay still for a second and
felt Jakob's hand groping my breast.

"Jakob," I hissed as his fingers pinched my nipple. I
shifted away and groaned as I realized that I was firmly en-
sconced in his arms. "Jakob, are you awake?" I murmured,
but there was no response from him.

I lay there for a second, wondering what I should do,
when I heard a light snore coming from behind me. So he
was asleep—unless he was faking it. And I didn't think he was
faking it. I grabbed his arm and pushed it down to my waist.
My breast felt abandoned for a few brief seconds, but I soon
began to drift off again myself.

I was almost asleep, when I felt his fingers running back
and forth across my stomach. I felt slightly self-conscious as
his fingers unconsciously caressed me. I definitely didn't have
abs or a flat stomach, and that was obvious to anyone who
touched me. I didn't move his hand though. I enjoyed the
feel of his fingers against my warm skin. It was harmless, and
it wasn't like he knew. I smiled to myself as I lay there and
snuggled back into him.

I closed my eyes again and imagined what it would feel
like to make love to him. Would he be a skillful lover? I supposed he had to be. I imagined that he would be if his kiss
was anything to go by. He would probably be very alpha and

dominant. He seemed the sort to like control. I wondered if he was into BDSM or other kinky stuff. He had mentioned the Marquis de Sade to me earlier. What if he tried to take me over his lap and spank me? I shivered as I imagined his hands on my ass again. Only this time, he wasn't caressing my ass— he was being rougher.

I moved backward slightly as I felt myself becoming turned on. My dream was so vivid that I could almost feel his hands teasing and tormenting me. My dream became dirtier as his fingers moved from my ass to my panties. His fingers gently rubbed the skin at the top of my panties for a few seconds before moving forward and sliding between my legs.

He was testing the waters at first, because he slid only one finger gently down to my panties. My legs parted involuntarily as another finger joined the first one, and his movements grew rougher and more urgent. I moaned as his fingers rubbed against my panty-covered clit. I wanted to feel his fingers directly on my skin. I wanted to feel him inside me.

I waited for him to explore further, and I wasn't disappointed when, a few seconds later, I felt his fingers slip inside my panties and start to gently rub me. I spread my legs, trying to give him easier access, yet his hand felt like it was at an odd angle. I closed my legs slightly and trapped his fingers there.

I could feel myself growing wetter as his fingers moved roughly in the tight space. It felt so good. I smiled to myself as he played with me, and then I froze as something in my consciousness woke up. I wasn't dreaming.

My eyes fluttered open, and I realized that Jakob's fingers were in my panties, and he was rubbing my clit. I knew that I should push him away and sleep on my own, but I hesitated for a few moments as I felt my orgasm building up. The devil inside me didn't want it to end. It felt so good. His fingers knew exactly how to please me. I knew I should stop it, but I just wanted to feel it for a few more seconds.

I was about to push his arm away, when he woke up. I knew he had gained consciousness immediately because his breathing changed and his hand stilled.

"Bianca?" he whispered as he pulled his fingers out of my panties. His voice sounded tormented, and I could tell that he felt ashamed of what had happened.

"Yes?" I whispered back, though part of me told me to pretend to be asleep.

"You're awake!" He sounded surprised. "I'm so sorry about that," he muttered, and rolled me over to face him.

"I was about to push your arm away." I blushed defensively. "I just woke up."

"I'm sorry." His eyes gleamed at me. "I didn't even realize I was doing that."

"It's fine." I stared at his lips and noticed that he was breathing harder than usual. "Are you okay?"

"I'm hard," he muttered, and groaned.

"Oh." I bit my lower lip, wanting to look down but not wanting him to see me looking.

"You were wet again." He winked at me, but I didn't laugh. My panties were completely wet, and it was no laughing matter. He reached his fingers up to his mouth and sucked them, his eyes still staring into mine. "Though you taste better than the sea," he groaned as he licked his fingers clean.

I stared at him for a few more seconds, and then I did something that surprised both of us. I reached down, rubbed the front of his briefs, and then gingerly grabbed his cock.

"You weren't joking." I smiled at him. "You're very hard."

"I never joke." His eyes darkened as he looked down at my hand and then back up to my face. "I think we should go back to sleep now."

"Okay." I nodded and stared at him, my hand moving away from his hardness.

"Good night, Bianca." He kissed my forehead and brought me into his arms.

"Good night, Jakob," I whispered and looked up the beach.

I could see Steve sitting up and looking in our direction. I wondered how much he'd seen. I shivered and rested my head back down next to Jakob. I closed my eyes again and snuggled next to his chest. This time, I fell asleep and didn't wake back up until just before sunrise.

~⊃

The next morning, I woke up before both men and walked to the ocean to think. It was still dark, but the sun was just beginning to rise. I was confused about my growing attraction to Jakob. My body and mind reacted to him in ways I'd never reacted to anyone before. There was some sort of instant chemistry between us that I couldn't break. Every time he was close to me, I felt as if there was a slow buzz of electricity running back and forth between us. It was like he made me feel more alive, only I wasn't generally one for romantic epithets and foolish thoughts. I almost wished that I'd met him online or in the real world somehow. That way I'd be able to trust him more and we'd have been able to get to know each other in normal circumstances.

"The ocean looks like a magnificent creature in the beauty of the day, does she not?" Steve's voice interrupted my thoughts and I nodded without looking at him.

"She looks magnificent at night as well though."

"Indeed she does, but at night, her treacherous waves are dark and subtle. During the day her hidden danger lies right before us but eludes us with its magnanimity."

"I suppose so." I agreed again, not really sure what he was talking about. If he wanted to say the ocean was dangerous, why didn't he just say so?

"The ocean plays an illusion on our minds." He continues. "It is so easy to perceive her wrongly."

"What do you mean?"

"On the surface, the water looks calm, does it not?" He took a few steps in and touched the water. "And even here, the water is gentle." He splashed around a little. "She is able to deceive us with her gentleness. However, if I were to go farther in, if I were to attempt to swim out in her graceful waters, I'd realize that looks can be deceiving. I'd be caught up in her currents. The undertow would suck me in. I'd be lucky if I made it out of the water alive."

"Well, of course you have to be careful how far you swim in the ocean. Everyone knows that. That's why they have buoys at the beach saying don't swim too far. You never know when the undercurrent is going to sweep you away."

"Exactly. That's the perfect phrase." He nodded. "You never know when the ocean is going to sweep you away. It is much better to avoid the possibility, don't you agree?"

"I'm not going to venture in too deep, so that's not a problem."

"If only it were that simple." He gave me an odd little smile and stared at my face. "Long night? You don't look like you slept well."

"It's hard sleeping on the sand." I shrugged. "My back's not accustomed to it."

"I've slept on the floor for the last five years of my life. This feels like heaven to me." He smiled and stretched. "Though, in the light of the day, I do have more questions as to how I got here and why."

"So you no longer think you're on the same island as your resort?"

"Considering how sparse this setting is, I'd say I'm pretty definitely not on the same island."

"So what do you think happened?"

"I think that someone's playing a sick trick on me."

"A trick?" I frowned. Who on earth would pull a trick like this? And why was he still acting so calm as if it were perfectly normal to wake up on an island with two strangers who had been kidnapped?

"You know. A trick? Also known as a prank." He shrugged.

"Who were you at the resort with?" I frowned.

"My wife." He paused, and I could see something going through his head. I was almost certain that he was lying—I was pretty confident he wasn't married. He wore no wedding band and there was no tan line on his wedding finger. The way he stared at me was also too interested. I mean, I understood that there are married men everywhere who still have their eyes open to other women, but this felt different. I was almost positive that he wanted me, in a very obvious way.

"Have you been married long, then?"

"No, this is our honeymoon." The lie slipped easily out of his mouth and I wondered why he would make up such a story.

"I'm sorry your wife played a prank like this on your honeymoon." I replied smoothly, and I saw the expression in his eyes change slightly. He knew that I wasn't swallowing his story. I stretched my arms and yawned. "You'll have to excuse me. I think I'm going to go lie down again. See if I can catch some more sleep before Jakob wakes up."

"He's lucky to have a girl like you." Steve called after me

as I walked away. "There aren't many things I wouldn't do to call someone like you my girlfriend."

My pace increased as I walked back to Jakob, and I lay down next to him with my heart beating fast. What had Steve meant? Was he threatening me? I shivered as I cuddled up next to Jakob and closed my eyes. I could feel that Steve was watching the two of us and so I gave Jakob a quick kiss on the cheek before wrapping his arms around me. Even though I was wary of my attraction to Jakob, I still knew in my heart that, of the two men, he was the one I'd much rather be aligned with.

six

There's a certain hollowness you feel when you're all alone in nature. It's an empty feeling that rattles in your head as you realize that you're all alone, even if you're with someone else. It's that feeling that pops up in all of us sometimes. The feeling that makes us ask the ultimate question—what's the point of it all? That's how I felt as I stared out at the ocean in her ominous glory. For while she was beautiful, she was still treacherous. The crashing waves against the rocks told me that if I were to swim out too far, I'd get stuck in her currents and washed out to sea. Not even Jakob could save me then.

Not that I wanted him to save me. I still wasn't sure how I felt about him. There was something in his blue eyes that reminded me of the ocean—seemingly so open yet so deep and dark that it couldn't be trusted. That didn't mean that I wasn't attracted to him. How could I not be? He was gorgeous. There was something so primal and raw about him, though I suppose that came from being on a deserted island.

I started laughing then. I was surely going crazy. I'd been close to tears just a few moments ago, and now all I could think about were Jakob's muscles.

"Bianca!" He shouted my name as if he knew I was thinking of him.

"Yes?" I answered, glad to be away from my thoughts.

"Where are you?" he called, his voice sounding closer.

"I'm at the shoreline!" I shouted back, staring once again at the ocean.

"What do you think you're doing?" he ran toward me and then hissed, annoyed. "You can't just disappear like that." He slowed his pace as he walked up to me, and I could see the displeasure in his stern face.

"We're on a deserted island." I rolled my eyes. "I wouldn't worry so much."

"We don't really know where we are." He grabbed my hand roughly and pulled me toward him. "Steve came out of nowhere; we don't really know if anyone else is here with us. We need to be careful." His fingers dug into my skin and I glared up at his face. I could see that his stubble was thicker today. Without thinking, I reached up and ran my fingers across his jawbone. His hair was prickly beneath my fingers, and he stilled as I touched him. He released his hold on my other hand, and I reached my other fingers up to touch his lips. I gasped as he opened his mouth slightly and sucked my finger in like a vacuum. He bit down on my finger and then nibbled it gently, his eyes never leaving mine. My other hand moved from his jawline up to his hair. I pulled my finger out of his mouth slowly, and he grabbed my head and tilted it up to him.

"Taste me," he grunted, and I looked up at him with a perplexed expression. Then he nodded toward my finger. I looked down and suddenly understood his comment. I reached the finger that had been in his mouth up to mine and slowly parted my lips and sucked on it. We stood there staring at each other as I sucked on my finger slowly and intently. I was mesmerized by the look of lust in his blue eyes. I took a step back from him, hoping that a little distance would stop my legs from trembling and my heart from beating so quickly. After a few seconds, I removed my finger from my mouth and then licked my lips slowly.

"The tide's coming in. You could have gotten stuck." He finally spoke and grabbed my arm again and pulled me toward him. "And I have no idea where Steve is. I was worried about you. Don't just disappear like that again. Are you stupid?"

"Let go of me." I looked up at him, annoyed, and tried to ignore the burn on my skin where he had touched me. "I'm not a little kid."

"You could have fooled me." He stared at me lips. "I ought to kiss you and show you that you can't go around just doing what you want."

"Did you come to harass me?" I sighed and crossed my arms. His eyes fell to my chest and lingered there, and I could feel my insides burning up at his stare. "I woke up, and you weren't there. I thought we were going to get up early so we could explore before Steve woke up. But I woke up, and both you and Steve were gone." I gave him an accusing look. "So I decided to take a walk."

"You should have waited for me." He crossed his arms. "What if something had happened?"

"What's going to happen?" I rolled my eyes. "At least we know where the rocks are." I shivered as I stared at the sharp treacherous rocks as the waves crashed into them. The water definitely was not as calm down here.

"For the record, when I woke up, you were still asleep. I didn't want to wake you, because you looked peaceful." He sighed and his eyes narrowed. "And Steve was already gone when I woke up."

"What?" I frowned. "Gone where?"

"I don't know." He shook his head and reached out to me. "I looked for him in the jungle, but I didn't see him."

"How could he just disappear?" I shivered.

"Like I said before, he seems to know his way around quite well." He grabbed my hand and squeezed. "That's why I've been telling you to stay close to me."

"You're the one that left me this morning." I was indignant at his authoritative tone. "It's not like we're in the Twilight Zone; nothing's going to happen. Like you said before, monsters aren't coming and I'm sure the Last Mimzy isn't coming either."

"Stranger things have happened." He looked away from me, and I gasped as I saw a cut on the side of his face, right next to his ear. There was a large bloody gash that looked like it was quite deep.

"Are you okay?" I frowned as I stared at the dried blood on his face. My fingers gingerly reached up to his face. "You're cut."

"I'm fine." He stepped away from me and ran his hands through his hair. I looked at his hands carefully. They looked dirty and bruised. I shivered as I remembered his fingers touching me the night before.

"What have you been doing?" I questioned him, not wanting to think about what had happened the previous evening. "Why do you have a cut on your face? Why are your hands bruised?" I whispered. My brain was screaming the question I was too scared to ask: *Did Steve really just go on a long walk by himself or did you do something to him?*

"I was in the jungle, looking for branches. I thought you'd like to have proper shelter tonight." He shrugged and walked away. "Apparently I was wrong."

"Don't tell me—you found a Marriott?" I attempted a joke to diffuse the tension in the air, but he gave me a derisive look that made me shut up.

"If it rains tonight, we're going to get soaked." He spoke matter-of-factly, and I stared at him silently. "I thought we could create a makeshift rooftop for shelter with some palm and coconut branches that are lying on the ground."

"Where?" I looked over to the bushes and shivered. There was something about the jungle behind us that scared me.

"We can set it up in the sand."

"How?" I frowned, not really seeing how that would be possible.

"Come with me and I'll show you." Jakob started walking away from me.

I couldn't stop staring at his strong, muscular legs. They were so tan and hairy. The white of his boxer shorts complemented his skin tone, and I swallowed hard as I stared at his butt. It looked firm, and I wondered if it was as tan as his legs. Or maybe it was pasty white like a baby's bottom. The thought made me giggle, and Jakob turned around and gave me a glance. He raised an eyebrow as if to say *Come on,* and I laughed even louder. It was hard for me to take him seriously as an autocrat when all I could think about was the whiteness of his ass.

"What are you laughing about, Bianca?" He didn't look amused, and I tried not to roll my eyes. He seriously was the most annoying man I'd ever met. He just did not seem to have a sense of humor.

"Do you really want to know?"

I gave him a quick smile, and he paused for a second. I saw a flash of something pass through his eyes as he stared at me. He looked unsure of himself for one split second, and then he frowned. I could feel that I was starting to lose it. Part of me was scared to death and the other part of me couldn't stop thinking about how sexy he was.

"What I want to do is get this shelter ready."

"I'm coming." I sighed and ran to catch up to him. "I was going to try to wash the sand off my body." I mumbled as I caught up with him.

"Oh." He looked at me, and there was a gleam in his eye. "I suppose you have sand in all sorts of cracks and crevices."

"I'm not an old house, Jakob, but yes, I do."

"So do I." He grinned. "And yes, it's a bit uncomfortable. If you want, we can go in the ocean and clean ourselves off before heading into the jungle."

"I suppose." I frowned. It sounded like a good idea, but I knew that I had to go completely naked to get the sand out of everywhere.

"What's wrong now?"

"I was just thinking that it's going to be hard to get the sand out everywhere." I shrugged and looked away from him. I didn't want him to see me blushing, though, I supposed it could be mistaken for sunburn.

"That's not a problem." He grinned and ran back to the ocean. "Just take your clothes off." I watched as he ran and pulled off his briefs. My breath caught as I stared at the creamy-white paleness of his taut bottom. I laughed at the contrast it made against his deep golden tan. "What's so funny?" He stopped and turned around and my breath caught as I realized he was facing me completely naked.

"Nothing." I called back to him and stared at his face. *Do not look down, Bianca.* My brain was screaming at me. *Do not look down.* Of course, my eyes didn't listen. I looked down and gasped. His penis was slightly erect and standing at attention. I looked back up at his face and he was grinning.

"Like what you see?" he shouted at me, with a slight laugh in his voice.

"I'm not sure what you're talking about." I looked down at the ground. "I didn't see anything."

"Pity." He laughed and turned back and ran into the ocean. I walked up to the water behind him and watched as he jumped in the waves and splashed himself. My eyes narrowed with jealousy as I imagined how good it would feel to strip off my underwear and go into the ocean as well. I hadn't been lying before. I literally had sand everywhere.

"What are you waiting for, Bianca?" Jakob turned around to face me. "Come on in." I stared at his silhouette in the ocean and tried not to fall in love with him then and there. He looked like Poseidon, king of the ocean, god of the sea, protector of all waters and me. His chest was built and strong, and it glittered like gold in the sunlight. I watched the water drops clinging to his chest and felt envious. In that moment, I would have liked to be a water drop, clinging to him for dear life.

"I can't come in." I shook my head. "I'm not running in naked."

"Don't be scared, Bianca." He teased me. "I won't bite." His grin showed off his perfectly white teeth, and of course now all I could think about was him biting every little part of my body. "Unless you want me to."

"I don't want you to and no, I'm not scared." I glared at him.

"It will feel good to get all the sand out, Bianca. Trust me."

"Fine." I walked into the ocean and moved away from him. "Don't come near me." I glared at him and then reached down and pulled my panties off. Immediately the water surged up and I felt weird but liberated.

"Bra next?" He shouted at me, but he hadn't moved closer to me, so I just ignored him. I held on to my panties tightly and then undid my bra. The water felt like heaven against my naked breasts, and I sighed happily. He was right. It felt absolutely amazing to be naked in the water. I used my hands to scrub down my body. Even though the water would leave a residue of salt on my body, I felt that was preferable to having sand and sweat hanging on to me all day. I scrubbed every inch of my body, trying to remove every grain of sand and dirt that I could.

"She's going to wash that man right off of her skin; she's going to wash that man right off of her skin." I heard Jakob singing, and I looked over at him.

"What are you doing?"

"Making a song up for you."

"You didn't make that up. That's a variation on a song from *South Pacific*."

"So you do know your movies, then." He raised an eyebrow at me and then swam toward me, and I froze.

"What are you doing?" I took a step back.

"I wanted to know if you needed help with your back."

"What help?" My heart skipped a beat as I imagined his strong hands on my naked back.

"I could help wash off whatever clinging sand grains remained." He shrugged and stopped about two feet away from me. "And you could do the same for me."

"You're too close." I glared at him and looked down in the water to ensure that my breasts weren't showing.

"Don't worry, I can't see much." He laughed.

"What does that mean?"

"I can see boobage, but I can't see nipple."

"That's more than I wanted you to see."

"Do you want me to scrub your back or not?" He moved closer, and I could see his blue eyes laughing at me. He was enjoying making me feel uncomfortable.

"I don't think that I do." I shook my head and froze as he moved even closer to me. His body was within inches of mine, and all of a sudden my heart was racing with excitement. I could feel the electricity in the water between us. My body was humming in anticipation. If I took just one step forward I would be in his arms and my naked body would be crushed against his. If I wanted to, I could reach down and touch his cock. I could see if it was as magnificent as it had looked earlier.

"Turn around." He commanded me, breaking our momentary silence.

"Sorry, what?"

"I said turn around, and lift your hair up. I'll be able to get your back better if it's facing me."

I'm not sure why I did it, but I turned around. His hands touched my skin lightly at first. His fingertips rubbed me gently, and I felt like I wanted to melt.

"You can scrub a bit harder." I muttered, wanting to feel the strength of his hands on me.

"I was being soft at first, in case you had a sunburn. I don't want to hurt you," he whispered in my ear as he stepped closer to me. I swallowed hard as I felt something brush my ass. I didn't ask what it was, because I already knew. He increased the pressure of his fingers, and I felt my body trembling as he scrubbed my back. His fingers moved in swift circular motions until he moved up to my shoulders. I felt his fingers squeezing my muscles, and I sighed as he worked to release the tension. "I hope you don't mind me giving you a massage," he whispered again, but I didn't answer. I could feel his chest against my back, and I was suddenly aware of just how close he was to me. He massaged my shoulders for another couple of minutes, and then he went back to rubbing my back.

"I think that's good enough." I murmured as his hands started scrubbing my sides and accidentally rubbed the side of my boobs.

"Don't worry, Bianca. I'm nearly done." I could hear the grin in his voice. "I just have one more spot to take care of." I gasped as his fingers fell to my ass and scrubbed it down.

"What do you think you're doing?" I shouted, and took a step forward.

"I'm making sure all of you is sand-free." His hands moved up to my lower back, and he scrubbed there. "I thought that's what you wanted."

"I didn't want your hands on my ass," I retorted angrily.

"My bad." His hands worked up my back again. "Okay, I'm nearly done."

"Good."

"Just one last place." He said softly, and before I knew what he was doing, I felt his fingers slide down the middle of my ass cheeks.

"What the fuck do you think you're doing?" I pulled away from him and turned around to glare at him.

"Sorry, you did say you had sand in all your cracks and crevices."

"Uh-huh." My eyes narrowed at him. "I'm going to shore now. I suggest you stay here until I get my bra and panties back on."

"What about my back?" He pouted, and I laughed.

"You're on your own, mister."

"Thanks a lot." He made a face, and I splashed water at him. "Hey, what's that about?" He sputtered and spat out some of the ocean water that had gone in his mouth.

"That's a warning. Don't try to pull a fast one on me again," I said lightly, and started to walk away from him.

"That's a pretty pathetic warning," he shouted at me, and I felt a huge wave of water crashing over me.

"Are you joking?" I turned around and glared at him, my face dripping with water. "You just splashed me?"

"What are you going to do about it?" He grinned, and I narrowed my eyes.

"This." I put my hands down in the water and created a huge wave to splash at him. He splashed me back, and we continued splashing each other for the next few seconds. Without my realizing it, Jakob had swum up to me and I felt his arms around my waist.

"What are you doing?" I gasped as I tried to splash him in the face.

"Nothing." He shook his head and leaned toward me. I

felt his lips pressing down on mine softly. His mouth was salty and hard. He brought me in closer to him, and I felt my breasts crush against his chest. I moaned against his lips, as I felt his manhood pressed against my stomach. He slipped his tongue into my mouth, and I sucked on it eagerly, running my hands up to his head to play with his hair. I felt his hands on my back pinching into my skin, and I pressed myself into him closer. His hands then fell to my ass, and he squeezed my butt cheeks together. I moaned again and then froze as I felt his fingers going down my ass crack, trying to get in between my legs. I stepped back quickly, with my heart racing.

"What are you doing?" I swallowed hard and stared up at him.

"Sorry, I got a bit carried away." He licked his lips and stared back at me. "We should probably get out now."

"I agree." I nodded.

"You go first. I'll wait here with my back turned so you can put on your bra and panties."

"Thank you." I swam away from him quickly and ran out of the water. I wrung as much water as I could out of my underwear and slipped them on. They were cold and clammy, but I knew they would dry out quickly in the hot sun. I also knew *not* wearing them was not even a possibility.

"I'm ready." I called out to Jakob and watched as he swam back to shore. He moved like a champion swimmer, and his body was made for the water. I stared at him as he exited the ocean, and this time, I didn't tell myself not to look. I gasped as I saw his cock was hard and jutting out.

Jakob looked up at me as he put his briefs back on, and we stared at each other for a few seconds before he walked over to me.

"Ready to go to the jungle?" he asked me lightly, and I nodded, grateful that he hadn't made a comment about my checking him out.

~

We walked in silence toward the jungle. I could feel my heart racing as I realized that I was about to enter the un-known. I thought back to one of my history classes where we'd talked about American Indian tribes who had never had contact with Westerners.

"I really hope we don't happen upon any native tribes who want to kill us." I shivered.

"Don't be stupid, Bianca." Jakob shook his head.

"Fine. I hope we don't happen upon any native tribes who want to kill *you*." I glared at him.

"Keep your eyes open and your ears keen, then," he re-sponded pompously. "If anyone is waiting to kill us, it's Steve."

"What do you mean?" I frowned at him, still feeling an-noyed by his imperious nature.

"Don't worry about it. I'll worry about Steve." He gave me a condescending look. "Just keep your eyes open for water, and your ears as well." He spoke slowly and arrogantly, and I wondered how I had allowed myself to be even slightly intimate with him. "At the same time, let me know if you see any Indians with bows and arrows."

"You're an asshole."

"I'm an asshole who doesn't want us to get further dehydrated."

"You really think we're going to find fresh water?"

"We're pretty screwed if we don't." He looked at me then and sighed. "Please don't cry."

I stared at him for two seconds before ignoring him and increasing my pace. He was such an asshole. *Please don't cry,* my ass. I hadn't cried since we'd been here.

"Wait up." He hurried behind me and grabbed my arm. "I told you already that you need to wait for me."

"You're not the boss of me." I shrugged his hand off. "And the last I heard, we weren't colonists. *We* didn't start a democracy, and I didn't vote for you to be governor or president." I gave him a haughty look. "So in case you don't get it, I'm not listening to what you say."

"Bianca," he started, and half-smiled.

"What?" I snapped, and then tripped over something and fell to my knees. "Ouch." I landed on the sand with a thud, my face burning up in shame.

"You okay?" He reached his hand out to help me up. "I was trying to warn you about that branch."

"I'm fine." I jumped up, ignored his hand, and then brushed the sand off my legs. I looked up and found Jakob staring at me with darkened eyes.

"Is it going to be like this the whole time we're here?"

"We're not here to repopulate the planet, so I wouldn't worry about it," I huffed out, and then paused. "Oh my God, you don't think we're here for some secret project? Maybe they want us to start a new colony and repopulate a new population to see if we can survive on another planet."

"Another planet?"

"You know, somewhere other than Earth."

"We're on Earth, Bianca."

"Duh. I meant, maybe they plan on sending us to another planet after we have kids." I sighed as if he were the slow one and then started laughing. "I'm joking, Jakob."

I could see his lips trembling as he listened to me, and I could tell that he wanted to join me in my laugh. Finally, he couldn't stop himself and he started laughing as well. We laughed for a good couple of minutes, and I felt tears running out of my eyes.

"Okay, I know how ridiculous that sounded," I finally choked out through laughs. "You should have seen your face when you thought I was being serious."

"I'm glad you realized that we don't have to worry about life on Mars, though I wouldn't be averse to trying for the kids." He winked at me, and my face flushed. "What say you?"

"I say no." I marched ahead of him, and he grabbed my arm.

"What are we going to do to get off of the island?" His voice was serious, and I knew that the joking part of the morning was done. "We also need to think about how we're going to protect ourselves. Just in case."

"Oh God, I feel like I'm Katniss and you're Peeta. Only, I don't know how to shoot a bow and arrow. Not that I have a bow and arrow, and I don't think you know how to bake bread."

"What?" He looked annoyed. "Who are Katty and Peter?"

"What?" I responded back at him. "You never saw *The Hunger Games* movies? I mean, the books were better, but I thought most people saw the movies at least. The second movie was much better than the first one though."

"Bianca," His voice was growing impatient. "I need you to focus on the matter at hand. I don't know *The Hunger Games*, and unless that movie is going to provide us with some answers we can use right now, I don't care to know either."

"Well, the main characters were in a similar situation to us, so I was trying to think about what they would do in such a situation."

"They were kidnapped and placed on an island as well?"

"Not exactly." I made a face. "I mean it's kind of similar. They knew what they were signing up for, only, they didn't really know." I shook my head. "They had no real concept of what they were going to be faced with."

"Bianca, I do appreciate the fact that you're a walking movie machine. You might even be the next Ebert, but right now I don't give two shits about any of your random movies. This is serious. We need to figure out a plan."

"I know that. Trust me, I know that. I don't know what we're going to do. I'm sorry that you chose to sit at a table with me and now you've been dragged into my mess." I pushed past him and started walking quickly away from him. I hadn't appreciated his tone or words. Movies were my answers to everything. They always had been. Movies had been my teaching guides as I'd grown up. They were easy to fall back on. I often talked about characters from movies as if they were people I knew in real life.

"Wait." His voice wasn't humorous anymore. "Don't walk ahead of me."

"Are we going to go—"

"Bianca." His voice rose. "Enough."

"What?" My jaw dropped open in shock. Was he seriously speaking to me as if I were a kid? Again?

"I said enough. We can't have you just . . ." He started lecturing me and I felt like a petulant kid as I stood there silently. His lips looked so luscious as he stood there mumbling about something. I'd already tuned him out and was admiring his chest. His abs looked so pronounced, and I had an urge to run my fingers down each ripple. I wonder what he would do if I stepped forward and ran my fingers all the way down? I chastised myself silently at my dirty thoughts. I was about to interrupt him, when I saw something moving in the bushes. I gasped and blinked quickly to make sure my eyes weren't deceiving me. There were two empty dark eyes staring back at me. I screamed out and the face backed away from sight. My eyes watched the branches shaking in front of me; I felt my heart stop as leaves fell to the ground. I heard a loud thud, and then I screamed again loudly, pushing past Jakob to make my way back to the sandy beach.

I ran back to the beach as fast as I could, my legs moving swiftly, while my mind thought back to what I'd seen in the bushes. "Bianca, slow down!" He chased after me and grabbed ahold of me when he caught up. "Bianca!"

"I saw something!" I gasped. "I saw two eyes looking at me." I stared at him with wide eyes as I tried to control my breathing. "Oh my God, we're totally going to die."

"Bianca!" He took a deep breath and pulled me into his arms. "Take two deep breaths and calm down."

"How am I supposed to calm down when Godzilla is on the island with us? Ready to eat me!" My voice was dramatic, and my hands rose to the sides of my face. "I have very sweet blood, you know. Predators can smell me."

"Really?" His lips started twitching again.

"Yes! I eat a lot of chocolate." I closed my eyes and took two deep breaths. "I'm not going back in there." I shook my head and fell to the sand. "I'm not going back. No way, José."

"Bianca, I'm sure all you saw was a bug or something. Or maybe it was Steve spying on us."

"Steve has blue eyes." I shook my head. "And I'd like to know what bug has big white irises and black-red eyes?"

"Black-red eyes?"

"You know what I mean." I glared at him.

"Not really." He sat down next to me and leaned back. "So you're too scared to go back into the jungle today?"

"I don't want to die today."

"So you'd rather die tomorrow?"

"I'd rather not die."

"Bianca." His voice was serious. "If I could go into the jungle and carry back what we needed without you coming with me, I would. If I felt safe leaving you on the beach by yourself, I would go. Unfortunately, I don't know where Steve is and I'm scared what he might try to do, especially if he is tracking our movements. We can't be apart from each other. So I'm going to need you to be a big girl today. I need your help."

"You're such a condescending asshole."

"Thank you, but you don't even know me yet."

"I think I do."

"I could be a lot worse." His lips were thin as his eyes stared into mine with an intense light. "I could be more than an asshole." His voice dropped, and his fingers ran down my arm.

"Get your fingers off of me." I shook him off me and moved back.

"My fingers can't do as much as other parts of my body," he said smoothly.

"What's that supposed to mean?" I furrowed my eyebrows together, and then my face flushed. "You're disgusting."

"Not as disgusting as I can be." He leaned toward me, and I was almost positive that he was going to kiss me. Instead, his lips moved to my ear and he whispered softly, "Only, you won't think I'm being disgusting. You'll be screaming out my name, begging me to never stop."

I jumped up then and walked toward the jungle. "You're so inappropriate. You know that, right? I just had the fright of my life and you're trying to seduce me. Let's go!" I shouted without looking back at him. "If you need my help, let's go."

"I thought that would do the trick." He jumped up off the ground and laughed. "There's nothing that scares you more than sex, is there, Bianca?"

I ignored his question and kept walking. Though he was wrong. Nothing about sex scared me. It was what happened after sex that turned my brain upside down.

~

"I don't know if we're going to find any water." I sighed as we kept walking through the shrubbery. "I'm getting tired and thirsty."

"I can crack open some coconuts if you want." Jakob touched my arm. "If we bash them hard enough into the rocks we can split them open. We have to find the green coconuts though, the ones still in the shell. The brown coconuts are hard already."

"It's okay. I can wait a little bit." I shook my head. "It's weird that we haven't seen any trace of Steve, isn't it?" I stared at the gash on Jakob's face and bit my lower lip.

"I guess." He looked away from me. "Let's stop for a moment so you can rest."

"Thanks." I rolled my eyes. "I'm the only one who's exhausted, right?"

"Let's stop so we both can rest. Is that better?" He gave me a look that made me feel like a little kid, and I turned away. "Wait here. I'm going to go—"

"Jakob," I whispered softly as my eye caught something. "Jakob," I said again, harder this time, and grabbed his arm.

My breathing was coming faster, and my words sounded slightly excited.

"Yes?"

"I see something." I stared ahead, not sure if I was seeing things. I rubbed my eyes and looked again.

"Not another alien or gorilla." His eyes twinkled at me.

"Funny—not." I glared at him. "I think I see a building."

"What?" His eyes narrowed, and he stared at me. "Where?"

"Look." I pointed to a spot between a gathering of trees. "Over there." His face turned to look in the direction I was pointing, and I saw him looking hard.

"I don't see it."

"Look between the two trees." I grabbed him again. "I think there's some sort of shack. It's covered in shrubbery, but there's a small window. Do you see it now?"

"I see it." He nodded and started walking. "Let's go check it out."

I wanted to grab him again and tell him to stop. We didn't know what it was or who was there, and I was scared. I wished I hadn't complained now. I wished we had kept walking. I would have felt safer. Now I felt anxious and scared. What was waiting for us in the cabin? I took a deep breath and tried not to start screaming. What if Steve was in there with a gun?

The shack in front of us was small and wooden. It would have looked comfortable in the middle of a horror movie, a fact I kept to myself as we walked toward it. My heart was beating rapidly, and I could feel the fear in the tips of my fingers and bottoms of my feet. My face was flushed with heat, and I followed behind Jakob, scared of what we were about to see.

"Do you think someone lives here?" I whispered.

"I don't know." His voice was stiff, and I had a feeling that he was as shocked as I was. "I'm surprised that there's a shack here. We've seen no other signs of the island being inhabited, aside from Steve showing up."

"And this one looks like they tried to hide it. There's shrubbery all over the front and back."

"Yeah, it looks like they tried to camouflage it." He looked back toward me. "Stand back while I go in. If you hear me shout, run back to the beach."

"And do what?" I mumbled, but he didn't answer.

I watched as he opened the door to the shack and took a step in. I followed him slowly, not wanting him to go in alone and not wanting to stand outside by myself. While I was worried about what was in the shack, I was also worried about the creature I had seen in the trees earlier.

"Jakob," I spoke softly as I stepped into the sparse shack.

"Someone's been waiting for us to find this place." He looked at me with a thoughtful expression.

"Huh?" I stared at him in confusion. "Do you think it was Steve?"

"I don't know." He sighed. "Look." He pointed to the corner of the room at a table.

On the small wooden table, there were two white envelopes. One envelope was addressed to Jakob, and the other envelope was addressed to me, Bianca London. I froze as I stared at the envelopes.

"Here you go." He handed me my envelope.

I opened it slowly and read. My fingers trembled as I read the short message, and I felt my heart stop.

"What does yours say?" Jakob's voice interrupted my thoughts.

"I, uh . . ." My voice shook, and I looked up at him with wide eyes.

"Mine says, "'Everyone has a price. Every action has a consequence.'" He frowned and looked at me.

"'Your life may be saved in death.'" My voice trembled, and I pressed my palm to my forehead to reassure myself that everything was okay.

The letter was printed on the same paper as the first note that had arrived at my apartment a week ago. My skin felt cold even though the sun was extremely hot outside, and the hairs on my arm stood on end as I shivered. I reread the note, trying to figure out if there was a clue I had missed on the page.

What was the connection between this note and the one I'd received before? What was I being saved from? Who was doing this to me? And why bring me here with Jakob? Why leave him a note as well? I didn't understand him. Some parts of the day, he was light and friendly, while at other times, he seemed guarded and thoughtful. There was a look in his eye that scared me—a look that said no matter how long we spent together, he would still have his walls up.

A part of me was hurt that he seemed so closed off. I felt stupid for being hurt. Rationally, I knew that I didn't know him, and he didn't know me, yet it was still hard for me to let go of the fact that I wanted to feel closer to him. I'd already opened up to him partially about my past. Yes, I hadn't told him the whole truth, but he knew more than anyone else. I'd told him more than I'd even told Rosie. And then there was the attraction I felt to him. Sexually, there was a magnetism to him that made me want to touch him and feel him on top of me. When he touched me, my skin lit up like a stove that had just been turned on. I craved his touch. I wanted to taste him. I wanted to feel him inside me. My time on the island was bringing out very primal urges in me. I felt like I was living each hour as if it were my last. For the most part, I enjoyed our banter. I felt like he really cared about me. I could see the concern for my safety in his eyes, and I could hear it in his voice. I knew that he legitimately felt something for me. I just wished that he trusted me as much as I'd already trusted me.

"Are you okay?" His voice interrupted my thoughts, and I looked up to see him frowning.

"The letter just took me aback." I nodded slowly, not ready to tell him about the other note I'd received. Not until I felt like I was getting more from him.

"I understand." He sighed. "We will get to the bottom of this."

"How?"

"We'll figure something out."

"Do you think we're going to die?"

"Only if we have to kill each other." His words were soft, and I froze.

"I'm confused." I spoke slowly, as if I were just now thinking about the question I was about to ask.

"About what?"

"Why would they leave you a note?" I scratched my head. "I mean, it just doesn't add up. They see you with me once at a coffee shop and all of a sudden you're prime suspect number two?" I licked my lips and studied his face carefully. I could see throbbing in his throat as he stared back at me. "What's the point of leaving you a letter? And such a deep letter as well?"

We stared at each other for a few seconds in silence, and I could tell that Jakob was thinking hard about something. I knew this was the turning point for us. He needed to tell me more than he already had, which was really nothing. I hadn't wanted to push him when we'd first arrived, but now that we'd been here for a few days, I needed more.

"So I guess now's the time I should tell you that I wasn't at that coffee shop by mistake."

"What?" My voice echoed in the small shack.

"It's not what you think." He sighed. "I received an e-mail that morning from a business colleague. She said she wanted to meet me there to discuss something about a business I'm in the process of trying to acquire."

"Okay . . ."

"There weren't any other tables, so I sat with you." He took a step toward me. "I chose to sit at your table on purpose."

"Why?" My body stilled.

"Because I wanted to flirt with the cute brunette I spotted typing away," he smiled. "Only, you ignored me when I approached the table."

"Sorry," I bit down on my lower lip as I watched him talking.

"It's okay. I felt like a bit of an idiot, so I took my book out of my bag and pretended to read instead."

"I felt like a bit of an idiot for being so rude, if that helps." I smiled at him. "I was trying to finish an article and only had a few minutes left. Normally I'm not so rude."

"That's okay, Pip is one of my favorites, so I was happy to sit there and try to read while I waited on my colleague to show up."

"Pip." I kept my composure as I stared at him. "Like Pip and Miss Havisham?"

"Yes. I told you I love Dickens, right?"

"Yeah." I nodded slowly. "You did."

"*Great Expectations* is one of his best novels, if I do say so myself. I read it in high school and it really touched something in me. I try to read it every couple of years."

"The movie was pretty good as well," I babbled. "Not the one with Ethan Hawke and Gwyneth Paltrow so much, but the one from the forties with Anthony Wager."

"Oh, not sure I saw that one."

"So you came to the coffee shop that day to meet someone and decided to sit with me on purpose because you thought I was attractive?" I tried to keep my tone even, but I was finding it hard not to panic. Why had he lied about the book he'd been reading? Unless he was just recalling it incorrectly? "Anything else?"

"No, not that I—"

"You told me before that you were reading *A Tale of Two Cities*." I cut him off, unable to keep it in. "So what was it, *Great Expectations* or *A Tale of Two Cities*?"

He didn't even flinch at my words. Either he was a good actor or it had been a genuine mistake. "I must have gotten confused. I love all of his books. Cliché I guess. I'm a rags-to-riches guy. I suppose I resonate with the characters in a way." He ran his hands through his hair and then stretched. "There's one more thing, Bianca."

"Yes?"

"My colleague never showed up that day. When I called her, she said that she'd never sent me the e-mail. I didn't think much of it until we were kidnapped." He paused and then looked around before continuing in a lower voice. "And the company we were going to discuss, the company I've been interested in acquiring, is Bradley Inc."

"What?" Several emotions hit me then: shock, distrust, and curiosity.

"I didn't want to say anything. I didn't realize that it had that much importance, not until you told me about your father's letter."

"You should have told me before." I gazed at him. "This means that it wasn't just a case of mistaken identity for your kidnapping. This means you likely weren't kidnapped because you were sitting at a table with me. This means that Mattias Bradley, if he's the one responsible for the kidnapping, wanted you here as well."

"I think you're right." He nodded. "Mattias is playing a game with both of us."

"Have you met him, then?" I asked him curiously, wondering why he would have kept all this from me when I'd spent half the previous night spilling my heart out to him.

"Stand still," he whispered suddenly, instead of answering. He moved toward me slowly, and his eyes narrowed as he moved his hand up swiftly. I took a quick step back as I saw something in his hand. My heart skipped a beat as his fingers continued their ascent. I felt the blood drain from my face as he stepped toward me again.

"Don't!" I gasped. "Please don't."

"Don't what?" His hand brushed something off my shoulder. "There was a mosquito on your arm."

"Oh." I looked at his palm and saw nothing there. It must have been a trick of my mind.

"They like sweet blood." He grinned suddenly. "And I remember you telling me that your blood is very sweet."

"Yeah, it is." I nodded, trying to catch my breath. I felt like my romantic suspense adventure was slowly turning into a psychological thriller. "Thanks. Mosquitoes love to suck on my skin."

"And so do I."

"You like blood?"

"No." He started laughing. "I messed that up. I meant to say I like sweet lips."

"There's a big difference between sweet blood and sweet lips."

"Yes, there is." He took a step toward me and gazed into my eyes. My heart started beating rapidly again, but this time, it wasn't because I was scared. "Do you like being kissed, Bianca?"

"As much as every other woman."

"Do you like it when I kiss you?" He took another step toward me.

"Why are you asking me this?" I swallowed hard but stood my ground. "I want to know what our notes meant. I want to know what else you're hiding from me."

"What do you think the consequences of my kissing you are?"

"Stop changing the subject. I don't care about the consequences of you kissing me. Last time I checked, it won't get me pregnant."

"My note said 'Everyone has a price. Every action has a consequence.'" His voice was dry. "I kiss you because I can't resist your lips, but there's a voice in the back of my head that says I should be stronger. I wonder what the consequences of my ignoring that voice in the back of my head are."

"I don't know," I whispered. "And I don't care. I doubt the note was talking about us kissing."

"You're mad at me, aren't you?"

"What do you think? I don't take well to people lying to me."

"I didn't lie. I just didn't tell you everything. Just like you, I didn't know if this was a setup. I didn't get to my position by trusting every pretty girl who flutters her eyelashes at me."

"You're so offensive. I know in movies, that might be cute to some women, but I'm not the sort of woman that needs a man who puts me down. I don't find that sexy."

"I'm glad to hear it."

"Goddamnit, Jakob." I pressed my hands against his chest. "What's going on here?"

"I really don't know, Bianca. I'm as confused as you are." His fingers covered mine.

"I don't know if I believe that," I whispered.

"Do you think it's wrong for a woman to trick a man into falling in love with her?" He leaned down and pressed his lips against mine lightly as he spoke. "Do you think that women use sex as a way to trap men?"

"I don't know," I whispered again, frozen and unable to move.

"What do you think should happen to gold diggers?" His tongue darted out and licked my lips. "Should they be punished?"

"I . . ." I swallowed hard as my heart raced. "I don't know."

I moaned as Jakob grabbed the back of my neck and pressed me toward him. His lips pressed down harder on mine, and his tongue slipped into my mouth as he kissed me, hard. All of a sudden, my cold skin had turned hot, and I kissed him back with abandon. His lips were unrelenting as he devoured my lips and sought the secrets of my mouth. His hands squeezed the back of my head as his fingers ran through my extremely tousled hair. His chest felt warm against my fingers as I caressed his skin and held on to his back. My legs were trembling as his fingers lightly ran up my stomach and over my breasts.

I was breathless as he pulled away from me. He stared down into my eyes, and his eyes looked angry. He took a step back from me and ran his hand through his hair before he spoke again.

"Whoever brought us here has a plan." He paused, then looked at me again. "And it seems very calculated. I think we must be connected in a much more direct way. Our only link can't be that we're both interested in Bradley Inc., that's just too broad."

"I wish we knew exactly what was going on. I'm so frustrated."

"You'll have to tell me more about your father. Maybe when we talk a little more we can figure some stuff out."

"I guess so."

I spoke reluctantly. I didn't really want to tell him more about my father. I didn't want to give him any more information until I was more confident in my trust for him. "Do you think someone else is on the island besides you, me, and Steve?" I licked my lips lightly and watched his eyes follow the movement of my tongue. If only we were here for a different reason. If only I could concentrate on the attraction we had for each other. Things would be so different then. Now, I felt guilty. My attraction to Jakob felt slightly dangerous. I felt like every kiss was playing with fire, and I was getting closer and closer to being consumed by his flames.

"No." He shook his head. "I don't."

"Then how did these letters get here? Do you think it was Steve?"

"Perhaps. I think whoever did this planned it out very carefully." He looked around the shack. "It doesn't look like anyone's been sleeping in here. For some reason, Steve doesn't strike me as a particularly delicate person."

"I wonder who built it."

I shivered and stared at the sparse shack. There were some pieces of material on the ground and in some boxes, but I hesitated to go through them. I was scared that it might be a trap. What if the boxes were full of snakes and spiders? I shivered at the thought.

"Who knows?" He shrugged and his expression changed. "Read your note to me again."

"'Your life may be saved in death.'" I shuddered as I read the letter. "Do you think they're trying to tell me that they're going to kill me? Is Steve going to kill me?"

"I don't think so." He shook his head. "It doesn't sound like a death threat. Anyway, I won't let Steve hurt you. I think we need to find Steve and figure out what he knows." His eyes stared at something in the corner of the shack, and I could see a nerve in his forehead throbbing. "We need to find

Steve. We need to find out why he's here." He grabbed my hand. "Come on, let's go."

"Do you think he's still alive?" I asked as he walked ahead of me.

"I don't know." He stopped and looked back at me. "Bad things happen to bad people when they least expect it all the time." He smiled at me then. A weird, sad smile. "But then bad things happen to good people all the time as well, don't they?"

"Yes, they do." I thought back to my mother's death and the grief my father had lived with for the rest of his life and pulled my hand back from his grip. "I wish I knew what the notes meant. What are they trying to tell us? I feel like my note is some sort of threat. And what about yours?" I thought back to his note. "Are they saying you did something bad? Did you take money for some shady deal and your being kidnapped is the consequence of your actions? Do you think Mattias is trying to warn you to stay away from trying to take over his business?"

"I try not to be shady." He gave me a half smile.

"Most rich people have been shady at some point in their lives," I said bitterly.

"Does that make you mad?" He looked at me keenly. "Do you feel like rich people owe you something?"

"I don't know any rich people." I stared at him and kept my voice even.

"Aside from your ex-boyfriends."

"Whatever." I glared at him. "I don't care if you have

money, Jakob. I'm sorry that some girl, who was obviously a gold digger, tried to date you, but she's not me."

"I won't say the obvious." He started, but I cut him off.

"Good." I handed him my letter. "You can keep this. I'm going to go look for some water."

"Wait." He grabbed my shoulders and pushed me against the wall. His eyes glared down at me, and I could feel the warmth of his body against my skin. "I don't think it's a good idea for you to just run off by yourself."

"What do you care?" I struggled to push him away from me, but I couldn't move him.

"Bianca, listen to me. I think we should stick together until we find out who brought us here and who left these letters for us."

"Then stop being an asshole to me."

"I'll try," he sighed. "I'm sorry if you think I'm being rude. I'm just on edge."

"You don't think I'm not on edge? Someone just threatened to kill me."

"Bianca . . ." He let go of my arms and stepped back. "I'll take care of you."

"Thanks." I looked around the shack again and froze. "Oh my God." I made my way past him, ran to the corner of the shack, and pushed aside the trash on the ground. "There's a bag." I kicked the medium-sized black leather bag gingerly, and screamed when a small lizard ran out.

"You're going to give yourself a stroke if you keep that up."

"I'm not doing it on purpose," I snapped back at him, and tried to control my breathing. "I didn't expect a huge lizard to almost attack me."

"Yeah, I wonder if he's related to Godzilla?" he quipped, and I looked up to see him smiling.

"It's not funny." I smiled, unable to stop myself. "I know I overreact a bit, but I just hate insects and creatures that aren't cats and dogs. I'm a bit of a frightened rabbit when it comes to bugs."

"Whoever chose to kidnap you must not know you very well, then." He laughed, and I froze at his words.

"Or they know me really well." My mind started racing. "I guess it depends on why I'm here. If it's for revenge, well this is perfect." I bit my lower lip. "This is like hell on earth for me."

"Who knows how much you hate wildlife?"

"Just my dad and Rosie." I sighed. "And my dad's dead."

"Do you think Rosie could have something to do with this?"

"No." I shook my head vehemently. "There's no way that Rosie would do this to me." My voice rose, and I watched as Jakob picked up the bag and placed it on the table. "It has to be someone else."

"Or it's just a coincidence." He opened the bag slowly.

"Or it's someone I spoke to online." I rubbed my forehead. "In my online profile, I stated that my worst date would involve camping because I hated bugs."

"I thought you never met anyone online?"

"I didn't." I sighed. "I spoke to a couple of guys, but they all turned out to be psychos."

"Were you looking for anyone in particular?" He looked up at me then, and I saw his expression change.

"What do you mean? I wasn't looking to get a husband. At least not right away."

"You had a type though? A certain somebody you were hoping to meet?"

"Of course. Who doesn't?" I shrugged, and he turned away.

He changed the subject. "It looks like there is a God after all."

"Why do you say that?" I walked toward him and gasped as he pulled out a bottle of water. "Oh, please tell me there's more than one bottle."

"I never thought I'd see someone so happy to see a bottle of water."

"Shut up and open it."

I stopped in front of him and eagerly took the bottle from him, drinking the water sparingly. It tasted better than the most expensive champagne, and I immediately felt refreshed as I drank it. I made sure to take only about four gulps before handing it back to Jakob.

"What are you doing?" He frowned as he took the bottle from me.

"Aren't you thirsty?"

"You've had only a few sips." He tried to hand the bottle back to me.

"I'll wait until you have some first." I shrugged. "We don't know how many bottles are in the bag."

"Thank you." He nodded and took a couple of swigs. "That was really thoughtful of you."

"I'm not selfish, you know."

"No, I don't believe you are." He handed me back the bottle. "Have some more. There are a few more bottles in the bag." He reached into the bag again and pulled out five bottles.

"That's it?" I pulled the bottle away from my mouth. I swallowed hard as I surveyed the bottles and mentally calculated how long they would last.

"It's okay. There's a lighter in the bag as well." He pulled out a pack of BIC lighters and grinned.

"This helps us how?"

"We can cook and we can boil water."

"What water? Not ocean water." I made a face, recalling the water we'd drunk the day before.

"If we find a waterfall, we can probably drink that water as is, but if we want to be safe, we can boil it."

"Safe from what?"

"Cholera and other parasites."

"Cholera?" My eyes widened. "I thought that disease no longer existed."

"It's a waterborne disease and yes, it still exists. It's quite prevalent in the West Indies and Southeast Asia."

"So you think we're in the West Indies or Asia?"

"I would guess." He shrugged. "Seems about right, the

weather and environment seem to fit. If I had to hazard a guess, I would say the West Indies more so than Asia."

"Have you been to the West Indies a lot, then?"

"No." He looked at me for a second and then looked back in the bag. "I've never been before."

"I wish I knew why we were both here." My voice cracked, and I could feel my body shaking. I could feel that I was about to lose it.

"Someone wants us to disappear." His voice was low. "We both know that we've been keeping secrets from each other." He paused and looked at me. "There's obviously some sort of deeper connection between us. If we want to figure it out and get off of this island, we need to explore our connections. Maybe we'll find that we'll be able to help each other."

"Help each other how? I don't have any secrets." I looked down at the ground and walked out of the shack feeling apprehensive. I stared up at the dark sky and shivered at the ominous gray clouds that taunted me.

"So it's a mistake that you're here?" He followed me out with the bag in his hands.

"I don't know how we can help each other." I sighed. "And I'm not keeping any secrets. What secrets are you keeping? What secrets are you keeping that I can help you with?"

"I'm not." He licked his lips, and I couldn't stop myself from watching the pink tip of his tongue as it slid along his lips. My stomach flipped as I thought about kissing him. "Let's go and find Steve, and then we can talk again soon."

His words made me thirsty, and I walked faster ahead of him. "Thanks for once again providing me with a satisfying answer." I made a face at the jungle in front of me as my brain screamed out for water. *Take that, monkeys and wild animals in the trees*, I thought as I glared into the unknown.

"I'm not here to make you feel better." His voice was short.

"I don't need you to make me feel better. I need you to answer my questions. I need you to be honest with me. We've been here for several days, and you only now decide to tell me that you have a connection to the Bradleys? The same people I tell you I think are after me!"

"I'm not just going to reveal everything because you have, Bianca. I don't know you from Adam. Let's be fair, I don't know if your story is true or not."

"That didn't stop you from kissing me."

"My attraction to you has nothing to do with my confiding in you."

"You're really cold, aren't you." I turned around and stared into his eyes searchingly. "Who hurt you so badly?"

"My mother always used to tell me, 'Don't give anyone the power to make you cry.'" He reached out and touched my cheek. "No one has the ability to hurt me. You shouldn't worry so much about others and what they do to you. Ultimately, you have the power in your life."

"I don't worry about others." I sighed. "I'm just saying that someone must have hurt you because you're so hot and cold. I never know if you're going to be nice to me or not."

"Life and love and even sex are what you make of them."

He looked to the sky and frowned. "It's going to rain. We need to make some sort of shelter—or we should go back to the shack?"

"What about Steve?"

"There's no point in our getting soaked looking for him. Let's go back to the shack, it's closer."

"I'm not going back to that shack." I shook my head and started walking again. "Let's figure out something else."

"We're going to get wet."

"I don't care." I frowned. "How did it get so gray already? The sun was bright and hot just minutes ago."

"That's the tropics for you."

"Weird," I muttered, happy when I saw the white sand of the beach in the distance. I didn't like being in the jungle.

"Bianca." Jakob grabbed my shoulders and stopped me. "I wanted to apologize to you. I should have told you about my connection to the Bradleys in the beginning. I don't want you to think that I don't want to find out the truth. I want all the answers I can get. This is more complicated because I'm attracted to you. I don't want you to think that my attraction to you is false. In a different situation, who knows what could have happened?"

"I'm sorry I snapped at you. I'm still freaked out by the letters and Steve's disappearance. And yes, I'm annoyed that you kept things from me, but I suppose I understand why."

"We could make love right now, and I could make you forget all your worries." His voice was low and seductive, and I felt my face growing warmer.

"You know, I was thinking about something." A thought suddenly hit me. "There is one person who hates me. Someone who could have set up a kidnapping as well." I changed the subject. "Though, I don't know if she would go to these lengths."

"Who is that?"

"My ex-boyfriend's ex-girlfriend." I sighed. "She hated me."

"Because you stole him from her?"

"No!" I exclaimed, and then paused. "Well, not really."

"What does *not really* mean?"

"It means not really." I looked into his eyes before I spoke again. He looked back at me with an intense expression. "I didn't know he was dating someone when we met."

"Didn't know or didn't care?"

"What does that mean?"

"Well he was handsome, rich. You felt like you won the lottery, right?"

"No!" I glared at him again. "You really think I'm some sort of gold digger, don't you."

"Like I said, you wouldn't be the first I've met." He shrugged.

"Money isn't everything."

"Tell me about this girl who hates you."

"Her name is Bridgette."

"Bridgette?" He frowned and leaned forward. "Do you know her last name?"

"Moore," I answered. "Her name is Bridgette Moore, and

she hates me because she thinks I stole David from her. But I didn't know that they were dating."

"You really liked David, it seems."

"He was very handsome and sweet to me." I circumvented his unasked question. My dating David had nothing to do with how much I liked him.

"Typical woman." He rolled his eyes.

"What's typical?"

"The number one trait you list is handsome."

"What's wrong with that? At least I didn't say rich."

"When he kissed you, did you feel as if your soul was on fire?"

I shook my head. "No."

"When I kiss you, do you feel like your soul is on fire?"

"Well, you're from hell, so it *would* feel that way," I retorted quickly.

"Yet you feel comfortable enough with the devil to let him touch you?" His fingers trailed across my collarbone and then to my cheek.

"I never said you could touch me," I whispered softly, not wanting him to stop.

"Sometimes an assent doesn't come from the mouth, it comes from the eyes."

"My eyes told you it was all right to touch me?"

"Your eyes told me it was all right to fuck you." His face moved toward mine, and I could feel his breath on my lips. "Your eyes are begging me to kiss you." This time, as he spoke, his lips trembled against mine.

I closed my eyes and waited to feel the firmness of his lips against mine as he kissed me, yet nothing happened. I slowly opened my eyes again, but I was disappointed. My breath caught as I realized that he was gazing intently into my eyes.

"I think . . ." he began with a small smile. "I think we have a connection."

"Oh?" My heart started beating fast at his words. I didn't know how much I liked him, but I was definitely attracted to him. "I agree." I nodded, my face flushing. I didn't know what was going to happen next, but I was excited to find out.

"I think I know Bridgette as well."

"What?" I blinked at him, not comprehending what was going on. I had been expecting him to take me in his arms, not to keep talking.

"I said, I think I know Bridgette as well." He smiled at me slightly, and his eyes appeared to mock me. "I think that's a second connection that we have. There was a Bridgette Moore who used to work for me."

"There was?" I mumbled as my brain started racing. He knew Bridgette? Bridgette Moore had hated me with a passion. The last time I saw her she was screaming at me and threatening to ruin my life. I hadn't taken her seriously. I'd figured her words were those of a heartbroken ex. David had told me that he was about to dump her before he met me. I hadn't thought she was seriously going to come after me, but now I wasn't so sure. Could this have been set up by Bridgette and not by Mattias?

"Yes, but I fired her." His fingers trailed up my neck and

circled it. For a moment, I thought he was going to strangle me as his fingers pressed in deeper and his expression changed. "I'm not the sort of man anyone should mess with." His voice was hoarse, and I swallowed hard. "Do you understand that, Bianca?"

"Yes," I whispered, my heart thudding with fear.

"Good." He smiled and he leaned down to kiss me. "Bridgette didn't seem to get that memo," he whispered against my lips before he kissed me.

I held on to his shoulders and softly kissed him back. There was a buzzing in my ears as we kissed, and my brain was screaming at me. The kiss lit something up in me, and I ran my hands through his hair, but all the while, I was thinking to myself, *Did I made a mistake in trusting Jakob? Is this man going to kill me?*

I pulled away from him and breathed a deep sigh of relief as his fingers left my throat. I took a step back and my fingers found the spots where he had been gripping me and rubbed gently. It struck me that maybe Jakob was hiding more than I'd even suspected. If Bridgette had been his assistant and Bridgette had dated David, wouldn't he have known David, or at least heard of David? And if he knew who David was, why hadn't he said anything?

seven

There's something about sexual attraction that makes your brain turn to jelly. Factually, I knew that it's the process of what happens when chemicals are released in your brain that affects your mood. The chemicals are the reason why, when you see someone you're attracted to you, you lose all sense. However, I still didn't understand why I always seemed to lose my mind around Jakob. I knew he was the sort of man most women would fall for. I'd just never expected to find myself lusting after a man who was handsome but also potentially dangerous. I wanted to ask him more about Bridgette, but I knew that I had to time it well. I didn't want him to think that I was making too many connections. Not yet. There had to be a reason why he wasn't being straightforward with everything. I just didn't know why.

I stared at his bulging biceps as he gathered coconut palms and tried not to lust after him too obviously. I watched the muscles in his back flexing and swallowed hard. The hot sun was already deepening his tan, and I could see sweat glistening on his skin. Hard work had never made a man look so sexy before. After Jakob had kissed me, we'd noticed piles of fallen coconut branches and stopped to pick them up to take back with us to the sand. I had no idea how we were going to put them together to make a shelter, but I'd leave that up to him to figure out.

"You okay?" He looked back and caught me staring at him.

"Uh, yeah. I was just looking for the ass," I mumbled as I stared at his butt.

"You're what?" He grinned and turned toward me.

"I was just . . ." I stopped talking as I realized what I'd said. "I'm gathering stuff for the house." I looked down at the ground with a red face. *Damn you, jelly brain.*

"What house?" He walked toward me.

"You know what I mean. The shelter."

"I see. I thought you were gathering keepsakes for when you get back home."

"Not quite." I rolled my eyes and then swallowed as I looked up and saw his crotch right in front of my face. "What are you doing?" I sputtered, and jumped up.

"I came to make sure you were okay."

"I already told you, I'm fine."

"I wanted to make sure." He gave me a small smile. "You've been gathering branches for a while now, but you have only one in your stack." He looked pointedly at the pathetic coconut limb beside me, and I frowned.

"Why don't you pay attention to your own pile before worrying about mine?"

"I'm concerned about both of our needs, Bianca." His tone dropped, and his eyes moved to my heaving chest. "You should put your shirt back on when we return to the beach."

"It's too hot." I shook my head and straightened my shoulders. I was no longer self-conscious that I was only in my bra and panties.

"Or you can take them off." He grinned and licked his lips. "I wouldn't tell you that's a bad idea."

"It's not your place to tell me anything," I snapped back, annoyed.

"I'm just concerned about you." He took a step toward me and ran a finger along my shoulder. "I don't want you to get sunburned."

"And being naked will help prevent that how?"

"My body will shield you from the sun. I can make sure that all you have is a healthy glow."

"That sounds really comfortable."

"I don't think you'll be complaining." He took another step toward me, and I could feel his chest brushing against my breasts. "In fact, you might even find that you like it."

"I don't think so." My words were barely a whisper as I stared up at him. My fingers were aching to reach out to touch his taut stomach. His abs were mocking me with their perfection.

"I can take your mind off your worries." His eyes crinkled

as he stared at the top of my breasts. "You have so little on, yet still I feel you are teasing me with your modesty."

"My modesty?" I laughed. "I'm in a bra and panties."

"A full-coverage bra and panties." He sighed.

"Sorry I didn't wear my thong and half-cut bra in anticipation of getting kidnapped and meeting you."

"That's okay." He smiled at me. "The anticipation is what makes it sweeter."

"The anticipation of what?"

"Seeing your body." His tone was gruff. "When I finally see all of you, it will—"

I cut him off. "You're not going to see all of me!"

"No?" He laughed as his arm reached around my waist and pulled me toward him. This time, my breasts were crushed against his chest and I could feel his growing manhood pressed against my belly. "You're so hot," he whispered against my ear as his hands fell to my ass and pulled me to him.

"Thank you." I gazed up at him, barely able to hide my lust.

"Why did you have to be so hot?" His voice deepened as his fingers massaged my behind. "I like a girl with a big butt." His lips whispered against mine as he squeezed.

"I don't have a big butt," I muttered back indignantly.

"It makes doggie style so much more enjoyable." He winked down at me as his fingers moved up my hips and held on to my waist. "Don't you think?"

"I don't know." I was starting to feel feverish by his closeness. I wanted him to make a move, but I didn't want him to know how badly I wanted him to touch me. "Wait, what?" I glanced up at him. "Did you say 'doggie style'?"

"Don't you like it?" He cocked his head and grinned.

"You're disgusting. Do you really think I'm just going to sleep with you? Do you think that I—"

"I like it when you're feisty." He took a step back. "Now that you've gotten your energy back, it's time to work."

"Excuse me? I was working, I was just—"

"Try not to stare at my ass too much this time." He walked away, laughing, and I turned away with a red face before starting to gather more branches.

"Ass," I muttered to the ground, and tried to ignore the rumbling of my stomach. I was starving, but sick of bananas, too. "It's starting to rain."

"Are you sure you don't want to go back to the shack for protection?" He walked over to me. "Though, I don't think it'll rain that long."

"I'm positive. Why do you think it won't rain long?"

"Rain comes in short bursts in the tropics."

"Okay." I nodded. "And no, I don't want to go back to the shack ever again. That place is spooky."

"You think it's haunted?"

"I don't think it's haunted, but I also don't want to come face-to-face with some crazy person."

"Like Casper the ghost?"

"Very funny—*not*. Casper was a friendly ghost. I'm talking about Freddy Krueger or the Sandman. If I saw either of them, we'd be rescued pretty quickly, trust me."

"Why's that?"

"Because if I saw them, my screams would be so loud that they'd hear me in outer space."

"I wonder if I can make you scream that loudly."

"When? During Halloween?" I asked stupidly, only realizing my idiocy after I spoke.

"When I take you and make you orgasm." He took a step toward me. "Maybe we should see right now? Feel free to scream as loudly as you want as I enter you."

"No, thank you." I blushed.

"Maybe after we find Steve?"

"Yeah, that'll happen."

"If we go back to the shack, we might catch Steve there, then we'd know that he left the notes for us."

"Not right now, thanks. You can go if you want."

"Wouldn't you like to know why Steve is here?"

"Not right now. Maybe after some food and when I have my clothes back on." I gave him an arch look. "I need energy to do my kung fu moves. If I want to take Steve down, I'll need to be fully prepared."

"You know kung fu?"

"Well, not technically kung fu. More like karate."

"Karate?" He looked impressed. "What belt are you?"

"You mean like black belt?"

"You have a black belt in karate? Wow." He bowed down to me. "I guess you can take care of me, then."

I blushed as I realized he'd misunderstood what I was saying. "I don't have a black belt in karate."

"Tae kwon do?"

"I don't have a black belt in anything." I shook my head. "Well, I do own several black leather belts. Some aren't real leather, but you can't really tell."

"Sorry. What?" His eyes narrowed, and his expression became confused.

"I thought they were leather, but they weren't," I continued, but I could see him starting to look impatient. "Anyway, my point is I don't actually have any vast experience in the martial arts, but I did take a weekend self-defense class with my friend Rosie. I also had a boyfriend in college who was into Shaolin movies, so I've seen quite a few."

"Bianca." His voice was controlled. "I think you missed your calling. You should definitely go into the profession of spouting absolutely useless random facts from movies."

"That's offensive." I made a face at him. "And factually incorrect. I didn't tell you anything about the Shaolin movies. I was just trying—"

"Though," he said, cutting me off, "I suppose that it's better than you saying you learned karate from watching *The Karate Kid*."

I kept my mouth shut even though I wanted to tell him about the move I had learned from watching Mr. Miyagi.

"Wait, don't tell me. That's how you know about the aliens, right? You saw them when you had an out-of-body experience?"

"You're going to have an out-of-body experience if you don't shut up." I turned toward him and caught him laughing at me. "I'm glad you think it's funny to make fun of an innocent, kidnapped woman who is trapped on an island with two psycho men."

"You got part of that sentence wrong."

"What?" I frowned.

"You should have said innocent kidnapped man who is trapped on an island with a psycho man and woman."

"Whatever, asshole."

"You really like my ass, don't you." His hands fell to the top of his briefs. "I can show it to you if you want."

"No!" I exclaimed a little louder than expected. However, my gaze didn't falter. If he wanted to show me, I wasn't going to miss it.

"Let's fish." He suddenly released his waistband and grabbed my hand, and I jumped.

"What?" I looked at him in confusion and disappointment.

"We're both hungry. And it's raining. It'll be easier to catch fish if it's raining."

"Really?"

"Yes, really. They will be jumping more and they'll be closer to the shore."

"I guess." I bit my lower lip. "I don't know if I'll be able to catch them with my hands. They seem like they can swim fast."

"Catch them with your hands?" His lips trembled.

"I don't see any rods or bait. Do you?" I snapped at him.

"Nope." His eyes were laughing at me.

"What's so funny?"

"Grab your branches and follow me."

"Where are we going?"

"To catch our dinner."

"More like breakfast, lunch, and dinner."

"Would you like fries with that whine?"

"Funny joke—not. I used to say that when I was a kid."

"Last year, then?"

"I'm twenty-five, ass."

"You're a twenty-five-year-old ass?" He seemed to be in good spirits now as we walked back to the sand with our arms full.

"I'm going to have so many muscles by the end of this trip." I stopped then and made a face. "Well, I guess this isn't a trip, but you know what I mean."

"I know what you mean."

"So we're going to fish instead of building the shelter?"

"If you don't mind getting wet." He nodded. "We can build the shelter later."

"I don't mind."

"So tell me more about you. Do you have any brothers and sisters? Do you often compare your life to movies?"

"No brothers and sisters, no." My voice trembled slightly as I thought about my parents. "My dad told me that he and my mom wanted more kids, but it never happened, and then she died."

"How did she die, again?" His voice was soft, and I kept my eyes ahead.

"Car accident." My words were short. "What about you? Any siblings?"

"I grew up as an only child with my mom." His voice seemed to turn emotional. "She was a great mom. She did everything she could to give me the best life she could."

"She was a single mom?" I looked at him in surprise.

"Yes." His voice was curt. "She was a poor single mother, and I was her life."

"So you didn't grow up rich?"

"No, I didn't. I was around rich people due to my mother's work. She was a maid, but we weren't rich. I got to where I am by my own blood, sweat, and toil."

"Sounds ominous."

"Maybe because it is." He shrugged. "You don't become a billionaire by being gentle."

"You've done bad things?" My eyes narrowed, and my breath quickened as I thought about his acknowledging that he would kill someone if he had to.

"Let's just say I'm loyal to those I think I should be loyal to."

"How do you make that decision?"

"Family, business, life." He shrugged. "My mom always told me it was important to hold off judgment until I knew someone personally. Though, of course it's hard in certain circumstances."

"Why is it hard?"

"Because sometimes loyalties are so strong they can't be broken." He paused. "And then there are people who can break loyalties in a second, if the price is right."

"Is that why you fired Bridgette?" I interjected smoothly. "Was she disloyal?"

"Bridgette liked to carry information, yes." He nodded. "Once someone shows me who they are, I don't give them a second chance to break my trust."

"What did she do?"

"She valued her relationship with David more than she valued her job." His eyes grew distant, and he didn't notice my sudden intake of breath. So he did know David.

"You didn't like that?"

"It was a stupid game for someone in her position to play. She thought she bet on the right brother. She had no idea."

"What do you mean?" My voice was sharp, and I watched his face change into an impenetrable mask.

"Nothing." He shook his head. "Bridgette is one of those women I've been telling you about. She's nothing but a gold digger. She decided to betray me because David is a fool."

"She played you?"

"She was just looking for someone to marry her." He shrugged. "I wasn't about to marry her."

"You slept with her?" I felt my stomach tense up as I thought about Jakob being intimate with Bridgette.

"She meant nothing to me. I would never marry someone like her. I think the bond of marriage should be sacred. I don't think it is for many people. I don't find that people go into marriage for the right reasons anymore."

"Oh."

"So to answer your earlier question, my loyalties are related to blood, duty, and trust."

"It's hard to know when to trust people." I dropped the branches on the ground, grateful that we'd finally arrived back at our spot. I wanted to confront him. I wanted to tell him I didn't trust him, but I didn't know how that would help. I didn't think that confronting him would lead me to any new answers related to the kidnapping. However, I was starting to wonder if perhaps he couldn't provide other answers. He obviously had access to Bradley Inc. in some capacity. Perhaps I'd be able to use him to gain access to the corporation when we got back to the States. Whenever that was.

"Yes. Sometimes it's easy to be deceived." He looked up at the sky and then back at me. "It's about to start pouring. We should gather some leaves and tie them together, see if we can weave some sort of bowls. That way we can catch some of the rainwater. Are you prepared to get wet?"

"I'm grateful for the rain on my skin, to be honest. It's so hot here." I put my face up toward the sky and grinned as drops of water crashed down on me. "It feels wonderful."

"Yes, it does." His voice was soft, and I looked toward him. He was staring at me with an odd expression as I danced around in the rain.

"Everything okay?" I asked him softly.

"You have many pieces to your puzzle, don't you, Bianca London."

"Yes, I do, Jakob." I nodded back at him seriously. If he only knew how many pieces I had, he'd be a lot less cocky.

"Come. Let's go in the water." He grabbed his shirt and two branches in one hand and then grabbed my hand with his free one.

"We're going to swim?"

"We're going to catch dinner."

"Oh." I laughed as we ran to the ocean. "I guess we're not going to be using our hands?"

"You guessed right." He smiled. "We'll tie the arms of the shirt to the branches, and then we'll scour the water with the shirt and treat it like a net."

"I hope it works," I said as my stomach grumbled. "I'm so hungry."

"I hope it works too." He gave me a reassuring smile, and my heart melted for a second as I stared at his water-drenched face. His hair was wet and slick, and he had never looked sexier. "If we don't catch any fish, I'll go back into the jungle and see what fruit I can find. I'm pretty sure I saw some more banana trees, and we already know there are coconuts. I think I even saw some five-finger."

"What's five-finger?" I shivered, wondering if he was talking about real fingers.

"It's a fruit. You might know it as star apple."

"Is it like Granny Smiths?"

"No." He laughed. "It's nothing like Granny Smiths."

"Oh, okay." I took one side of the shirt and tied the arm tightly to the coconut branch. "So what are we going to do?" I looked at him for guidance. "Just drag it in the water?"

"What?" His eyes narrowed, and he looked at me intensely.

"Are we just going to drag the shirt through the water?" I repeated breathlessly as he continued to stare at me.

"Yes." He nodded, but his eyes didn't leave me. "Your bra is getting wet," he said after a few seconds, and I looked down at my completely soaked bra, now molded to my skin.

"Yes it is." I nodded and looked back at him. "So are your briefs."

"Enjoying the view?"

"There's not much to see." I shrugged, and he laughed.

"We can change that." His hand grabbed the top of his briefs and he started to pull them down.

"What are you doing?" My voice rose.

"Wanted to give you a view you could see better."

"No thanks."

"Aww." He laughed. "I was hoping it would be tit for tat."

"Excuse me?"

"My briefs for your panties."

"You wish."

"Yes, I do." He stared at me suggestively again, and I felt my skin burning up.

"Let's just concentrate on this fish." I turned away from him and started moving the shirt in the water.

He grinned at me. "Follow my movements. We can't go charging through the water or we'll scare the fish. We have to stand still."

"Aren't they going to see us standing there?"

"They won't pay attention to us if we stand still. They'll think we're just part of the landscape in the water."

"Really?" I was surprised. "I didn't know that fish were that dumb."

"I don't know if they are, but it sounded good." He laughed.

"You're a goof."

"Yay, I'm moving up in the world. I've gone from ass to goof."

"Hopefully you can move up from goof to predator," I responded without thinking.

"I don't think I have to move anywhere to be called a predator," he replied softly, and I pretended that I hadn't heard him.

❧

I became bored after about ten minutes. Standing there waiting for fish to approach was one of the most tedious things I'd ever done in my life. My arms were also growing tired, though, I didn't want to tell Jakob that.

"So how long are we going to just stand here?" I asked softly.

"Until we catch something to eat."

"That could be all day," I moaned. "We're just standing here in the rain. I don't see any fish jumping, and we haven't caught anything yet."

"Well, we just need to concentrate harder."

"I can barely see." I blinked the water out of my eyes. "And I'm started to get cold."

"Let's just wait another ten minutes and see if we get anything."

"Uh-huh. Maybe a big trout will just jump into your shirt and save us some time." I rolled my eyes.

"You never know." He grinned.

"How many times have you been fishing, Jakob?" My eyes narrowed, and I stared at him.

"Once when I was a young boy. And no, I didn't catch anything."

"Oh, this is great," I groaned. "How do you know they're going to be jumping in the water, then?"

"I don't."

"What?"

"It sounded good though, right? Like I knew what I was talking about?"

"So you really had no clue?"

"I really have no clue, Bianca." His tone changed, and so did his expression. "Shh." He put a finger to his lip. "I think I see a school of fish swimming toward us."

"Are you sure?" I whispered back excitedly, and stared into the water. I could make out a dark shape moving toward us, and I prayed that it was fish and not the fourth coming of Jaws.

"I'm pretty sure." He nodded, but he didn't move his eyes from the fish. "When I say go, drop the shirt, push it forward and lift."

"Okay." I stood as still as possible and waited for his command.

"Go!" he yelled, and we dropped the shirt into the water and pushed it forward to scoop up the fish.

"We got some!" I cried out in excitement as I saw some fish trying to jump out of the shirt.

"Beginners' luck." He grinned at me as he tied the shirt into a little bundle.

"I can't believe we caught four fish!" I exclaimed as we made our way back to the sand. "How are we going to eat them? Not live?"

"No." He laughed. "We have the lighters, remember? We should be able to start a fire, and we can grill them."

"Oh, that sounds amazing." I made my way with him to the shore, and we both laughed as my stomach growled.

～

"That tasted really good. Almost as good as if it were made in a restaurant." I licked my lips and leaned back. "Thank you."

"I'm glad you enjoyed it." He patted his stomach. "I feel pretty satisfied myself."

"So what do you think happened to Steve?" I asked him curiously. My eyes watched his every move to see how he reacted.

"I don't know. Maybe he's playing some sort of game." He frowned.

"Do you think we should look for him now? I feel like we both keep delaying the search."

"I think that's what he wants." Jakob moved closer to me.

"He wants us to come to us. You ever study military history as part of your degree?"

"You think he wants to ambush us?"

"I think he has an agenda."

I closed my eyes and sighed loudly. "I wish I knew what was going on."

"We should talk again." His hand reached out and grabbed mine. "See if we can figure out anything else."

"You mean the Bridgette connection?"

"Yes, the Bridgette connection."

"I don't know how that would be of any help." I shrugged. "She dated my ex before I did." I debated asking him whether he knew David, but he spoke before I could decide.

"Bianca," he said my name slowly, and I looked at him. He was frowning and his expression looked annoyed. "There was something else in my envelope."

"Oh?"

"A photograph."

"A photograph of what?"

I watched as Jakob stood up and walked over to his pants. He pulled out both of our letters and a photo, which he brought over to me.

"Can you explain this?" He dropped the photo in my lap, and my body froze. The photo was of me and Bridgette smiling at a party about a year ago.

"I . . . I . . ." I stumbled over my words. "It's a long story."

"Bianca, I'm going to ask you a question, and I want you to be honest. Did you steal your ex from Bridgette?"

"No," I shook my head. "I swear I didn't know they were dating when I met them."

"Who did you meet first?"

"Technically I met Bridgette first, but I thought they were just friends."

"Did you have a plan to meet him?" he asked me softly, and my heart sunk.

"Yes." I nodded. "I had a plan." I paused and reached out for his hand. "It wasn't because I was a gold digger though."

"So you weren't after the Bradley family money?" His eyes narrowed, and I shook my head.

"How did you know David?" My heart started beating rapidly as I decided to stop chickening out. "When I mentioned my ex was David Bradley, why didn't you say anything?"

"I didn't make the connection. My brain was still contemplating the fact that I'd been kidnapped. Bridgette was my assistant. Yes, we slept together a couple of times. It didn't mean anything. I knew that she started dating someone else, but I didn't care," he said with a shrug. "She was my secretary. Nothing more. It was only when I found out that she was sharing classified information with David that I fired her."

"So you know David?" I persisted with my questioning. I wasn't going to allow him to distract me from this questioning.

"Not very well." He shook his head. "I know of him. I like to keep to myself."

"I guess that makes sense, what with you being so rich." I lay back and asked softly, "How did you make your money again?"

"I'm in venture capitalism. Buying small businesses and selling them for a profit was how I started. Now I buy larger companies and either sell them for a profit or maximize their business productivity and keep the profits for myself."

"So you don't care about the businesses?"

"Some of the businesses have their uses. I don't do anything based on emotion. Every act in my life has a purpose."

"You sound so driven. It seems so boring."

"It's not always boring. Sometimes I buy some cool companies. Last year I bought a vineyard and a chocolate factory."

"I love wine and chocolates."

"I love the money both companies are now making me. I keep companies based on the value they add to my portfolio."

"That sounds like a lot of hard work."

"I like hard work. My mom taught me that the only thing that matters in life is hard work."

"What about love?"

"Love is for fools." His tone was derisive. "All love does is make people weak."

"So you don't believe in true love?"

"There is no true love. One person always loves the other one more. One person always gives up something. Human beings will do more for money than for love."

I thought about his words and felt sad. "My parents were really in love, but it was cut short."

"Death is a sad part of life."

"Yes, it is." I sighed. "I still believe in love though."

"You're the sort of girl who could make me believe in love as well," he whispered into my ear. "But don't start getting any ideas."

"Are you becoming a softy, Jakob?" I smiled at him, and my insides felt warm.

"I don't think anyone could ever accuse me of being soft." His hand rubbed my back. "Not inside the office and definitely not in the bedroom."

"You're a regular lothario, huh."

"I don't sleep around, if that's what you're asking."

"You don't sleep around?"

"I don't do relationships, but I'm not a man whore. I'm not in and out of bedrooms. I don't have a revolving door or a little black book."

"That's hard to believe."

"Why?"

"You seem like you'd have a lot of ladies," I mumbled, feeling slightly taken aback by the intense expression he had on his face as he stared at me.

"Why would you think that?"

"You're so handsome." I shrugged. "And you're rich."

"Those are the two least important qualities in a man."

"I never said they were important. They're not what I look for in a man."

"Good." He leaned down and kissed me. "I don't look for those qualities in a man either," he joked, his eyes glinting with amusement.

"Are you mad that I didn't tell you I knew Bridgette better than I let on earlier?"

"No, I understand why you didn't tell me." I bit my lower lip and stared at him for a few seconds.

"But . . . ?" His eyes narrowed as he surveyed my face.

"You're making it hard for me to trust you, Jakob. First, our accidental meeting at the coffee shop might not have been so accidental, then we both get kidnapped, then I find out you're in the process of trying to buy Bradley Inc., then I find out that your ex-assistant is my ex-boyfriend's ex-girlfriend who hates me. And then to make it all worse, I find out that you actually kind of know David. To top it off, there's another guy on the island with us that has just disappeared into thin air. And we're getting more threatening notes."

"What do you mean, *more*?"

"Nothing."

"Bianca?"

"I got notes before I was kidnapped as well."

"What sort of notes?"

"Threatening notes."

"Like death threats?"

"Not exactly." I shook my head. "And I guess, I shouldn't say notes, it was one note."

"What did it say?"

"Something about two people, one surviving and one being destroyed."

"I see." I watched as his shoulders stiffened and his hands squared into fists.

"It's fine. It didn't scare me."

"We need to get off of this island. I promise, I'll help you find out whatever you need to know."

"What do you get though?"

"I get the truth."

"I'm worried about Steve." I looked at the dark green mysterious jungle behind us. "What if he's lost?"

"I doubt he's lost."

"What do you think happened to Steve?" I whispered again, and touched the healing cut on his cheek.

"I don't know, but I promise I won't let him harm you."

"He didn't seem dangerous." I shivered and moved forward to kiss his cheek.

"Looks can be deceiving. We can't be too careful."

"I know." I yawned. "I just wish I . . ." I stopped talking as his hand reached out behind my head and pulled me toward him. His eyes sought mine and I stared at his lashes and eyebrows. They were perfectly groomed. His stubble had grown in even more, and he was close to having a beard. He looked even sexier with his rough look. All of a sudden I wasn't so tired anymore. I reached up and brushed some sand off of his shoulders. His skin was hot beneath my fingertips, and I enjoyed the slight shock that vibrated through my body each time I touched him. I looked down at his chest and held my breath; his body showed off a perfect bronze tan, and I was envious of how smooth and silky his skin felt and looked.

"Are you tired?" His fingers ran down my cheek and to my lips.

"A little." My tongue darted out and licked his finger as it trailed across my lower lip.

"That's good," he said, and then leaned down toward me, gathering me in his arms as he lowered both of us to the ground. As soon as we hit the sand, his lips descended onto mine. His tongue entered my mouth smoothly, and my fingers ran through his hair eagerly. He groaned against my mouth, and I felt his fingers tracing down the side of my body as he lowered himself on top of me. He grabbed me and rolled me onto my side, and his hand pushed my leg up as he slid one of his legs between mine. I could feel his hardness pressed up against me, and I moaned.

"You're so sexy," he muttered, and I felt his fingers undoing my bra. He slid the straps down my arms and then threw it onto the sand. He pulled away from me for a second to stare at my breasts, and his breathing became loud and raspy. His fingers reached for my breasts and touched them gingerly. I closed my eyes and rested my head back on the sand as he caressed my nipples.

"Oh!" I cried out as he lowered his lips to my right breast and sucked. A feeling of desire ran through my stomach as he nibbled on one breast and squeezed the other one with his fingers. Then he kissed back up my chest and to my neck, before licking a trail up from my collarbone back to my lips.

"I could taste you all night," he groaned as he kissed me again. My hands ran to his back and then to his chest. My fingers ran down his abs and then along the side of his stomach, enjoying the hard yet silky feel of his skin. He pushed me

onto my back, and his fingers slipped between my legs, rubbing me softly over my panties. My legs parted more at his
touch, and I moaned as his fingers increased their pressure
against me. His eyes stared into mine as he slipped his fingers
into my panties, and his finger rubbed my clit. "You're so
wet." He groaned against my lips and increased the pressure
of his fingers. "I have to taste all of you." He slipped his fingers out of my panties and kissed down my stomach and
stopped right below my belly button. He glanced back up at
me, and I nodded eagerly, not wanting to think too hard
about what he was about to do. His mouth continued kissing,
and he caught my panties between his teeth and tugged them
down. I lifted my hips slightly so he could pull them off more
easily, and I felt a whoosh of fresh air down below when he
succeeded. He sat up slightly to pull my panties off my ankles,
and then he leaned forward and spread my legs apart.

"This is okay?" He looked down at me with a questioning
look, and I nodded up at him. Within seconds his face was
buried between my legs, and his tongue was lapping up my
juices eagerly. I groaned and closed my eyes as I reached
down and grabbed the top of his head.

"Oh, Jakob," I cried out as his tongue entered me and his
lips sucked down on me. I gripped the top of his hair and
bucked my hips under him. I felt so wet and his tongue felt so
good inside me. He moved his tongue in and out furiously,
and I could feel the climax building up inside me. "I'm going
to come!" I cried out, and spread my legs even wider. That
seemed to turn him on even more, and his hands grabbed my

hips and pulled me even closer to his face. He withdrew his tongue from inside of me and flicked my clit back and forth with his tongue before entering me again. I screamed as I came, my body shaking and trembling as the climax took over.

He backed away from me and grinned, and I watched as he yanked his briefs down. His cock stood at attention, and I gazed at his magnificent hardness. He lay back down next to me and kissed my cheek as his fingers once again played with my nipples.

"I knew you'd taste like heaven," he whispered in my ear before kissing me again.

"You have a way with your tongue," I whispered against his lips, and moaned as I felt his fingers between my legs again. "Oooh." I spread my legs as his fingers rubbed my clit.

"You're already wet again," he groaned as he continued playing with me. He repositioned his body, and I felt his cock between my legs. He kissed me again hard, and my body exploded in pleasure as I felt his tongue in my mouth, at the same time he started pinching my nipples. His fingers then left my nipples and moved down toward his cock. He grabbed it and placed it at my entrance and rubbed the tip of his cock against me gently. I squirmed beneath him and he groaned. "I want to fuck you so badly," he whispered in my ear, and I felt the tip of him enter me slowly. I froze, and my eyes popped open in fear. As badly as I wanted him, this didn't feel right. My body wanted him, but my brain still wasn't sure if I trusted him. There had been too many revelations that had come out recently. I didn't want to sleep with him and regret it. I was a romantic at heart, and while I wanted to feel him inside me, I wasn't sure that now was the right time. He looked at me for a second and then withdrew his cock from me and groaned.

"I'm sorry," I whispered, and leaned over and ran my fingers down his chest.

"Don't be sorry," he groaned, and closed his eyes. "Good things come to those who wait."

"Thank you." I reached up to kiss him, and he pulled me into his arms.

"No, thank you." He kissed the top of my forehead, and I snuggled into his chest and closed my eyes. The fact that I hadn't had to ask him to stop made me feel more comfortable with him. The fact that he'd known from a look on my face that I wasn't ready spoke words to me. He was in tune with my feelings, and he respected me enough to not try to talk me into it. I lay in his arms knowing that I wasn't a complete and utter fool. Jakob was a good guy. I knew it in my soul. Though, that didn't stop me from thinking about Steve. Why hadn't Jakob seemed more worried about his disappearance? And what role did both of them play in our being here? I felt my calmness seeping out as I lay there listening to Jakob snoring. I was no closer to finding out what had happened to my mother. In fact, I was even farther away than I had been when I'd first found my father's letter.

eight

"Wakey, wakey, sleepy Bianca." Jakob's warm voice whispered in my ear, and I stretched out and smiled. "I have breakfast for you." His voice spoke again; this time I felt the tip of his tongue tickling my inner ear.

"Morning." I opened my eyes slowly and saw Jakob's face a mere inch from mine. "Oh." I blinked rapidly as my eyes focused in on his lips.

"Good sleep?"

"Yes." I nodded and smiled.

"Hungry?"

"Absolutely."

"Limited vocabulary?" He grinned, and I sat up and rolled my eyes.

"I'm not even going to respond." I stretched my arms and reached for my bra.

"You don't have to put that on. I bet that won't be feeling

too comfortable right now." Jakob's face reminded me of a lascivious wolf, and I ignored him.

"Thanks for your concern." I laughed as I slipped on my bra. "You got up and brought breakfast to me?" I stared at the fruits lying on the large green palm leaf. "That was really thoughtful of you."

"You looked so peaceful lying there. I didn't have the heart to wake you up."

"Who knew you had a heart?"

"Don't get used to it." He sat down next to me. "After last night I wanted to make sure you got a good rest."

"I almost forgot we weren't here by choice." I gave him a small smile. "And how much I hate the wilderness."

"It's not so bad when we have nights like last night." He handed me a peeled banana. "Try this; it's firm and sweet."

"Thank you." I took it from his hands and nibbled on it. "It's delicious." I gobbled up the rest of the banana greedily and then licked my lips. "Best breakfast I've had in a long while."

"Do you enjoy breakfast, then?" He sat back and watched me as I reached for another banana. I felt slightly self-conscious that he was just sitting there watching me eat, but I soon got over it.

"I don't normally eat breakfast," I mumbled between bites. "I'm the sort of person who waits until lunchtime and then gobbles up everything in sight."

"That's not healthy." He frowned.

"It's just how I grew up." I shrugged. "My dad was the

same way. He kept really odd working hours, and I guess it caught on with me."

"So what was your dad like?" he asked casually, grabbing a banana.

"He was really wonderful. He was devoted to me. Though, he was very forgetful when he was working on a new invention. I can't tell you how many times I waited at school after the last bell because he was late to pick me up."

"Why didn't he just hire a nanny?"

"He didn't have money for a nanny." I stared down the beach. "He never made much money from his inventions."

"I thought he created the self-painter."

"He did." I gave him a wry smile. "That's part of the reason why I'm trying to get access to Bradley Inc."

"I see. That makes sense. What's the other part of the reason?"

"I think that David's father had my mother killed."

"What?"

"My father didn't believe my mother died in an accident." I decided to tell him almost everything. I figured I couldn't be mad at him for holding back, when I was holding back as well. "When he died he left me the letter I told you about, but he also left me some business papers. Papers that would lead someone to believe that the timing of my mother's accident was too coincidental to have been an accident."

"So that's the real reason why you're trying to gain access to the files?"

"Yes." I nodded. "I just want to go through all the files from that time period. I want to go through the financials. I want to know if the corporation would have been okay if my father had left. I want to know when and why it changed from Bradley, London, and Maxwell to Bradley Inc."

"I didn't know." He pursed his lips and looked toward the ocean. "I wish I'd known."

"It's okay." I shrugged. "I didn't tell you."

"This has nothing to do with the money for you, does it?" He cursed under his tongue. "I'm sorry for my earlier comments."

"Don't worry about it. But no, I'm not investigating so I can get a whole bunch of money."

"I'm going to help you, Bianca." He threw the banana peel on the ground. "It's a shame that your father wasn't compensated properly by the company."

"Yeah, it really was." My mind flashed back to the all the different patents I'd found in my father's box, and I looked back at Jakob. "It's surprising as well, because he was really quite brilliant. I'm not sure why he just walked away without demanding his cut. I mean, I know he loved my mother, and he was devastated by her death, but I never thought he'd just walk away from something like that. I guess he just didn't care about money."

"Isn't that always the way? The brilliant ones never seem to make much money. Such is the life of a genius." He shrugged. "Even though many of them seem to be chasing the money, karma always catches up with them."

"Yeah, I guess so. I can't say I know any geniuses that are chasing money," I said with a sigh. "Do you?"

"I know men who *think* they are geniuses." He scratched his right eyebrow. "I know men that will do anything for money. I know men who figure out on their deathbed that their love of money got them nowhere."

"Who are you talking about?"

"No one in particular." He shook his head.

"What's your father like?" I changed the subject, hoping I could find out more about this man I was starting to fall for. At first, it had been all about the physical attraction, but now, as each day passed, I realized that I liked who he was as a person. He was genuinely caring, and I believed he had my best interests at heart. It was just so hard, because he was so reserved and closed off. I still didn't really know anything truly personal about Jakob. He was still essentially a stranger. A stranger I wanted to get to know better.

"He's dead." His voice was curt.

"I'm sorry."

"Don't be; I didn't know him very well, and we weren't close."

"Did you never meet him, then?"

"No, I knew him all my life." He gave me a twisted smile and lay back on the sand. "I've been thinking."

"About what?"

"Everything." He looked up at me, but he didn't smile. "I wonder what's going on in the real world."

"We are in the real world." I laughed. "Unless you think we're in some sort of twilight zone or time warp or something."

"I don't." He groaned and rested his face on his hand. "So who in the real world is worried about you right now?"

"Rosie must be freaking out." I lay down next to him. "I bet she's gone to the news media and everything. What about you?"

"I can't say that anyone will be worried about me." He shrugged and moved a few strands of hair from my eyes.

"That's sad." I reached out and removed a small leaf from the side of his ear. "You know what you never told me?"

"What's that?" he asked curiously, and ran his fingers down my cheek.

"You never told me where you were the night we got kidnapped." I was testing him. I still remembered what he'd said when I'd asked him before, and I wanted to see if his answer was going to remain the same.

"I was leaving work," he said smoothly as his fingers ran along my lips.

"You must have been deep in thought to not have noticed two men following you."

"Yeah, I guess I was."

"Had you had any alcohol earlier that day?" I whispered as his fingers moved to my neck and then to the valley between my breasts.

"No." He shook his head. "I wasn't drugged, at least not via alcohol."

"How did they get you . . ." My voice trailed off as his

fingertips ran along the curve of my breasts. "What are you doing?"

"Touching you." He leaned in closer to me. "You can touch me too."

"I don't want to," I mumbled as my fingers flew to his chest.

"Liar," he whispered.

"I'm not lying." My eyes widened as his fingers worked their way to the back of my bra. "I thought we were going to look for Steve this morning."

"He can wait." He grinned and bit down on my shoulder. "Can I?" His eyes fell to my breasts as his fingers paused on my bra clasp, and then he looked back up at me. I nodded, and he grinned as he undid my bra. "Do you want to have a bath?" He pulled away from me and smiled at me. I was grateful that he wasn't staring at my breasts or attempting to get into my panties. I knew that I wouldn't be able to tell him no if he did. I could still remember the pleasure he had brought me the night before, and I wasn't sure I'd be able to stop him from going all the way again.

"I'd die for a warm luxurious bubble bath right now, with some Epsom salts." I rested my head on the sand and sighed. "And then I'd like a nice massage. Someone with nice firm hands."

"I can't guarantee any bubbles, and I can't guarantee that the water will be warm, but I'm willing to give you a massage."

"What?" I sat back up and felt my breasts falling forward.

"What?" he repeated as his hands fell to my breasts and played with my nipples.

"Jakob, you were telling me you were going to give me a massage!" I closed my eyes and withheld a moan as his fingers played with my breasts.

"I am." His deep voice sounded hoarse, and I knew he was feeling horny without looking down to his briefs.

"I'd like my back massaged, not my breasts," I whispered before moaning loudly. His lips were sucking on my right nipple, and his teeth were nibbling on it as if it were a carrot and he was a hungry rabbit.

"You taste so sweet." He groaned as he pushed me back to the ground and fondled my other breast with his fingers. "I almost forgot."

"Don't you mean salty?" I replied breathlessly.

"I mean divine. Your breasts almost make me forget my hunger."

"Jakob." I pushed him back slightly. "Why don't you seem concerned about finding Steve?"

"What do you mean?"

"He's been gone for over a day and yet, we haven't even gone to look for him." I nibbled on my lips. "Did you hurt him? You can tell me. I just need to know."

"I didn't touch him. I swear to God. I haven't done anything to him."

"So why haven't we gone to look for him?"

"I promise we'll go later today. I don't know why we haven't gone as yet. I guess I've just enjoyed spending time with you."

"How are we going to get off of this island, Jakob?" My voice cracked. "I don't know what we're going to do."

"Where there is a will, there is a way."

"That's not tangible. I don't see how that helps me—us." I was starting to panic and I took a couple of deep breaths. "I think I need to relax. What were you saying about a bath?"

"I'm pretty sure there's a river somewhere close by. I heard running water when I went to pick the fruit."

"Oh." I made a face. "I don't know if I want to go back into the jungle."

"There's nothing to be afraid of."

"Besides the fact that there might be a psychopath on the island with us."

"I think if he wanted to kill us, we'd be dead by now. And we don't know that he's a psycho."

"That's comforting." I bit my lower lip as I shivered and cuddled up next to him.

"Don't be scared, Bianca. Come on, let's go. I think we'll both benefit from a nice dip in some non-salt water."

"Okay. You're going to massage me, right?"

"Try to stop me."

"Can I ask you a question, Jakob? If you grew up poor, and you never knew your father, how did you make your money? Is it all legitimate?"

"Just through business, like I said." His voice was short, and he jumped up. "I need to go wash this salt water and sweat off my skin. We can talk more as we bathe if you want."

"You'd leave me here by myself if I said I didn't want to go?"

"I thought you felt safe on the beach."

"I feel safer being with you," I acknowledged lightly.

"I see." He grinned and pulled me up to join him. "I'm happy to hear that." His arms went around my waist, and I stepped toward him so that my breasts were crushed against his chest. His fingers fell to my ass and cupped my butt cheeks. "Don't you want to feel fresh and clean as well?"

"Are you saying I smell?" I raised an eyebrow at him, and he chuckled.

"I wouldn't kick you out of bed, if that's what you're asking."

"No, that's not what I was asking." My hands reached up around his neck, and I pressed myself into him, enjoying the warmth of his body next to mine.

"I think I saw some yucca plants when I was gathering bananas."

"Okay?" I waited for him to continue. "And?"

"If I recall correctly, the yucca root can be used as a natural soap, and so can the leaves if we rub them with some rocks a little bit to release their oozy gooeyness."

"Why didn't you tell me this before?" I groaned and touched my hair. "I'd love to shampoo my hair. I must look a right mess."

"You look beautiful." He gazed into my eyes without smiling. My breath caught as he leaned down to kiss me hard. His hands pushed me against him hard and slid up to fondle my breasts while his hardness moved against my stomach. My mouth opened slowly to let his tongue in, and I wasn't disappointed when I finally felt our tongues collide in a game of absolute passion. I melted against him as he sucked on my tongue, alternating between a soft feathery suction and a harder, more arduous action.

"Jakob." I pulled away from him, feeling slightly mesmerized by him. "Let's go find that waterfall."

"Oh?" His eyes jumped in happiness and I laughed happily at his excitement.

"You're still willing to give me a massage?" I smiled up at him shyly, knowing that I was ready for the massage to lead to more.

"Yes." He grinned. "If you'll let me give you a full-service massage."

"What's a full-service massage?" I asked innocently, though my body was burning up at the places my thoughts were going.

"A naked massage."

"I'm practically naked already."

"There's one very important piece of clothing that needs to be removed." His fingers fell to the top of my panties, and his thumb traced my belly along the top of my underwear.

"If the massage is good, I think that can be arranged." I winked at him, and he burst out laughing.

"You're full of surprises, aren't you."

"Well, you know." I licked my lips. "When in Rome." I stared at his lips and then his chest and reached down and ran my fingers over his abs. It was unfair that his body was so perfect. In comparison, I felt slightly nervous and unsure. I definitely didn't have defined abs or a picture-perfect body.

"What's wrong?" He frowned as he stared at me.

"What do you mean?"

"Your expression changed."

"Wow, you're perceptive."

"Are you nervous? Am I moving too fast for you?"

"No." I shook my head and looked down. "I was just thinking how perfect your body is and how I could stand to lose a pound or twenty."

"You'd be a stick if you lost any weight."

"Yeah right. A stick with some extra pulp."

"I like pulp." He grinned and licked his lips, and I rolled my eyes at him.

"Let's go find this waterfall." I turned away, and he grabbed me. "You might find that I'll repay last night's favor if my massage is good."

"Last night's favor?" His breath caught as I reached down and rubbed the front of his briefs and smiled.

"Hold on." He handed me his shirt. "You should put this on before we leave. I'm not sure we'll make it to the waterfall if you're walking without a top on."

"Why, aren't you thoughtful." I pulled his shirt on and did the buttons up. "I bet you never thought about how useful this shirt would turn out to be when you bought it." I grinned at him. "Catching food, covering strange women, providing cover and warmth at night."

"I don't think the girl who bought it for me considered any of that, you're right."

My stomach churned with jealousy at his words, and

part of me wanted to pull the shirt off. "Who bought it for you?"

"No one important." He grabbed my hand and we started walking toward the jungle. It was a nice day today; there were no dark clouds, and the sun was already beating down on us murderously. The setting was once again idyllic and serene, and I wondered at what point I would stop thinking about ever getting off the island. Being here made me forget all my everyday worries and concerns. It almost made me forget my father's letter, my investigation, and Steve.

"What are we going to do about Steve?" I asked softly as we walked through the jungle. I wasn't as scared as I'd been the first day. The trees that had seemed so tall and full of mischief on the first day seemed majestic and full of life today. The swaying branches and leaves no longer carried scary creatures but food and sustenance. I was accustomed to the different thuds of monkeys swinging and other animals. This was their habitat, and it was beautiful. We walked carefully through the thrush, making sure we stepped over the broken branches that lay in our way. The ground was relatively firm, and the sun had dried out the wet mud from the day before. Jakob held my hand as he led me through the bushes, and I felt safe in his company.

"We'll look for him after we have a bath." He squeezed my hand. "Is that okay?"

"I guess so." I nodded. "I hope nothing bad happened to him."

"I'm almost positive nothing bad has happened to him." He stopped and closed his eyes.

"What are you doing?"

"I'm listening to the sound of the water to see which way to go."

"Oh?" My stomach lurched at his words. I no longer felt as safe in his company, though, I knew I was being ridiculous. It's not as though I thought he had a map to guide us.

"Close your eyes and listen." He suggested. "You'd be surprised at all the noises you notice when you don't have the sense of sight."

"I guess." I closed my eyes and waited. At first, I heard nothing, but then I relaxed. First, I heard two birds that seemed to be chirping to each other as though they were in love. The sound reminded me of the opening scene from *Cinderella*, and I realized that the birds were happy. Their chirps were happy, and that in turn put a smile on my face. Then I heard the sound of dragonflies as they flittered around. I was surprised at the sound, as I hadn't even noticed any since I'd been on the island. I was about to open my eyes, when I heard the sound of running water. It reminded me of the sounds I'd heard at a spa Rosie had taken me to once. She'd paid a couple hundred dollars for our entry and here I was enjoying the same experience for free.

"So, where do you think we should go?" Jakob asked me as we stood there, and I concentrated on the sound of the water for another minute before opening my eyes.

"I think we should walk forward and then try to head toward the left." I pointed ahead. "Is that right?"

"I'm pretty sure it is." He smiled and me gently, and we

continued on our way. I started to feel excited as the sound of flowing water grew louder and louder.

"I have to say, I'm feeling pretty proud of myself." I grinned at Jakob as we increased our pace. "I never would have believed I could locate a waterfall just by listening for it."

"You can do whatever you want to do." Jakob sounded like a motivational speaker as he responded to me, and I wanted to tease him. Then I realized that teasing him would ruin the moment. And this was a moment I didn't want to ruin. "We're here." He stopped and pointed directly in front of us. I could see a small waterfall through the trees and I ran closer to get a better look.

"This is beautiful." I looked back at Jakob for a moment and then stared at the waterfall in front of us. "Who knew this existed on the island with us?"

"Many Caribbean countries have waterfalls." He grabbed my hand and pulled me toward him. His hand started unbuttoning my shirt and I held my breath. "Though, I don't know if it is as beautiful as you."

"You're just saying that."

"I would never lie." He shook his head and pulled the shirt off my arms before reaching back and massaging my shoulders for a few seconds. The tension crept out of my pores as his fingers banished it, and I moaned at the feeling of calmness that was overtaking my body. I closed my eyes for a second, wanting to think about nothing other than his hands squeezing my muscles, when his fingers crept to my stomach and then up the middle of my body. His hands cradled my breasts, and he squeezed them tenderly.

"Shall we go in first?" I moved closer to him, enjoying the sexual thrill that was once again racing through me. "The water looks so inviting, and the rocks look so smooth. I think I could lie down and sunbathe on them easily."

"I don't know if I can wait." His voice was raspy, and he took a step toward me.

"Oh?"

"I've been thinking about the promise you made me on the beach the whole time we've been walking over here."

"The promise?" I looked at him questioningly, and then blushed as I remembered what I'd said.

"You don't have to, if you've changed your mind." His fingers pinched my nipples, and I squeezed my legs together.

"I haven't changed my mind." I shook my head and reached down to his briefs. My fingers rubbed the outside of his hardness, and I gasped as it moved against my palm.

"He's telling you he wants to be released." His laughed at me, and I smiled. I grabbed his briefs and pulled them down his legs, and then he kicked them off his feet. I reached down and held him in my hands and ran my fingers down the length of him. He groaned as I squeezed the tip of his cock and I moaned as I felt his precome on my fingertips. I made a circle with my thumb and finger and ran it back and forth on his cock, stopping to squeeze and play with his balls every once in a while.

"I want to feel your mouth," he grunted, and pulled me toward him for a kiss. "I want to feel your hot little mouth sucking on me as I come." His teeth bit my lower lip, and I smiled at him as I lowered my body to the ground. I took him into my mouth eagerly and gently at first. I felt giddy with power as I heard his loud gasp as I sucked on him, taking his hardness as far into my mouth as I could.

"Fuck, you're hot." He groaned as I bobbed up and down. His fingers played with my hair as he pushed my face against him. "Shit, I don't know how long I'm going to last." He groaned, and I felt him thrusting himself forward as if he were fucking my mouth. "I'm close to coming, Bianca." He groaned, and I moved my tongue back and forth on him as my lips sucked him hard. Within seconds, Jakob exploded into my mouth and I kept sucking him as I swallowed his salty climax. A part of my brain wasn't sure what I was doing, but the other part of me was high on lust and passion.

I stood back up then, and Jakob grinned at me with desire-filled eyes. "I need to fuck you." He groaned and reached for my panties. I stood still as he pulled them down. His fingers immediately reached in between my legs, and he cried out in a tone similar to a howl as he felt how wet I was.

"I'm not on the pill," I whispered.

"I don't have any condoms." He groaned as he continued playing with me. "I'm clean though. I had my last checkup three months ago, and I haven't been with anyone in six months."

"I'm clean too." I pressed my breasts against his chest and ran my fingers down his back.

"I can pull out." He leaned down and sucked on my neck. "When I'm about to come, I'll pull out."

"Okay." I nodded, even though I knew that wasn't fool-proof. Jakob took my hand, and we walked to some rocks at the side of the waterfall.

"Have you ever had sex in water before?"

"No."

"Good." He grinned. "That'll be our second time."

"Second time?"

"First time will be on the rocks." He sat down and pulled me toward him. "Straddle me," he commanded, and pulled me on top of his lap, my breasts rubbing against his face. He took one of my nipples into his mouth, and I moaned as his fingers squeezed my ass and pushed me forward.

"You're hard again already." I sighed with pleasure as I felt his cock pressed up to my wetness.

"You do that to me." He nodded and ran his hands up to my hair. "This feels so primal and so right. I can't wait to feel myself inside of you."

"I can't wait to feel you inside of me," I whispered in agreement, and he groaned.

"Say that again," he muttered as he kissed my lips

feverishly. His fingers squeezed my breasts together, and I moved back and forth on him, slightly gyrating my hips as I rubbed myself up and down on his hardness. "Tell me you want me to fuck you, Bianca." He pulled my hair harder. "Tell me you want to feel me inside of you, deep and hard."

"I do," I whispered against his lips, and he grabbed ahold of my hips.

"Tell me what you want me to do," he muttered as his lips fell to my breasts and sucked on my nipples. This time his teeth weren't so gentle, and I cried out slightly as he bit down on them and then sucked.

I closed my eyes and concentrated on the pleasure coursing through my body. His cock was positioned at my opening, and all I had to do was move forward slightly and then he'd be inside of me. "Bianca . . ." His voice cracked with desire. "What do you want me to do?"

"I want you to fuck me, Jakob!" I screamed out as he lifted my hips up and brought me back down on his hard cock. He entered me smoothly, and I tensed slightly as he moved deep inside of me. It had been a while since I'd had sex, and he was larger than any other man I'd been with.

"Am I hurting you?" he whispered, his eyes concerned.

"Not at all." I grinned and sat back and moved my hips back and forth as I rode him.

"Oh, fuck, Bianca." He grabbed my hips as my pussy walls

tightened on his hardness. "Don't stop." His eyes blinked up at me, full of lust. "Whatever you do, don't stop."

I continued to rock back and forth on him, allowing my breasts to brush aggressively against his chest. After a few minutes he groaned and lifted my hips off him.

"What are you doing?" I pouted as he placed me on the rock next to him.

"I had to stop you," he grunted and shook his head. "I was about to come."

"Oh." I moaned and looked down at his cock still standing at attention.

"You feel so tight and wet." He growled loudly. "It felt so good. I had to stop. I know you haven't climaxed yet."

"You didn't have to stop." I shook my head and watched as he moved over so he could get on top of me.

"I care about your needs more than my own." He grabbed my hips and forced me up. "Get on all fours," he commanded me, and positioned himself behind me.

I kneeled and then laid my hands flat on the smooth rock. The rock felt hard against my knees, and the position was slightly uncomfortable. "I'm not sure this is going to work," I murmured back at him, but then he grabbed my hips and pulled my ass back toward him, and I forgot all about the hardness of the rock. I was more concerned about feeling his hardness inside me as I felt his fingers between my legs, and I groaned as he rubbed my clit.

"So wet," he grunted, before sticking a finger inside me. "And I don't think it's just the water this time."

"Jakob." I groaned, dying from the anticipation of feeling him inside of me again. "Please."

"Please, what?" His voice was playful as his fingers left me. I felt him rub the tip of his cock at my entrance.

"Please fuck me again!" I screamed, and was rewarded by the feel of him entering me. This time felt different. He was in charge of the movements, and his strokes were long, deep, and hard. He held on to my hips tightly as he thrust in and out of me, and I thought I was going to pass out from all the pleasure.

"Oh!" I screamed as I felt his cock pushing down on that spot continuously.

"What is it, Bianca?" He grunted behind me as one of his hands played with my breasts.

"It feels so good," I cried out. "It's never felt this good before," I whimpered.

"That's because no one's ever fucked you this good before." His voice was hoarse, as if that turned him on more, and his strokes became harder and deeper. I felt my body shaking as my climax was about to explode.

"I think I should pull out now." He groaned, and I shook my head.

"No! I'm nearly there." I screamed and backed my ass back into him as he fucked me. "I'm coming," I cried out as my juices exploded in the biggest orgasm of my life. I felt Jakob's cock slide in and out of me and then into me one last time with such force that he had to hold on to my hips tightly. I felt his explosion inside of me as our bodies shook

together, and all I could think about was how absolutely perfect the moment had been. Jakob pulled out of me and
groaned as I turned around to face him.

"I'm sorry, I couldn't stop in time."

"It's okay." I leaned forward and kissed him. "I should
have let you pull out when you wanted to."

"Let's go in the water." He grabbed my hand, and we
stood up awkwardly and made our way into the small waterfall. My body was tingling, and I felt more alive than I'd ever
felt in my life.

"This is perfect." I kissed him as he pulled me toward
him, and he smiled.

"I'm glad you think so." His hands ran down my spine.
"I'm so glad that you're hap—"

"What was that?" I froze and stared at him with wide
eyes.

"It sounded like a gun." He jumped up quickly and pulled
me with him. "We need to move."

"Who has a gun?" My eyes widened. "Do you think Steve
has a gun?"

"It has to be Steve, unless someone else is on the island."

"I'm scared, Jakob." I clutched his arm, and I could feel
tears welling up in my eyes for the first time. "What's going
on?"

"I'm not sure. Look, put this on." He threw his shirt to
me and pulled on his briefs. "Ready?"

"Yes." I nodded, suddenly feeling very scared.

"Hold on." He grabbed a my shoulders and looked me in

the eyes. "Everything is going to be okay. I'm going to take care of you." He gave me a deep kiss and held me close for a second. "I promise." I nodded my understanding, and he grabbed my hand and started running. I tried to keep up with him as best as I could, but all I could think about was the loud gunshot we'd heard. Was it smart for us to be running toward the man with the gun?

nine

We made it back to the beach in record time, and there was no one there.

"Where do you think he is?" I whispered, feeling even more scared.

"I don't know." Jakob's face looked hard and angry.

"It was a gun we heard, right?" I shivered, and he hugged me close to him.

"I think it was a gun." He nodded and then took a step back to look around the beach. "I don't know what game Steve is playing."

"Anyone miss me?" a voice cried out, and we both froze. I looked to the right slowly, and there I saw Steve hobbling toward us. His hands were empty.

"Steve?" I called out to him weakly. "Where have you been?"

"I'm not sure." His eyes looked blank, there was a manic expression on his face, and his shirt was ripped.

"Did you hear the gunshot? Are you okay?" I took a step toward him, but Jakob grabbed me and pulled me back.

"I heard a loud noise." Steve nodded. "I was worried about the two of you. That noise gave me the energy to get up and start walking again."

"Where have you been?" I frowned and looked at Jakob. His eyes were narrowed, and I could see his chest heaving.

"I got lost in the jungle." He offered me a smile. "I wanted to surprise you both with breakfast yesterday, but my leg made it hard for me to get around. So I sat down and took a nap." He paused. "Then I felt something hit me hard, and I blacked out. When I came to, I was disoriented and lost."

"What hit you?" I stared straight ahead, not wanting to see Jakob's face.

"I don't know." He shook his head and reached out to grab my arm. "Sorry. I hope you don't mind my holding on to you for support."

"No, of course not." I held my arm out to him.

"Thank you. I was so thankful when I found you both." He looked up at Jakob then. "I would hate to think what would have happened if I hadn't."

"I hate to think what will happen now that you have." Jakob's voice was low, and he walked over to our makeshift water bowls and grabbed a branch we'd found the previous day and handed it to me. "Take this, Bianca." He pushed it into my hand.

"Okay." I nodded.

"The battle has only just begun," he muttered under his breath. "You might need it."

～೨

"What are you doing?" Jakob's voice was loud and angry as Steve hobbled toward us. His eyes narrowed and I could feel his heart beating fast next to me. "What game are you playing?"

"I don't know what you're talking about." Steve's eyes were wide as he stopped in front of us. "Right now, I'd love something to eat. Do you have anything?"

"You should have gotten some fruit in the jungle," Jakob responded coldly.

"We can try fishing again." I squeezed Jakob's arm. "Maybe we'll catch some more."

"I guess." He sighed. "If you want some." I nodded, and we walked toward the ocean.

"So what are we going to do with the fish? Make sushi?" Steve hobbled along behind us as we walked, and I felt him poke me in the back.

"You good with knives?" Jakob looked back at him.

"Maybe as good as you are with a rock," Steve shot back, and silence filled the air. I slowed my pace down slightly and waited for him to catch up.

"Are you okay?" I whispered to Steve as he walked next to me.

"He tried to kill me." His eyes looked scared. "He left me for dead."

"What? When?" I frowned. "Why did you come back if he tried to kill you?" My eyes widened.

"I wanted to make sure you were okay," he whispered hurriedly. "I know why you're here, Bianca. I know the—"

"What's going on?" Jakob stopped in front of us, and he stared at me. I stared at the gash on his face and wondered if he had really tried to kill Steve. And if he had, why? What did Steve know that I didn't?

"I was just asking Bianca if she minded my holding on to her arm as I walked. My leg is playing up a bit."

"I don't mind." I smiled weakly and offered Steve my arm while I avoided Jakob's intense gaze.

"Are you okay, Bianca?" Jakob gave me a look of concern, and I nodded uncertainly. I wanted to tell him what Steve had said. I wanted to hear his response, but I was scared. What if Steve had been telling the truth? Would he try to kill both of us, then?

"We'll have to start another fire." Jakob stared at me thoughtfully. "You think you can go and fish by yourself?" He stood there and nodded toward the ocean. "Then we can grill the fish right away."

"What about the bones?" Steve questioned.

"Bones won't kill you."

"But you wish they would, don't you," Steve mumbled under his breath, and my breath caught. Something had definitely changed since the last time we'd all been together. The two men weren't even pretending to like each other now.

"Bianca, come with me. I need your help gathering wood." Jakob waved me over to him.

"Be careful, Bianca," Steve whispered. "I know about your mother. I know about David."

"What?" I gasped as I looked back at him.

"Be careful," he mouthed as Jakob grabbed my arm. "You can't trust him," he whispered into my ear as I walked away.

"Let's go." Jakob pulled me along with him, and I shook him off me.

"Don't touch me! What did you do to him?"

"I didn't touch him, Bianca."

"I don't believe you."

"I didn't touch him." His eyes bored into mine. "I'm telling you I don't know where he went, and I don't know why he came back."

"You tried to kill him."

"He told you that?" His eyes narrowed.

"Yes." I nodded. "He told me he knows David as well."

"David Bradley?"

"Who else?" I gulped. "I'm only going to ask you this one more time, Jakob. Do you know David more than you've let on?"

He paused then, and I saw him thinking hard. "Yes, I do."

"Oh." I felt the blood drain from my face. I hadn't expected this answer.

"I can't tell you now." He grabbed my hands. "I need you

to trust me. I will explain everything to you once we make it off of the island."

I didn't want to trust him. I was so angry that he'd kept something else from me. Yet, I didn't hate him. "Answer me this," I asked him softly, my eyes flashing. "Did something happen between you and Steve yesterday?"

"I didn't try to kill him."

"Do you know who he is?"

"I don't know who he is." He looked me in the eye. "I can tell you honestly that I have never seen that man before in my life."

"Jakob—" I swallowed hard and stared at him for a few seconds before asking him the question that was on my mind. "Can I trust you?"

"Yes, you can trust me." He grabbed my hand. "I promise that I didn't try to kill Steve yesterday."

"I didn't date David because I liked him. In fact, I orchestrated our meeting." I was hesitant to say much more, for fear that Jakob was going to judge me. "I wanted to meet and date Mattias, that was the initial plan, but you'd think that man was the head of the KGB. No one knows anything about him."

"Oh?" His eyes narrowed.

"I wanted help. The Bradleys have access to information that I don't."

"Why are you telling me this now?"

"I think Steve knows something." I took a deep breath. "I think that Steve knows the truth about what happened.

He says he wants to tell me something about what happened."

"I don't understand what you're talking about." He rubbed his temples and stared back at Steve. "Do you think Steve knows David and Mattias are working together?"

"No, but . . ." I paused and looked at him. "What did you say?"

"Huh?" He frowned and took a step toward me.

"Nothing." I shook my head. "We should be careful with Steve." I attempted a smile, even though my brain was screaming at me. Why had he said David and Mattias were working together? I'd not mentioned anything that suggested that. What was it that he knew about David that he wasn't telling me? I could feel my heart racing as another thought hit me. Did he know Mattias Bradley as well? I knew that I needed to speak to Steve and find out exactly what he knew. "Let's go back to him now, so we can keep an eye on him."

"I don't trust him." Jakob's eyes narrowed. "I think we should go into the jungle."

"Now?" I shivered at the thought of going into the jungle with Jakob.

"We need to make sure we're safe."

"I think it's smarter to be closer to him, so we can keep an eye on him." I offered him another weak smile. *Please agree with me,* my brain was screaming at him.

"Yeah, I guess that's true." He nodded and then sighed.

"I just want you all to myself. I can take care of you better, then."

"I know." I looked away and tried not to throw up. My brain kept replaying what he'd just said. He'd asked me if I thought Steve knew that David and his brother, Mattias, were working together. Why had he said that? As far as I knew, David was not working with Mattias. As far as I knew, David was still my friend, and he was slightly afraid of his older brother. Why had Jakob said they were working together? What did he know? I stared at his bulging biceps and swallowed hard. What if the man I had given myself to was the man I should be running from? "You go ahead and see if you can find some wood in the jungle for a fire; I just want to wash my face off in the ocean."

"You can do that later. I want us to go and get this wood together." He stood resolute. "I'm not leaving the beach without you."

"Okay, fine. I'm coming." I took a deep breath and looked back at Steve, who was standing by the water, staring at us. "Let's go and get this wood."

"I'm going to ask you something, Bianca, and I want to make sure that you don't take offense, okay?

"Go ahead."

"Are you sure your father was sane when he died?" His voice sounded jaded. "Maybe he regretted the fact that he was dying and had no money to leave you. Maybe he regretted the fact that he'd been a poor businessman."

"My father would never insinuate or state a fact like that unless he believed it to be true," I said indignantly.

"Okay, I was just checking." He kicked the ground. "So your dad was partners with David Bradley's father?"

"Yes." I nodded. "This I know to be true."

"And David Bradley knows this?"

"It's a long story. He knows some of it."

"Does he know about the patent paperwork you have and the incorporation papers?"

"No." I stopped. "Though, I think someone knows."

"Why?"

"Just some funny things have been happening since I started investigating." I looked over at him. "I think that David's brother, Mattias, has been behind the kidnapping. I think that he's willing to do anything to get that paperwork away from me." I laid my cards on the table and waited to see his reaction.

"You have a very bad opinion of someone you've never met." His voice was grim, as he stared at me. I could feel the tension in the air.

"I don't know him. I've never met him before. But David told me things." I stepped forward and touched his chest lightly. "He's not a good guy. I don't think he's any better than his father. Don't lie to me, Jakob. Do you know Mattias as well?"

There was silence after I spoke. His eyes went blank, and I could see him thinking hard as we stared at each other. I could hear my heart thumping, and my body was shivering as I waited for him to answer me.

"I do." He nodded after a minute.

"So we have another connection, then." My words sounded accusatory as I tried to joke. "So is he capable of kidnapping?"

"Yes, I suppose he is. I didn't know . . ." His voice trailed off.

"You didn't know what?"

"I think we're in danger." He changed the subject.

"How do you know the Bradley brothers, Jakob?" My fingertips squeezed his arms tightly, and his fingers reached up to mine. He was silent for a moment, and I could feel his heart pounding through our embraced fingers.

"I don't know them well, I'm afraid." He shook his head and stepped back. "Let's gather the wood." He walked away from me and I felt my heart thudding in my stomach. This man that I'd given myself to was still hiding something from me. I was sure of that. Why would he be hiding something from me? Would I ever be able to fully trust him?

We gathered the wood in silence and then walked back to the beach. "I'll be right back. I dropped some branches." Jakob called out to me as he turned around and walked toward to the jungle.

"Okay," I mumbled, and watched him hurry away. I jumped as Steve appeared next to me. "You scared me." I took a step away from him, suddenly feeling apprehensive of him.

"Sorry, it wasn't my intention to scare you."

"It's okay." I shrugged. "Just try to make a bit of noise when you approach someone. I didn't even hear you."

"Sorry, I'm used to having to be quiet in my line of work." He smiled with a wry look on his face.

"It's fine." I wanted to ask him what line of work he was in, but I was pretty sure he wouldn't be honest about it anyway.

"Would you like to go for a walk, Bianca?" Steve offered me his arm, and I tried to think of a reason to decline.

"That sounds good, but let's wait for Jakob. Maybe he'll want to come with us."

"I was rather hoping that we could take a walk without him." Steve's eyes narrowed. "There are some things I wanted to talk to you about."

"Things like what?"

"Forgive me if this is an intrusion into your private life, but I can't help but think that you and Jakob aren't really boyfriend and girlfriend."

"Why would you say that?"

"I don't see any sexual chemistry between you. You seem awkward around him." He shrugged. "You know you can tell me anything, Bianca. I will protect you if you need me to."

"I don't know what you're talking about."

"Is Jakob your master?" He took a step toward me, and I frowned at him.

"My *master*? What do you mean?"

"Are you a slave, Bianca?" His voice lowered. "I remember you talking about trafficking on the first night, and I wonder now if you were giving me a clue."

"Do I look like I'm a slave?" I shook my head. Was Steve crazy?

"Like I said before, appearances can be deceiving." He grabbed my arm. "If you come with me, I can take care of you."

"I don't need you to take care of me." I shook my arm and his hand fell to the side. "Thanks for your concern, Steve, but I'm fine." I looked up the beach hoping I would see Jakob walking back toward us.

"Can I tell you something, Bianca?" He spoke urgently, and I looked at him in surprise at his tone.

"Sure, go ahead."

"Those who watch are the watched, those who listen are never heard, those who love are bound for heartache, and those who seek the truth are always lied to."

"Okay." I frowned at him. "What does that mean?"

"It means, my dear, that you're in danger." His eyes widened and he stepped away from me. My heart started racing, and I wanted to call out to him to ask him what he meant. There was something so off about him. He was starting to remind me of a wizard.

"Everything okay?" Jakob's voice carried down the beach, and I stood there unsure of what to do. As I watched him approaching us, I could see the distrust and anger in his eyes as he stared at Steve. He looked at me searchingly for a few seconds to make sure I was okay, and I nodded quickly. His expression changed to one of satisfaction, and I ran toward him, knowing that someone who wanted to harm me wouldn't be worried about my safety.

"Do you need any help carrying those?" I gave him a short smile and offered to take some of the branches from his hands.

"No, I'm fine." He frowned at me. "Your forehead is sweating. Are you okay?"

"I'm fine. It must be the sun," I lied, not wanting to tell him what Steve had said and the fleeting doubts I'd had about him.

"I shouldn't have left you alone." His eyes searched my face. "We have to be more careful about safety."

"It's fine. I can take care of myself."

"I want to make sure." He looked over at Steve. "There is something *off* about him."

"I know." I nodded. "But I don't think he would try to hurt me with you here. I think he's harmless. Or at least I hope he is."

"Everyone looks harmless in the beginning." He dropped the branches and walked over to his pants to pull out the lighter. "Pull the leaves off the branches, and let's get this fire started." He walked toward me again, and I couldn't help but stare at his legs once more, so sturdy and muscular. I wanted to feel his legs in between mine. I could remember the feel of them under me as we'd made love. I stared at his legs and then his chest longingly and tried to ignore how badly I wanted to touch him. The truth of the matter was that even though I was still angry at him I still wanted him. I just wanted to press my whole body against his and feel his warmth and comfort.

"Are you cold?" Jakob watched me as I shivered, and I nodded. "Let's get this fire started, then." He exclaimed and then dropped to his knees.

I didn't want him to know the real reason why my body was trembling.

ten

The fire added another dimension to the beach. It almost made me feel like I was out at a party on the beach somewhere. Almost, but not quite.

"I'm hungry," Steve complained, and I nodded in agreement.

"Shall we go and get some more bananas?" I looked at Jakob, hoping he had another suggestion.

"We can." He nodded. "Or we can see if there's some other fruit we can pick."

"How will we know if they're poisonous or not?"

"We just won't pick any fruits we aren't sure of."

"I saw some green berries in the jungle." Steve spoke up. "I think they looked ripe."

"What sort of berries were they?" Jakob looked at him, and Steve shrugged. "Berries are the worst types of fruit to just pick and eat. They can be highly poisonous. I'm going to say that we should stay away from berries. We don't know which ones may kill us."

"That sounds like a good idea to me." I nodded. "I'm not a huge berry person anyway; I always get the seeds stuck in my teeth, and it's a pain to get them out."

"If you need any help, I've got a super-duper tongue." Jakob grinned at me, and I laughed.

"I think I'll be able to manage."

"So are you two ready?" Jakob jumped up. "Let's go into the jungle."

"Should we just leave this open fire?" Steve frowned and remained seated.

"It'll be fine." Jakob's face was hard. "I suggest you come with us into the jungle if you're hungry."

"Fine." Steve stood up awkwardly, and we all walked into the jungle in silence. "So, Jakob," Steve began. "Tell me more about you."

"What do you want to know?"

"Why do you think you were kidnapped? You seem like a pretty big guy. Someone would have to be a fool to draw your wrath."

"There are plenty of fools in the world. Trust me; I'll have the last laugh."

"I'd be scared to get on your bad side, that's for sure."

"You don't seem very scared." Jakob stopped and turned toward him. "In fact, it seems to me that you're making it very clear that you aren't scared of me."

"I'm a good actor, I suppose." Steve laughed weakly, and I frowned as Jakob charged toward him.

"Jakob, what are you doing?" I took a step forward and placed a hand on his arm. "Don't hurt him."

"I'm not going to hurt him." Jakob's lips were in a thin line, and he looked grim. "I just want Steve to know that he's right to be scared of me. Not many people cross me and live." There was silence in the air as we all stood there. I could see the vein popping in Steve's forehead. I felt slightly bad for him, but then I noticed the expression on his face. There was a small sliver of a smile, as if he were happy that he had made Jakob crack. I looked away and frowned. Maybe Steve wasn't as scared as he had let on. Maybe Steve was playing a game with us and we were his unwilling pawns.

"He might have a gun, Jakob." *Back off and stop playing like you're a superhero!*

"What gun?" Steve frowned and looked scared. "I don't have a gun."

"We heard a gun the other day." I scratched a small ant bite on my arm and stared at him to see if he was telling the truth.

"Do you hear that?" Jakob's eyes were alert as he whispered and pointed to his ear. "Listen carefully." He put a finger to his lips and looked around quickly. I closed my eyes and listened carefully to see if I could hear what he was talking about. What I heard made my heart stop. Something was running. And whatever it was was running fast.

"What's that noise?" I grabbed on to Jakob's arm in fright, and he pulled me toward him.

"Listen," he said after a minute grinning. "Do you hear that?"

I closed my eyes again and listened. I heard an odd grunting sound. At first I thought it was the sound of a man out of breath, but then I realized exactly what it was.

"It's a wild boar," Steve exclaimed out loud, and Jakob nodded.

"Do you guys want to eat boar tonight?" His eyes glittered as he looked at me.

"What are you going to do?"

"Follow me." He grabbed my hand and started running toward the grunting.

"What about Steve?" I exclaimed as we ran.

"He'll be fine." Jakob let go of my hand and picked up a rock. "He'll just slow us down. Stay close to me, and it'll be fine." I watched him running ahead of me, and I struggled to keep up with him. It was then that the boar must have heard us, because I suddenly heard the grunting get louder and the sounds of branches cracking as the boar started to run again. I watched Jakob sprinting after the boar and ran as fast as I could to catch up with them both. I heard a crashing sound and then a loud cry in the distance and ran as fast as I could through the bush to see what had happened.

I stopped as I got to the gathering. Jakob was on the ground sitting on top of the boar and bashing the rock into its head. I cried out, and he froze.

"Look away, Bianca!" he commanded me from his stance on top of the animal.

"I don't want to hear it either." I felt like I wanted to cry as I stood there staring at the trees, trying to ignore the sound of the dead hog grunting and dying as his head got bashed in. I finally heard Jakob dropping the rock onto the dirt and I looked over at him

"You killed it?" I was shocked, and my voice was low as I stared at the dead animal.

"You wanted to eat something other than bananas tonight, right?"

"But you killed it." I got choked up as I stared at Jakob. His chest was rising quickly, and he was panting. His eyes looked manic, and his hands were full of dirt and blood.

"What did you think was going to happen, Bianca? Did you think I was chasing it for fun?"

"No." I shook my head and looked to the ground. I could feel tears welling up in my eyes. "I just didn't expect you to catch it."

"Bianca"—he walked toward me—"we're stranded on an island. We have to do what we can to survive."

"I just didn't expect to see you kill it." I stared at the boar and the rock on the ground next to Jakob. "It just feels so primal."

"It is primal." Jakob grabbed my shoulders and forced me to look up at him. "This is the situation we're in, Bianca. We're not on some resort, or competing in a TV show. We're not playing a game of *Survivor*. We're living it. We have to do what we have to do."

"But you killed it."

"And I would kill it again, if it meant we'd be able to eat." His eyes were hard as he looked into mine. "Am I a bad person for saying that?"

"No." I bit my lower lip and then leaned up and pressed my lips against his. "I'm not naive, Jakob. I understand the situation we're in." I closed my arms as his arms pressed me toward him. "I just never expected to see my dinner killed before my very eyes."

"Didn't you know that the fresher the meat, the better?" he whispered against my lips, before kissing me hard. I held on to him and kissed him back passionately. I felt like I was having an out-of-body experience; everything around me seemed surreal. I was here with a tall, dark, dangerous hunter, and I was letting him touch me and kiss me as if I didn't have a care in the world.

"We should get this boar back to the fire." He pulled away from me and stared into my eyes with a lighter expression. "Do you think you'll be able to help carry it back?"

I nodded and tried to hide my shudder. I really didn't want to touch the boar, but I knew that if I expected to eat some of the carcass, I should help in some way.

"Actually, it's okay." He shook his head. "I can carry it by myself."

"What?" I frowned. "No, I can help."

"I can see from your expression that you'd rather not touch it." He smiled and stroked my cheek. "And that's okay. I don't have these muscles for nothing." He flexed his biceps, and I groaned.

"Show-off." I rolled my eyes at him. "We could always go and get Steve to help you carry it."

"I'm sure we could." It was Jakob's turn to roll his eyes. "Hold on, let me just grab the boar before rigor mortis sets in."

"Doesn't it set in as soon as someone dies?"

"I have no idea." He crouched down and grabbed the dead animal.

"Do you think its brothers and sisters are watching us and planning their revenge?" I whispered to Jakob as he picked up the boar. It had suddenly gotten really dark, and I was starting to feel uncomfortable being in the jungle. I could sense that there were animals staring at us from the trees. Animals that had most probably witnessed Jakob killing one of their friends. Animals that were most probably scared that they would be next. It was *Watership Down* all over again, only, this world consisted of more than just rabbits.

"I think we're okay." Jakob walked ahead of me, carrying the dead animal as if it were as light as a feather.

"Did you ever read that book *Animal Farm* when you were growing up?" I followed behind him closely.

"I think everyone had to read it in school, right?"

"Yeah, I guess so. I mean I know it was an allegorical novel about society, but have you ever wondered what the world would be like if animals did decide to fight back?"

"Fight back?" His voice sounded amused.

"I mean, I'm sure they don't appreciate being killed just so we can get food and clothes."

"Are you a vegetarian?"

"No, no." I shook my head. "But I have to admit I have sometimes thought about what life would be like if animals decided to fight back. What if instead of running away from you, the boar had run toward you and tried to attack you?"

"That wouldn't be very unusual. Many wild boars attack people."

"You would have been scared, right?"

"I would have retreated."

"See, once animals figure that out, they will start fighting back."

"That's what they did in *Planet of the Apes*, I suppose." I could hear the laughter in his voice and frowned.

"You think I'm silly, don't you."

"Not at all. I think that you like to think out of the box, which is refreshing."

"I think it's because I grew up with a father who was always encouraging me to think outside of normal parameters."

"That makes sense."

"Sometimes, I don't wonder if I'm a little crazy."

"We're all a little crazy," he responded seriously.

"Were you going to hit Steve earlier?" I asked, hoping he wouldn't be mad at my question.

"I wasn't going to hit him, no."

"You looked like you were going to hit him."

"I was just giving him a warning."

"A warning or a threat?"

"He can take it whichever way he wants."

"Do you think he was scared?"

"Not as much as he should be."

"There's something about him that gives me the creeps." I admitted at last. "I feel horrible saying that, because I don't really know him, but there's just something about him that seems really off."

"I know exactly what you mean." He stopped still and looked at me for a few seconds before continuing. "I've got a bad feeling about him, Bianca. Please be wary around him."

"I will be." I nodded, and we continued walking. My stomach rumbled, and I could feel the tension in my back. I rubbed my arms as we walked back through the jungle and tried to get rid of the image that had just popped into my mind. I couldn't stop thinking about Jakob standing there next to the boar with the bloody rock in his hand. My brain was ticking, and all I could think was that maybe I should be wary around both Jakob and Steve. I was pretty certain that I was underestimating what both of them could and would do. I only hoped that their targets were each other.

~∽

Steve was waiting on the beach for us when we made it back with the boar. His eyes widened as he saw the beast, and I noticed an exchange of looks pass between him and Jakob.

"I'm going to get some sharp rocks to see if we can get this boar's fur off." Jakob glanced at me and walked away. I stared after him and wondered if he wanted me to come with him.

"I have something for you." Steve walked over to me quickly. His limp was more pronounced, and I wondered if he had injured himself even more by walking through the jungle with us.

"What is it?" I looked at him puzzled.

"I found this note in the jungle." Steve slipped it into my hand and walked away quickly. I looked down and read it.

Be careful of who you trust and fall in love with. They are deceiving you. You should run away as soon as you can.

I reread it again carefully, then threw it into the fire. I stood still as I thought about the note. It was on the same paper and had the same handwriting as the other notes. Only, this time it looked like it had been hurriedly scribbled. And the tone of the note seemed off. The advice in it was a little too direct, compared to the other notes. It was as if the writer of the notes was upset that I had become close with Jakob. My heart started racing as I realized that Steve might be the one responsible for leaving the notes on the island and the letter at my house. My head spun as I realized that I had no idea which way was up. However, I knew that if he was the same person who'd left all the notes, he might know exactly what was going on. I didn't expect him to tell me everything, but even a few clues would be helpful.

"Steve," I called after him. Where did you get that note?"

"I found it in the jungle, near the waterfall." He shrugged and turned away. I sighed and glanced down at the fire. Had he really found it near the waterfall? If so, how had it gotten there? And who had left it? Was there someone else on the island with us, or did I already know the man who had been leaving me the notes?

I didn't know if I could trust Jakob or Steve. Had Jakob tried to kill Steve, and was he out to get me as Steve was implying, or was Steve really the mastermind behind everything? The problem was that I didn't know why either one of them would want to harm me, unless this was just some sort of sick joke. I knew from watching *Criminal Minds* that sometimes there was no rhyme or reason as to how or why psychopaths chose their victims. I wanted to believe that Steve was the one who had been leaving the notes, but the fact was that Jakob was the one who had lied to me so many times. Why would he have pretended he didn't know the Bradleys? And it suddenly struck me that Jakob had disappeared every morning. He could have hidden the notes as well. In fact, he could have left the first note on the beach next to us. He'd been awake before me, both in the car trunk and on the beach. As far as I knew, he hadn't been drugged either. Maybe Jakob worked for the Bradleys. That would explain why he'd been at the coffee shop that day. Maybe he was the one in charge of trying to figure out where the papers were. Maybe his cat-and-mouse game was deliberate. He wanted to confuse me into trusting him. But then I looked back at Steve and saw the calculating look on his face and I knew that his goal was to make me doubt Jakob. Everything he had done and said was in the hope that I would no longer trust Jakob. I knew for a fact that Jakob hadn't told me the entire truth, but I knew in that moment that if it came down to Jakob or Steve, I was definitely choosing to believe Jakob. I looked back at Steve with narrowed eyes, and I saw the disappointment in his eyes as he walked away from me.

"You okay?" Jakob walked over to me and put his arm around my shoulders.

"I'm fine." I nodded. "I just wish we were off this island."

"Where's Steve?" His voice changed from caring to hostile.

"I think he went into the water." I kept my eyes ahead and debated telling Jakob about the note.

"I'm pretty sure he has a knife." Jakob's tone was low, and he leaned toward me.

"How do you know?" I swallowed hard.

"I saw it." He looked around. "I didn't want him to know that I knew."

"Why does he have a knife?" I shivered, and Jakob pulled me into his arms.

"Remember when I asked you if you could kill someone?" he whispered in my ear, and I froze.

"What are you saying?"

"I'm saying that I need you to get me that knife." His eyes peered into mine. They looked dark as night, and if they were any indication of his thoughts, I knew they were ex-treme.

"What do you want me to do?" My stomach dropped as I realized where this was leading. If I had been scared by his killing the boar, I didn't know how I was going to react if he actually did something to Steve.

"I just need you to get me his flask." His fingers gripped my arm. "I'm not sure if you noticed, but the bottom of the flask looked like it had something glued on to it."

"I didn't see any such thing."

"Just go and ask him for a drink. He trusts you. He'll let his guard down around you."

"I guess so." I closed my eyes to allow my nerves to settle.

"Just bring the knife to me when you have it," he commanded me. "Do you understand?"

"Yes." I nodded, unsure of what to do. If the note was right, then that meant that Jakob was after me. If I stole the knife from Steve and gave it to Jakob, I could be putting a nail in my own coffin. I felt Jakob's lips on my cheek, and I melted into him. I didn't think Jakob would hurt me, but I already knew that he was lying to me about something. He'd admitted knowing both David and Mattias in some capacity. He'd even made a comment about them working together. How could he know that? Unless, of course, he knew the two brothers better than he'd let on. And if that was true, maybe he was here to shut me up, to stop me from finding out exactly what had happened to my mother. There was a possibility that he had been put on the island to harm me, so that I'd be quiet forever. Part of me wondered if he was here to find out exactly what information I had. It would make sense, what with all the questions he'd asked about my father. Who else would be so concerned?

But as I stood in his arms and thought back to his gentle lovemaking and tender caresses, I began to doubt that he would ever want to harm me. If he was here to kill me, why would he admit that he knew Bridgette? Why would he have been kidnapped as well? Why would Steve be the one handing me a note on the same paper as the other notes I'd received? It didn't add up. It had to be Steve who was trying to play mind games and manipulate me. His plan was working, because he was making me begin to doubt Jakob.

"Don't be scared, my love." Jakob whispered into my ear as he caressed my back. "I won't let Steve harm you." My heart jumped at his endearment, and I looked up into his eyes. They were so sincere and full of emotion that I wondered how I could have doubted him for a second.

"Steve tried to warn me about you," I whispered against his lips as he moved in to kiss me. His face twisted, and he looked into my eyes questioningly. "He gave me a note," I whispered frantically. "It was like the other notes."

"What do you mean?" His eyes narrowed.

"It was on the same paper and while, I'm not positive, I think the same person wrote all of the notes and tried to change their handwriting slightly."

"What did it say?"

"It said to be careful of you. It said that I should run away from you."

"He's trying to split us up." He frowned. "He's trying to divide and conquer." He grabbed my hands tightly and took a deep breath. "I'm not trying to hurt you, Bianca. I promise. I'm just trying to get the truth."

"I know." I nodded. "I know."

"I wish things were different." He groaned and ran his hands through his tousled hair. "This was a mistake. I need to get to the bottom of what is happening."

"You'll be careful, won't you?" I whispered, suddenly feeling terrified. I wanted to get to the bottom of everything that was happening as well, but I didn't want to get hurt. I wanted to close my eyes and transport myself back to my apartment. I shuddered then as I realized that was a lie. I no longer felt safe at my own apartment either.

"Just get me that knife." His voice was ominous, and my heart stilled for a moment. The man in front of me was no longer my gentle lover; he was now a terrifying hulk.

"I'm going to go into the jungle," he whispered. "I'll stand at the outskirts, but you can tell him I've gone to the shack. That will give him a sense of false security."

"Do you think he'll believe me?"

"He will if you tell him that I left something there. Tell him that I went to look for something to skin the boar with."

"You said you were going to use rocks."

"Tell him the rocks I found didn't work."

"Okay." I bit my lower lip. "And then what?"

"And then you get the knife."

"How will I get the knife?"

"He keeps it in his back pocket. That's why he hasn't taken his pants off. You'll have to find a way to grab it from him. Maybe pretend to fall into him and grab it that way."

"That sounds like something a pickpocket would do."

"That's what you're trying to do." He grabbed my hands and stared at me intently. "You have to be careful, Bianca. You have to be *very* careful. If he suspects anything . . ."

"I'll be careful." I nodded. "I'll get the knife." I swallowed hard as another thought hit me. "Do you think he has a gun as well?" I thought back to the loud bang we'd heard at the waterfall.

"I think he has something, but I don't think it's a gun. If he had a gun, I think he would have pulled it on me a long time ago." His voice lowered. "I'll be watching as best I can." He held me close to him. "Call out if you need me."

"I don't know if I can do this." I felt my eyes growing heavy as I held on to his arms. My voice trembled, and I looked down to the ground in embarrassment.

"Then you don't have to do it." He shook his head. "I won't make you do it if you're too scared." He brought my face to his chest and stroked my hair. "I can take care of you, Bianca. I won't put you in danger." Something in his tone gave me the strength I needed, and I pulled away from him.

"I'm sorry. I can try." I swallowed and pushed my shoulders back. "I've always been a more passive person, but I'm trying to be stronger." And this was all for my dad. This whole situation was to find out what had happened to my mother. I couldn't allow fear to bring me down.

"Funny, that's what my mom taught me too." He gave me a wry smile. "Yet both of them seemed to take it and accept it."

I nodded without saying a word, and we just stared at each other. I watched as Steve came out of the ocean, and something in me snapped.

"Get away from me!" I pushed Jakob away and screamed. "You liar! Get away from me!"

"What?" He grabbed for me, and I reached over and slapped him hard. I beat my fists against his chest and shook my head like a crazy woman.

"You'll pay for this!" I screamed, and leaned forward. "Run to the jungle." My eyes implored him as I whispered hurriedly. "I'm going to get the knife."

He nodded his understanding and stepped back. "I'll be back once you calm down," he said loudly.

"Leave me alone!" I screamed, and ran toward Steve.

"Are you okay?" Steve's eyes were wide as he approached me. His expression looked eager and satisfied, and I knew that he had bought my little shouting act.

"I confronted him about the note," I told him, feigning outrage.

"You told him?" He grabbed my arms. "Why did you do that? He's going to be mad."

"I need to know the truth. I need to know why he's been terrorizing me."

"He's never going to tell you the truth, you stupid girl." Steve's voice changed, and he looked angry.

"Can I have a drink?" I reached my hand out, hoping he would hand me the flask without even thinking about it. "I really need one right now."

"Sure." He reached into his pocket and pulled it out. My eyes immediately fell to the bottom of the flask, and that's when I realized that the stainless steel at the bottom wasn't completely flush. Steve froze as he realized what I was staring at.

"I think I'll keep my alcohol to myself after all." He took a step away from me.

"I know you sent me the letters." I gasped, going out on a limb, wanting to know the truth and knowing I had to do something to distract him long enough to try to grab the flask away from him. "I know it was you."

"He told you?" He froze, and I saw his expression change to something unpleasant. "I can't believe he told you about the plan."

"You're working with David?" I frowned. "Why didn't you tell me?"

"David told you?" He paused and took a step toward me. "What did he tell you?"

"David didn't tell me about the notes." I hurried out. "I didn't know that this was part of the plan. He just told me that Mattias didn't want me nosing around Bradley Inc., He told me that it would be smart for me to disappear for a few days. I didn't know he was going to be the one to make me disappear."

"David? Or Mattias?" He frowned, and that was when I knew that Steve definitely wasn't here to protect me. If he didn't know about David or his involvement, that meant he wasn't here to try to help me. The fact that he brought up Mattias's name told me everything I needed to know. That meant he was the enemy. I took a step away from him and stumbled to the ground. Steve stood in front of me, looking down with a wild gleam in his eyes.

"I'm sorry, Bianca."

"Sorry about what?" I asked and tried to jump up. I fell back again in my haste, and we both froze as we heard footsteps running toward us. I turned around and saw Jakob approaching us. "What are you doing?" I shouted at him and jumped up. My heart raced in joy, and my stomach flipped over at the sight of him.

"I couldn't let you do this alone." His face was manic. "I would kill myself if anything happened to you."

"What are you two talking about?" Steve looked back and forth at us, and then his eyes narrowed as he stared at me. "You weren't really fighting, were you?"

"Did you think you'd get away with this, Steve?" Jakob's voice was loud and angry. "Did you think you could play this game with us?"

"You didn't know each other when you got to the island." Steve stared at me. "Listen to me, Bianca. This man is playing a game with you. None of this has been an accident. I'm here to protect you. I'm here to help you seek your truth."

"He's lying to you, Bianca." Jakob grabbed my arm and

pulled me toward him. "I promise you, this man is up to no good."

"Why don't you tell her why she's really here?" Steve stepped forward and pulled the knife off of the bottom of his flask before flinging the flask to the ground. He pointed the knife at me and it glittered in the moonlight, and I screamed as he ran toward us, knife high in the air.

"Shut up!" he shouted at me as I continued to scream. He lunged toward us, and I immediately noticed that he was no longer limping.

"Step back, Bianca." Jakob pushed me behind him and lunged toward Steve. He grabbed Steve's arm, and I watched as Steve kneed Jakob in the stomach. He doubled over, and Steve took the opportunity to right hook him in the gut.

"Jakob!" I screamed as I watched the two men fighting. I didn't know what to do, but I nearly dropped to the ground in relief when I watched Jakob stand tall and punch Steve in the face. He grabbed Steve's face and hit him again.

I stared at the fight and felt tears running down my face. I had never been so scared before in my life. Jakob definitely had the better build, but Steve had the knife. "Jakob, be careful!" I shouted as loudly as I could, trying to warn him as I saw Steve step forward to try to stab him.

"Run, Bianca." His voice was hoarse, and I saw both men fall to the ground. "Run!" he called out to me again, and he turned to look up at me. I stared at him in shock and watched as a suddenly very agile Steve pushed him down and held the knife to his neck.

"Stop!" I stepped forward to hit Steve on the head, but the look Jakob gave me froze me to the spot.

"Run!" Jakob commanded once more. "Don't worry about me, Bianca. You need to run and hide." I stared at the two of them fighting for a few seconds and saw Steve look back at me. His eyes looked like evil slits, and I could see that he was no longer pretending to be a nice guy. "Run, Bianca!" This time I didn't hesitate.

eleven

As I sprinted up the sandy beach, I heard the two of them fighting, but I didn't look back. My legs were aching, and my mind was numb, but still I didn't stop. "Be okay, Jakob, please be okay," I mumbled to myself as I ran.

I ran to the jungle and through the trees on the path to the shack. My mind was blank with fear, and all I could think about was the look in Steve's eyes as he had watched me standing there. He was out for blood. I stopped as I thought about Jakob getting hurt. My breath came out fast and erratic, and I turned around. I needed to go back to the beach to help him. I needed to make sure he was okay. I couldn't leave him there by himself. Maybe if I jumped on top of Steve, I'd be able to distract him long enough for Jakob to grab the knife.

My breathing grew heavier as I thought about the knife. When had Jakob realized that Steve had a knife? Why hadn't he said anything before now? I collapsed to the ground, suddenly overcome by tears. I was scared, really scared. Maybe the most scared I'd ever been in my life. And I was also confused. Nothing was adding up, and nothing was making sense. I dropped to the ground and sobbed, not knowing what to do.

I heard a cracking noise above me and jumped back up. "Don't break down now, Bianca," I muttered to myself, and jumped up and down for energy and then dusted off my legs. I looked back toward the beach and thought for a moment. "Self-preservation, Bianca." I started running farther into the jungle. "You can't figure out the truth if you're dead." My heart wanted me to run back to the beach to help Jakob, but my brain was telling me to look after myself. I ran toward the shack, anxious to get to the hideout. I ran so fast that I tripped over some small rocks and went flying into the bush. I scraped my knee, and it started burning, but still I continued on. I almost cried in relief as I made it to the small building, which I'd been so afraid of returning to. I opened the door eagerly and hobbled inside. My eyes immediately went to the table in the corner. It was no longer empty. I walked over to it and saw a bunch of candy wrappers and a pen. I frowned as I stared at the table. I was positive that those candy wrappers had not been there before. I looked to the ground to search for anything else. There were a couple of pieces of paper that I snatched up, but they were blank. I leaned back against the wall and closed my eyes, trying to control my breathing. It was then that I saw something white sticking out of a piece of fabric lying on the floor in the other corner of the shack. I walked over to it and pulled the fabric up. I gasped as I saw that it was a photo. I grabbed it and stared at it, the blood draining from my face.

The photo was of my mother, my father, and me.

It was one of the only photos I had of the three of us. The last time I'd seen the photo, it had been in my father's box, in my apartment. I held the picture to my heart, which was racing now, and I was starting to feel claustrophobic. I looked around to see if I could find anything else as I waited. I surveyed the rest of the shack quickly, and all I found was some blank pieces of paper; the same paper that the notes had been written upon. Sinking to the ground, I closed my eyes and prayed that Jakob would defeat Steve. Steve was the man who had been writing the notes. He was obviously working with my kidnapper. The fact that there was a photo of my family in this room told me that someone had been in my apartment and through my personal belongings. Maybe the photograph was even a warning. Maybe this was Mattias's way of telling me to back off. I dropped the photo onto the ground and started crying. I picked the photo back up and stared at it for a few minutes before turning it over. It was then that my heart stopped again as I saw the message. How did Steve know I was going to see the photo? Unless, of course, it was part of his plan. Or a part of the plan that he hadn't gotten to carry out as yet. I walked to the door and opened it so that I could read by the light of the moon.

What do you see when you look at me? A happy family for
all to see. A man so consumed with greed and with spite,
that his children now suffer and live in fright. What do
you see when you look at me? An ominous picture of your
life to be.

I stared at the note and frowned. If the other notes had
made little sense, this one was even more confusing. I turned
the photo around again and stared at it. What did I see? And
why was he saying my father was greedy? My father was the
least greedy person I knew. He'd been swindled by his business partners and hadn't even done anything to get his money
back. I frowned and reread the words. Why was the photo
ominous? What did Steve mean?

I shivered as I stared at the photo. And then I blinked as I
studied it again. There was another couple in the photo. I'd
never noticed them before. The other couple looked just as
happy as my parents, and they were holding hands. I looked
at the photo again to see if there was anything else I had
missed. I couldn't see anything else in the photo but a surly-
looking boy standing to the right in the photo, looking at the
group next to him. It was then that I heard a loud crying
noise, and I froze.

I looked at the shack and at all the blank papers that were
in here. Papers and clues that hadn't been here the first time I
was here. This wasn't a safe place to be. I wouldn't even be
able to see if someone was coming. I ran out the door and
started thinking. "Where should I go? Where should I go?" I

muttered to myself frantically. I thought about going to the waterfall, but that would make me a sitting duck. If Steve somehow managed to take Jakob down, being at the waterfall wasn't going to help me. There was only one other option: I needed to be up high. The predator always needed to be watching from above. Only the prey stayed below and waited to be hunted. I looked around to see if there were any trees I could climb. Each tree I passed caused me to panic as I stared at the long trunks. There was no way I'd be able to climb any of these. Looking around, I took a couple of deep breaths. "Calm down, Bianca. Think. And pay attention." I closed my eyes and stood there. All I could hear was the sound of my own heartbeat and the faint sound of the water from the waterfall. "Look for the banana trees," I told myself. I knew that Jakob had climbed the banana trees to bring me breakfast, so I knew that it was possible to get up one. If I could find a tree that wasn't very high, maybe I could go from that tree and transfer to another one and climb higher up. "If a monkey can do it, so can you," I whispered to myself, and shuddered as I realized that I might come into contact with some other animals hidden up in the trees. My chest started heaving as I sobbed in frustration and terror. Then I heard a bloodcurdling scream, and my body went into panic mode. I'd never experienced anything like it before. It was as if my body was guiding me. My legs started moving of their own volition, and I found myself at a tree, attempting to climb it before I could even process what was going on. My feet brushed against something prickly, and I stepped back and bit my lip.

This was going to hurt. The tree trunk already felt rough against my skin, and my palms were already aching.

"You can do this, Bianca." I stretched my arms a few times and walked back to the tree. "Mind over matter. There is no pain." I kept repeating to myself as I attempted to climb the tree. However, I kept falling down. I realized that the photo still clutched in my hand was keeping me from grasping the tree tightly enough and my feet just weren't able to grab on to the tree trunk and stay there. I dropped the photo and stared at it for a moment before squaring my shoulders. "It's thigh time." I sighed and held on to the trunk. I wrapped my arms and legs around it as tightly as I could and then tried to shuffle up the tree. I didn't think I was going to make it. As soon as I shuffled up a couple of times, I kept sliding down.

But then I decided to close my eyes and pretend I was somewhere else. I counted to three and then attempted to climb again. I didn't open my eyes until I'd made it at least twenty feet above the ground. Then I made the mistake of looking down. My stomach dropped as I realized how high up I was. "Don't look down, Bianca," I lectured myself, and held on to the tree for dear life. The tree I was on didn't go much higher up than I currently was, and I knew I needed to get higher. I also knew that I wouldn't be able to remain on the tree very long in this position. My thigh muscles were already killing me.

I looked to the right and saw another tree, with thick branches that looked like they would be sturdy enough to support my weight. The only problem was how I was going to make it to the other tree. I took a deep breath and held on to the tree slightly. My mind wondered about the scream I'd heard. It sounded like someone was in a lot of pain, like they'd been stabbed. Maybe even killed. I swallowed hard as my heart dropped. I hoped Jakob was okay. I needed him to be okay. I needed to know what was going on. I looked at the other tree again. There was a branch about two feet away. If I could just stretch my feet out and stand on it, then I could use it for balance and attempt to make the move. I knew it would be easier for me to use my arms, but I knew that I couldn't hold my own weight. The only option I had was to try to use my feet.

"One, two, three, go," I whispered to myself, and let go of the tree trunk with my legs. swinging them to the branch on the other tree. My feet connected with solid wood, and I sent up a small prayer. I shifted my position slowly and used my balance to push myself off the other tree to the new tree. My fingers grabbed ahold of the branch on the new tree, and I gasped for air as I watched a bunch of leaves and bananas from the first tree falling to the ground. "Focus, Bianca," I muttered to myself, and looked for another branch to climb onto so that I could continue going higher. My legs wouldn't stop climbing until I felt physically exhausted. And then I stopped. I didn't look down. I knew that it would all be over if I looked down. I held on to the tree branch and closed my eyes and waited.

I wasn't sure how long I was up in the tree before I heard someone walking through the jungle. I felt my body trembling, and I pressed my lips closed so that no whimpers escaped into the air. I heard my name being called, and still I didn't answer. I wasn't even sure who was calling me. All I knew was that the voice was male.

"Bianca, where are you?" The voice sounded angry, and I shivered as I opened my eyes. I stared at the large expanse of dark blue sky through the tree branches and prayed that it wasn't Steve who had prevailed. "Please don't find me," I mumbled to myself, almost incoherently. The white-sand beaches looked so different from my vantage point and illuminated by the moon. The whole island looked so much smaller from up here. My limbs felt numb, but I was too scared to move even an inch. If he heard the rustling of leaves, he'd know where I was. I closed my eyes to block out my surroundings and tried to think about something happy. I imagined that I was on the Ferris wheel with my father, high up in the air and happily eating my cotton candy. *Just think of the cotton candy, just think of the cotton candy.*

"Bianca, this isn't funny." His voice was hoarse, and I heard his footsteps moving closer to me. "Bianca, if you can hear me . . ." He paused, and his voice changed. "Please don't make this harder than it has to be. I'm not going to hurt you." I still couldn't make out the voice, I was starting to feel tired, and I knew that I couldn't hold on much longer.

"Bianca," the voice shouted, "where are you?" Suddenly through the fog of my brain, I realized it was Jakob, but I was still in shock. My brain refused to allow my mouth to call out to him. I was still scared.

I heard a branch snap below me, and I knew he was close.

All he had to do was look up. If he looked up, he'd find me. This man who'd become my most intimate confidant was now my predator, and I his prey. I opened my eyes and took a deep breath before looking down. An involuntary gasp escaped from my mouth as I realized how high up I was. That was my first mistake. I felt my stomach drop as I stared at the ground beneath me. I would surely die if I fell.

"I've found you," he whispered as he looked up at me with wild eyes. "Thank God, I've found you."

"Did you hurt him?" My fingers started trembling as I looked back down at him. "Tell me, did you hurt him?"

"It depends on what you mean by *hurt*." He lifted his hands up, and I saw that his fingers were drenched in blood. I closed my eyes; I had my answer.

twelve

"What did you do, Jakob?"

"I did it for us," he said simply, and I felt my heart drop into my stomach. "Don't you trust me?" he asked me softly as he started to climb the tree. I saw the shiny glitter of the silver knife in his left hand before he dropped it, and my heart stopped beating for a second.

"I trust you." I nodded and waited for him to reach me. I decided to see if I could make my way down so he didn't have to climb so high. That was my second mistake. My fingers slipped, and I screamed as I grabbed ahold of another branch.

"Stay where you are, I'm coming up." His voice sounded panicked, and I felt all of the energy seeping out of me. "Stay strong, Bianca. I'll be there in a few seconds. You're going to be okay."

"I wasn't trying to escape from you," I called out, glad that he was safe and sound. "I was just scared." My voice broke as I started sobbing.

"Don't cry, my dear. It's okay. He can't hurt you now."

"Did you kill him?" I croaked out, scared to hear his answer.

"No. I wanted to, but I didn't." He made it up the tree in record time and grabbed my hands. "Thank God, you're okay." He squeezed my hands, and he leaned toward me. "Oh, Bianca." He reached out and wiped the tears from my eyes. "I was so scared that something was going to happen to you in the jungle. I thought you'd trip and hit your head or sprain your ankle. Thank God, you're okay."

"All I could think about was you," I sobbed. "I wanted to go back and help you, but I didn't know if there was anything that I could do that would help."

"I'm glad you didn't come." He held my hand, and I briefly closed my eyes. "I wouldn't have wanted you to see what happened."

"Was it bad?"

"There was a lot of blood." His brows furrowed, and he sighed.

"Are you okay?" I scanned his body to make sure he had no cuts.

"I'm okay." He nodded and squeezed my hand. "We're going to go down now. Do you think you can make it?"

"Yes." I nodded, still feeling slightly dazed.

"I'm going to go ahead of you. I'll make sure you make it down safely. Just hold on to my arm and follow me, and you'll be okay. Understand?"

I nodded again, and we made our descent to the ground.

~9

"Your feet are bleeding." Jakob stared at me with anguished eyes.

"It's fine," I whispered, trying to ignore the cuts and bruises all over my body.

"It's not fine." He shook his head and ran his fingers down my cheek. "Why didn't you go to the shack?"

"I went there first, but then I left. That would've been the first place Steve would've looked." I rubbed my eyes. "I didn't want him to be able to find me if he got the better of you."

"You thought he had a chance against me?" He raised an eyebrow at me, and I shook my head slowly as I stared at his bulging muscles.

"Not really, but he had the knife."

"The knife did give him false confidence."

"Did you stab him?"

"Yes." He pulled me toward him. "I don't want you to think about it," he whispered against my ear. "It's not anything I want you to imagine."

"I heard him screaming." I pressed my forehead against his chest. "I heard him screaming like he was dying." I could still hear the bloodcurdling scream tingling in my ears. I wondered exactly what Jakob had done to make him scream so loudly.

"I told you that I could murder if I had to." His voice was

still hoarse as he rubbed my back. "He would have killed both of us."

"So you killed him, then?" I asked him again, wondering if perhaps he didn't want to tell me the truth.

"I don't think he's dead." He shook his head, and his eyes gleamed. "I could have killed him though. I could have taken his life just like that."

I shivered at his statement. How easily he talked of death. He scared and fascinated me. "But what about all the blood on your hands?"

"I stabbed him in the thigh so he couldn't run away." He shrugged. "There was a lot of blood."

"It doesn't make sense though." My brain ached as I thought about everything that had gone down. "Why would he try to kill both of us?" I frowned and studied his face. "Everything in me tells me that this has to do with my mother's death, yet what role do you have in it?"

"Why do you think it only has to do with your mother's death?"

"When I went to the shack, I saw a photograph. It was of me and my parents and in the corner of the photo was another couple with a son. There was a note on the back of the photo. It alluded to my father being greedy." I paused as I felt the need to yawn and then continued. "Steve was clearly trying to send me a message that my family is greedy. Mattias must be worried that I'm going to try to take over the family business." I looked directly at Jakob. "The thing I don't get though, is how are you involved in all of this?" I stopped and tried not to show him the sadness in my face. My brain hurt as I tried to think why Jakob was on the island with me. It just didn't make sense. Even if Steve had been after me and the information I had on the Bradley family, why would someone kidnap Jakob as well?

Jakob studied my face and sighed. "Let's go back to the beach. We can talk more there."

"Where's Steve's body?"

"He's on the beach." He grimaced. "Don't worry though, he won't be able to do anything to us."

"How do you know?"

"I'm pretty sure he's unconscious."

"Oh."

"I found some other things in his pocket. Things I think you should see."

"Oh?"

"Let's get to the beach first." His hands moved down, and I jumped. "It's okay, Bianca. I'm just going to carry you."

"You can't." I shook my head and yawned. "It's too far. I'm too heavy."

"You're perfect, Bianca." He kissed my forehead. "Shh." He picked me up into his arms. "Close your eyes and rest," he whispered in my ear as I laid my head against his chest.

"You must be tired too," I mumbled, suddenly exhausted and unable to keep my eyes open.

"Just sleep, Bianca," he murmured, and continued walking. "Just get some sleep." His arms adjusted beneath me,

and I felt warmed and comforted by him. As he walked slowly
out of the jungle, I drifted off to sleep.

~

"Are you terribly sore?" he whispered in my ear as he set me
gently on the ground. I slowly opened my eyes and looked
around the beach. It was hard for me to believe that this tran-
quil spot had been the scene of a bloodbath just hours before.

"I'm okay." I touched his shoulder. "Honestly, I'll be fine.
That'll teach me to stop going to the gym."

"You don't strike me as a gym rat."

"Thus my comment that I don't really go." I grinned.

"When Steve and I were fighting all I could think about
was you." Jakob sat on the ground and lifted my head onto
his lap. "Every punch and kick that came my way meant nothing to me. It meant nothing because all I could think about
was coming to find you and save you."

"I'm surprised he got so many punches in." I frowned up
at him. "I'm not trying to be offensive, but he didn't look
that strong."

"I guess appearances can be deceiving." Jakob stroked my
forehead. "Turns out Steve had a wicked right hook."

"No way." My eyes widened with shock. I could barely
believe that puny, pale Steve had any real strength, but then I
supposed he would need some sort of skills if he did this sort
of thing for a living. I remembered something he'd said when
we'd first met. He had talked about traveling a lot for his job
and taking on different assignments. Maybe he was one of

those men who people hired to take care of difficult situations, like me.

"So you think he was working for someone?" I asked Jakob, my mind racing.

"That's what I think." He nodded. "I found two needles in his pockets."

"Needles?" I tried to sit up, but Jakob shook his head and pushed me back down.

"I don't know what he was planning to do with them, but I have my ideas." He pulled me into his arms. "I don't know how a man like that could even think of harming an innocent woman."

"I was so scared when I was up in that tree." My voice was soft as I remembered how scared I had been. "I couldn't even allow myself to think, because all I could think about was you. What if he killed you? What if something happened? What would I do? How would I survive? I couldn't even allow my mind to think about the possibility of your getting hurt. It scared me so much. My whole body shut down on me and went numb. I closed my eyes and waited for what seemed like an eternity. I couldn't even look down. I just held on to the branches and waited, thinking about nothing."

"I'm sorry." Jakob looked despondent for a few seconds, and then he leaned down and kissed me on the forehead. "I'm safe now, Bianca. You don't have to be scared anymore."

"I know," I whispered. "I'm trying."

"What can I do to help?" His fingers stroked my face.

"Just hold me," I whispered, and pulled him down next to me. "Hold me and talk to me."

"What do you want to talk about?" His arms slipped around my waist, and he pulled me toward him.

"I don't know." I closed my eyes and thought about the photograph. "I want to think of happy thoughts."

"What makes you happy?" he asked gruffly.

"Seeing you alive." I smiled at him. "And thinking about my parents." I sighed. It always came back to my parents.

"Tell me about them. What do you remember about them?"

"I remember that my mother used to love to bake." I talked idly. "Chocolate chip and oatmeal cookies. Every Sunday, she would make them." I smiled at the memory. "Even after she died, my father would take me to a bakery on the Lower East Side and we'd get cookies and milk."

"He really tried to keep her memory alive, then?"

"Yeah, though, I don't know if that was a good thing now." I sighed. "He loved her so much, and when she died, a part of him died with her. I always felt like he was just waiting to pass away so he could join her."

"He never dated anyone after that at all?"

"Never. A couple of times when I was a teenager, I tried to set him up, but he always told me no. He said that no one would ever have his heart but my mother and that it wouldn't be fair to date anyone else, because he knew no one could ever replace her."

"He seems like he was obsessed," Jakob commented, and I frowned.

"I wouldn't say he was obsessed." I shook my head but kept my tone light, as I didn't want to argue. "He was just a man very much in love."

"Your mother was lucky to find a man so devoted to her."

"Yes, yes, she was." I looked up at the sky and stared at the stars. "I think they were both very lucky to have found each other."

"Most people don't find love like that." Jakob's tone changed, and I turned to face him.

"Tell me about your mom. She must have been a wonderful lady to have a son like you. She must have been so proud of the man you became." I stared into Jakob's eyes, and he stared back silently. I wasn't sure if I had annoyed him with my question, as he didn't say anything. "I'm sorry, we don't have to talk about her if you don't want to."

"She was beautiful." His voice sounded distant, as if his mind were far away. "She was so beautiful that people used to say she should have gone to Hollywood. She would have been a big star."

"Describe her to me."

"She was tall and slender, with long brown hair and big blue eyes." He smiled at the memory.

"Do you look like her, then?"

"Yes." He nodded. "Thank God."

"Tell me more about her. What did she like to do?"

"She was a hard worker, dedicated to her job. She was also

a great provider. She never took a penny from my father, yet she managed to send me to the best schools. I was her pride and joy."

"She must have loved you very much."

"I suppose she did. When I was four a talent scout approached her. Offered her a chance to go audition for a movie in Hollywood. Only, she wouldn't have been able to take me with her, so she turned it down."

"Did she like acting?"

He nodded, and his lips pressed against mine softly before he continued. "She used to love singing and dancing."

"I bet that must have been nice. I can't really remember what my mom and I used to do together, aside from baking on Sundays, but I always used to imagine us putting on family plays and dancing and singing."

"My mom used to sing to me every night. She used to love making up songs. There was this one song that she sang that was so beautiful. Everyone would stop and listen when she sang it. I used to love it, and I would sing it with her every opportunity I had." He looked at me sadly. "That was until the day I realized what I was singing."

"Do you still remember the song?" I asked softly. I wanted to hear the song, and listen to his voice as it comforted me in the darkness of the night. He turned to look at me then, and the expression on his face made my heart melt.

" 'Will you remember me if you saw me on a dark, low-lit road? Will you remember me when I'm scatterbrained and old? Will you love me with your very last breath? Will you kiss me with everything you're worth? I'll remember you until the ends of my days. I'll love you until you're old and gray. I'll marry you and be yours always, for you were made for me and all my life is yours.'" He sang sweetly and I held my breath until he sang the last note.

"That was beautiful," I choked out as tears ran down my face.

"Don't cry, Bianca." He wiped the tears from my eyes with his fingers before kissing them away.

"It's just so sad." I sobbed. "Your mom loved your father so much, and she waited her whole life for him. Did she write that song for him?" I continued sobbing and wiped my nose with my hands.

"No." He shook his head. "The ironic part of the story is that my father wrote the song for my mother. It was his wedding gift to her."

"I thought they never got married." I frowned, trying to think if I had remembered what he said incorrectly.

"They didn't." His tone grew bitter. "My father ended up marrying a girl from a well-connected family. However, he didn't want to give my mother up, so he hired her as his maid. He sang that song to her the night he got back from his honeymoon."

"That's horrible." I stroked his cheek. "I'm sorry your mother had to go through that."

"When I was younger I vowed that I would make my father pay for breaking my mother's heart. I wanted him to feel the anguish and hurt he had given her. I wanted him to feel the pain that she felt, but I didn't want to do it while she was still alive. Lucky bastard got off easy, because he died before she did."

"Maybe that's for the best?" I ran my fingers down his chest and played with his chest hair. "Maybe your father was hurting as well."

"My father was a cold, ruthless man." His voice was monotone. "He had no backbone. He allowed other people to dictate his choices. He valued money more than love, you see."

"That's horrible."

"You think that's horrible because he put something above love, don't you?" His eyes gazed into mine, and I nodded. "I don't blame him for that. Love is a man-made emotion. We're not made to truly love someone else. My devastation comes from the fact that he put money before honor. Honor should always be number one."

"I agree that honor is important, but I don't think it's more important than love."

"That's because you're a romantic, and you're naive, and you trust too easily," he scoffed.

"I'm not naive." I glared at him.

"There are a million things I could show you and tell you to prove that you're naive, but I won't."

"Why not?" I could feel my face burning up at his words. I was so angry and annoyed. His childhood was sad, I gave him that, but that didn't give him the right to take out his issues on me. I knew I had to be patient. I couldn't expect him to suddenly just believe in love. Not after the life he'd had. I would have to show him through example. I'd let him see through my actions that not all women were gold diggers, and money wasn't the be-all and end-all in life.

"Because I want to make love to you instead."

"I don't know if I can—my thighs are too sore." I shook my head, wanting to be with him but not in this state. Not while I was still annoyed.

"I have a solution." He grinned and sat up. "Do you trust me?"

"I guess so." I nodded, and he lifted me up.

"Where are we going?" I looked at him with a puzzled expression.

"You told me you've never had sex in the ocean, right?"

"Well, I said I've never had sex in the water, but I guess that includes the ocean."

"You're not into it?" He looked disappointed.

"I'm just tired, Jakob." I touched his arm. "It's nothing to do with how into it I am."

"I'm sorry, I'm being selfish."

"All I know is that tonight you're my savior." I shook my head, and his eyes lit up.

"You think highly of me, don't you?"

"I think you're a pretty stand-up guy, yes." I gave him a hug. "I also think you're pretty sexy, but right now I think I just want to cuddle with you and sleep."

"Your wish is my command." We sat back down on the

sand, and Jakob took me into his arms. "Tonight, I'll let you sleep. We have plenty of time for lovemaking later."

"Thank you, Jakob." I ran my fingers down his chest. "You do know that I want to touch you and feel you, but right now I'm still so sore." My breath caught as Jakob grabbed my hand and held it tight.

"I understand, my dear, but if you keep touching me like that, I'm not sure I'm going to be able to stop myself from flipping you over and taking you."

I gasped at the dark smile on his face, and he laughed. He pulled me close to his chest and bent his lips down to my face. "Sleep, my darling." He kissed my forehead and held me close to him. I felt myself drifting off to sleep within seconds.

~

I woke up the next morning with aching limbs and a heavy head. I sat up slowly, feeling disoriented, and saw Jakob sitting there staring at me.

"How did you sleep?" His voice was light.

"Like a baby." I offered him a weak smile. "You?"

"Barely." He stood up. "I was on edge all night."

I looked around the beach to see if I could see Steve's body. My fingers were trembling as I braced myself to see his body.

"I moved him." Jakob shifted over to me. "I didn't think you should see him."

"Is it bad, then?"

"It's not pretty." He moved some hair away from my face, and I heard him gasp. "You've got bruises all over your face." He frowned and touched a spot on my cheek carefully.

"I guess that's what happens when you climb a tree and you're not super fit."

"You did a great job." He leaned forward and kissed my cheek. "I can't believe you're so bruised."

"What are you doing?" I reached out and touched the cut on his cheek.

"I'm kissing your boo-boos away." He picked my arm up and kissed a large bruise on my wrist.

"My boo-boos?" I smiled at him.

"It's something my mom used to do when I hurt myself when I was a kid." He smiled at me, and his eyes glazed over. "She would kiss each one and make the pain go away."

"She sounds like a fantastic mother. You must have loved her a lot."

"She was my world." He nodded and held my hand between his. "You know, talking with you last night brought back a lot of memories. When I was younger, I thought I was the luckiest little boy in the world. It was only when I reached my teenage years that I realized how sad and heartbroken my mother was, and that broke my heart."

"Your father sounds like he was a jerk."

"He was. He was a jerk who was easily influenced by his best friend."

"What do you mean?" I reached out and touched his shoulder. My heart ached for this Jakob. I was now seeing a more vulnerable side, and I was starting to understand why he didn't believe in love. If his mother had been hurt and he'd witnessed that heartache, it was understandable that he didn't know how beautiful it could be.

"My father was from a well-off family. He married someone from a well-off family. He strung my mother along her whole life." His voice was angry. "He promised her that he loved her, but he never did right by her."

"She waited for him?"

"She waited her whole life for him."

"And he never came around?"

"No, he never made an honest woman of her." He looked at me and frowned. "What would you think of me if I had no money?"

"Your money means nothing to me, Jakob." I grabbed his hand. "You know that, right?"

"You sought out David Bradley because he has money or as a way for you to gain access to money."

"It wasn't because he had money, I told you that." I shook my head. "You know it was because I wanted to find out more about my mother's death. I explained that to you."

"I know." He sighed and stretched his arms. "Forgive me, Bianca. It was a long night, and I'm antsy."

"I understand." I looked at him for a few seconds and then moved next to him. "What are we going to do now?"

"What do you want to do?" He gazed at me then.

"I don't know." I reached out and took his hand in mine. "I want to leave the island. I want to get to know you better.

I want to figure out what happened to my mom. I want to claim my inheritance back from the Bradleys."

"Your inheritance?"

"It's a long story. I'll tell you later."

"What if you never get any money from them?"

"It's not about the money, really." I looked up at him. "It's about knowing the truth. I want to know the truth about what happened to my mother."

"This is hard for me to say, but I think I owe you an apology." Jakob's tone changed, and he grabbed my hands.

"Why do you owe me an apology?"

"I got you wrong, Bianca." His eyes looked sad. "I'm sorry for thinking that—"

The rhythmic thumping of an engine growing louder in the sky distracted me from what he was saying, and I gazed upward to see where the noise was coming from.

"Hey, do you hear that?" I ran toward the water. "I think I see a helicopter." I started jumping up and down. "Over here!" I screamed as I jumped. "We're here!"

"Bianca, I need to tell you . . ." Jakob walked toward me and I jumped into his arms in excitement and kissed him. He looked taken aback by my exuberance, but I put it down to shock.

"I think we're being rescued." I wrapped my arms around his neck. "I think this nightmare is about to end." I kissed him again and stepped back down to the sand. I moved up and down some more and waved my arms frantically in the air. "They're coming toward us." I grinned at Jakob. "I think they see us."

"Even if they see us, this isn't the end, Bianca. We still need to figure out exactly why we were brought here. We need to talk. I need to tell you what I know about David and Mattias."

"I know." I nodded. "And we will talk, and you will explain everything, but it will be easier once we are off this island."

"I hope so." He looked at me thoughtfully. "I hope we can figure it all out."

"Yeah, we will." I rubbed his shoulder. I knew I was going to have to tell him the whole truth about David, but then I remembered something he had told me the evening before. "Hey, didn't you tell me you found some stuff in Steve's pockets?" I glanced at him, and he nodded.

"I found a cell phone." He nodded toward the helicopter.

"Oh?" I frowned as the knowledge hit me in surprise. "He had a phone this whole time?"

"Yeah." He nodded. "So I think he was in contact with someone."

"Who?" I continued jumping up and down while trying to process the fact that Steve had a working phone the whole time. "Mattias?"

"That we still have to figure out." He reached out for me. "I think we need to stick together once we leave the island."

"What do you mean?"

"I think that we might still be in danger." He paused. "Think about it. Steve kept appearing and disappearing. We didn't understand it at first, but what if he was disappearing because he was calling someone? What if that someone was telling him what to do? What if that someone is waiting on his call right now?"

"Why don't we check the call history?" I bit my lower lip. "That way we can see the numbers he called."

"I already did that." He sighed. "There were no outbound numbers."

"So he hadn't called anyone?"

"Or he had and he deleted the numbers, just in case."

"Oh." I stopped jumping up and down. "That would have been smart."

"Yeah." He sighed. "So my point is, if someone went through all this trouble to get us here, they aren't going to be happy that we got off the island."

"What do you think they will do?" My eyes widened.

"That depends on why we were on the island in the first place, and we still don't know why."

"Did Steve say anything?" I ran my hands through my hair. "Did he give you any clue as to why you were here?"

"Nothing." He shook his head.

"What are we going to do?" My words tripped out of my mouth, and I was no longer as excited about being rescued.

"I think we should stick together. Not only because we need to figure this out, but also because I like you. I'd like to see how it goes between us." His eyes searched mine. "This time on the island has been crazy, but it's also been magical. I never thought I could feel this way about someone. I got you all wrong, Bianca." He frowned, and his fingers brought my face toward his. "I'm not sure what's going on, but I know I want to keep you safe, and the only way I can do that is if you are close to me."

"So you like me, huh?" I grinned at him, and he ran his hands over my shoulders and down my back.

"You have no idea."

"I think I like you too."

"I'd hope so."

"So who did you call to rescue us? Nine-one-one?"

"I called my secretary. She called our IT department, and they tracked the GPS of the phone and dispatched my copter."

"You have your own helicopter?"

"I'm a billionaire, Bianca."

"Oh yeah." I answered quietly, wishing that he wasn't quite so rich. It would have been easier to date him if he was poor. "So the police don't know we're here?"

"I didn't think we should call them." He shook his head. "Sometimes the people who are supposed to help us are the ones who harm us."

"Yeah, that makes sense. How would we even explain it to them?" I nodded and melted against him as he kissed me. "I haven't told them anything about what I've been doing. Maybe we can go to them if we find out my mother wasn't really in a car accident."

"I'm glad you understand." He nodded. "And we can do whatever you want, once we figure out the truth."

I heard the helicopter coming closer and pulled away from

him. I looked around the sand frantically. "Where are my pants?"

"Your pants?" His mouth twitched.

"I'm not going on a helicopter wearing your shirt and my panties." I made a face at him. "It's bad enough that my hair is completely frizzed out, and I've probably got a face as red as an apple."

"I don't care." He took a step toward me and tried to kiss me.

"I do." I glared at him as I pulled away from him, and he laughed.

"Okay, hold on." He ran up to where we had been sleeping and brought both of our pants back with him.

"Should we get Steve now?" I asked him hesitantly as I saw the helicopter coming even closer.

"No, I don't want you to see him." He shook his head. "We'll get you seated in the copter first, then the pilot and I will get him."

"Okay." I didn't argue with him, as I really didn't want to see Steve's body. I could only imagine how bad he looked. I didn't want to see the reality of his pale white body covered in stab wounds.

"Hold my hand." He grabbed hold of my hand, and I rolled my eyes at him as he pulled me to him without warning.

"Well, aren't you charming." I laughed at him as I fell back into him. All of a sudden I was feeling light-headed. The reality of our situation was finally hitting me. We were finally getting off the island. And even though we didn't really know why we'd both been taken there, I was confident that we'd be able to figure it out together.

I stood there in Jakob's arms watching the helicopter approach us faster now. I really felt like we had something special, and I was glad that he had admitted that he felt the same way. I admired his strength, and part of me was thankful he had been on the island with me. I didn't even want to think about what would have happened to me if I had been on the island with Steve by myself. Everything about him had been a deception. I shivered as I thought about how sinister the previous evening had been. I couldn't believe he'd had a knife. I couldn't believe that I had almost believed him and his lies. I thought about his warnings about Jakob, and I wanted to shake myself for almost doubting Jakob's sincerity and motives.

"You okay?" Jakob grabbed my hand again and pulled me farther back with him. "I don't want you to worry. I'm going to take care of you, Bianca."

"I know." I gazed into his deep blue eyes.

"I think we'd better move even farther back so we can give the helicopter space to land." We stood there in silence watching the helicopter descending.

"I'm so glad I'm here with you," I whispered as I waited to be rescued. "I never imagined I'd find someone I would trust like I do you in a circumstance like this."

Jakob looked at me then, and I saw a flash of worry in his eyes before he smiled. "I'm glad that you're here with me too," he whispered. "This is everything I could have hoped for."

At last the helicopter landed on the beach. I stared at the huge machine in front of us and thought how odd it looked in this idyllic environment. I got into the copter and buckled up, watching as Jakob and the pilot walked to go collect Steve and then decided to close my eyes. I didn't want to see them as they brought his body back. I opened my eyes one last time to stare at the beach and the jungle behind it. It didn't look so scary anymore, but maybe that was because I was now leaving it.

thirteen

I slept through the helicopter ride, and that disappointed me. I'd wanted to see the island from the air, but my body was so fatigued that it didn't matter what my brain wanted.

"We're here." Jakob nudged me awake.

"Are we back in New York?"

"Not yet." He shook his head and pulled me into his arms. "We're staying at one of my hotels on a different island."

"You have a hotel?" I yawned and smiled at him.

"Several." He grinned. "I have one of the most exclusive hotel chains in the Caribbean."

"Wow, that's cool." I stepped out of the helicopter, and my mouth dropped in awe. "This is so cool." We were standing on the roof of the hotel, and I could see the resort and beach around me. There was a huge pool, and I could see some people swimming. "I never thought I'd be so happy to see other people." I giggled.

"Are you ready to go inside?" Jakob asked patiently, and I gave him a questioning look. "They're waiting on us to leave before they pull Steve out."

"Oh." My face blanched as I recalled Steve. "Yes, let's go inside."

"So we're staying here and then flying to New York?"

"We can do whatever you want us to do."

"I want to find out why we were on the island."

"Let's relax for a few days first." Jakob guided me across the rooftop.

"That sounds good. I'll have to call Rosie to let her know I'm okay."

"All in due time." He smiled at me and directed me into an elevator. It went down one floor and stopped at the penthouse suite.

"They gave you the best suite?" My mouth dropped as we walked into the luxurious suite of rooms.

"I do own the hotel." He laughed and walked straight to the bar. "Would you like a drink? I think I need a stiff shot of whiskey."

"I'll have some whiskey as well." I nodded and looked around the room. There was a white linen couch in the center directly across from a huge flat-screen TV. I looked to the right and saw a door. I walked over to see what was behind the door and then gasped as I saw the king-size bed.

"Yes!" I cried out gleefully as took a running leap onto the bed.

"I see you've found my favorite spot already." He walked

into the bedroom as if he owned it . . . which I guess he did. I looked up at his dark, handsome face, and I felt my body purring. "Here's a small shot. I don't want to give you any more than this until you eat and have rest."

"I've just been sleeping for how many hours?" I protested, and drank back my shot quickly. It went down smoothly, and I felt the liquor heating up my stomach.

"Well, that's good. That means you'll have plenty of time for our activities tonight."

"What activities?"

"The ones that involve me on top of you, me inside of you, me making you come." He growled and collapsed into the bed beside me.

"What about the activities that involve me on top of you, riding you and making *you* come?" I wrinkled my nose as I realized that my little snippet was nowhere near as smooth and sensual.

"I'm happy to agree to any activities that include your riding me." He paused. "Long and hard."

"You want me to canter?"

"I want you to gallop." He winked at me, and I licked my lips slowly as I waited for him to kiss me.

"I don't mind if you try to buck me off."

"I would never try to buck you off." He grabbed the front of my shirt and pulled me toward him. "I want you to ride me for as long and as hard as you can." His lips crushed down on mine, and we fell back in the bed. "It's going to feel nice to make love to you on a bed."

"I know." I wound my hands through his hair and wrapped my legs around him. He ripped the buttons of my shirt open eagerly and I sat up so that he could take it off easily. He pulled it down my arms and threw it to the floor before brushing some grains of sand off my breasts.

"It feels weird being away from the island," I murmured. "It was like our own private paradise in a way."

"Yes, it was a surreal experience." He kissed down my neck to my breasts, and I closed my eyes in sweet anticipation. His teeth bit down on my nipple, and I froze as I remembered something.

"Hey," I whispered as he sent darts of pleasure through my body.

"Yes?" His tongue flicked my nipple back and forth.

"I thought you said you'd never been to the Caribbean before." I frowned as I tried to remember the conversation we'd had on the island.

"Why would I say that?" He looked up at me and looked confused.

"I asked you, and you said you'd never been to the West Indies."

"I must have misunderstood your question." He shrugged easily. "Maybe I thought you meant that particular island."

"Yeah." I smiled. "Or maybe I'm thinking of Steve."

"Yeah." He nodded. "I bet you're thinking of a conversation you had with him. I should punish you for getting us confused like that." He looked down at me with a wicked look in his eyes.

"How are you going to punish me?" I gasped as his fingers worked their way into my panties. "Oh, Jakob," I groaned as he rubbed me teasingly.

"You'll have to wait and see." He stood up and pulled my panties down and then pulled his briefs off. "Turn over."

"Turn over?"

"Are you questioning me, Bianca?"

"No." I lay on my back and stared up at him.

"Then why are you still on your back and not on your front?"

"Just because you say to do something doesn't mean I'm going to do it." I grinned up at him, and he fell back down into the bed and leaned on his arm.

"I wondered where disagreeable Bianca went." He licked his lips as he stared down at me and ran his fingers across my lips. He pushed his index finger into my mouth, and I sucked on it eagerly until his eyes started gleaming as if he had proved something. I promptly sunk my teeth down and nipped at his finger.

"Feisty." His eyes flashed at me in lust.

"You like that, huh?" I stared up into his face and tried not to squirm as his fingers pinched my nipples.

"You don't know how much." His lips fell to my forehead, and he kissed me softly. "I think I've met my match in you, Bianca. I think I've met my match, and I like it."

"What do you like?"

"I don't want to scare you away." His fingers trailed down to my stomach and then farther below.

"You think I'm easily scared?"

"I don't think you're easily scared at all." His lips followed the path his fingers had made, and he kissed down to my stomach. He stuck his tongue into my belly button, and I squirmed beneath him. His fingers reached up and grabbed my breasts as he lowered his mouth and went farther down my torso. I gasped as he spread my legs and I felt his tongue running straight down my slit.

"Jakob," I groaned as he alternated between lightly flicking my clit and sucking on it. I grabbed the top of his head and pushed him closer to me and squeezed my legs closer together.

"You're not so shy anymore, are you." He laughed against my pussy, and his cool breath tickled me and turned me on even more.

"Maybe you just bring out the wild side in me," I whispered, and then moaned as he pushed his tongue inside of me. I could feel my body trembling and my walls closing in on his tongue as he thrust in and out of me. My juices started flowing, and I gripped the sheets tightly as I waited for my first orgasm of the night to hit me.

"Oh no." Jakob pulled his tongue out of me and kissed back up my chest. "It's not going to be that easy."

"What?" I groaned, my eyes pleading with him. "Please, Jakob."

"Remember when I told you to turn over?" He kissed up to my lips.

"I'll turn over now," I mumbled against his lips, my pussy still waiting for fulfillment. "Please."

"Too late." He grinned and kissed me hard. His tongue entered my mouth and I sucked it hard, enjoying the taste of myself on his lips and tongue. I wrapped my legs around his waist again and shifted on the bed to try to guide his cock inside of me. "Oh, no, you don't." He laughed and pushed my arms down onto the bed and shifted his body so that he was straddling me. He sat there staring down at me, and I watched as the expression on his face changed from lust to something deeper. My breath caught as he brushed a lock of my hair away from my face, and his fingers brushed my eyebrows.

"I bet I need to get them waxed," I joked, trying to lighten the mood.

"They're perfect." He shook his head.

"Liar," I whispered up at him.

"Never a truer word has been spoken." His eyes lost focus for a moment, and I wondered what he was thinking about. "I really think you're someone special, Bianca London." His voice was husky as he spoke. "If I was a different sort of man, I'd be telling you I wasn't worthy of you right now."

"We don't have to do this now." I reached up and ran my hands down his chest.

"I just wanted you to know that I wasn't expecting to meet anyone like you. I wasn't expecting to feel like this." He sighed. "And it doesn't change anything."

"It's okay, Jakob. I'm not asking for a declaration of love." I leaned up and pulled him down and kissed him. "We can take it slow. See how it goes."

"You're too perfect for me." He groaned as my hands pulled his ass down toward me. "Or maybe you're a devil, like me." His hand reached down to my hips, and he lowered himself down on top of me. "You win." He growled as he guided his cock to my opening. "I can't resist you any longer." He kissed me again, and I felt his tongue entering my mouth at the same time his cock thrust into me.

"I could fuck you all day and night." He grunted as he thrust in and out of me. "I swear your pussy was made for my cock." His voice was hoarse as my pussy walls constricted on him. "You're so wet," he whispered in my ear.

"And you're so hard." I moaned as he increased his pace.

"That's what you do to me." He pulled out of me and then grabbed my legs and pulled them up to his shoulders. "Hold on tight." He grinned before he slammed into me again. I cried out in pleasure as his thumb rubbed my clit as he thrust into me. I could tell that he was close to coming, because his breathing was heavy and his thrusts were becoming more and more urgent.

"I'm going to come!" I screamed as I climaxed. My whole body shook as Jakob gripped my legs and orgasmed inside of me as well. He collapsed down on the bed next to me and kissed my cheek before lying flat on his back. We lay there side by side trying to recover from our amazing experience, and I smiled to myself at how good my body felt when we made love.

"I forgot about the condom." He rolled over and gave me a serious look.

"It's okay, I forgot as well." I turned toward him and bit my lip. "It's not your fault."

"I'll buy some condoms tomorrow." He ran his fingers across my face. "And if you get pregnant I'll be there for you."

"It'll be fine." I smiled at him and then yawned.

"You're tired." He jumped off the bed and pulled the sheets down. "We should sleep."

"I should call Rosie." I sat up, but he shook his head.

"It can wait until tomorrow." He picked me up as if I were as light as a feather and placed me on the clean sheets. "Tonight we sleep." He got into the bed beside me and pulled me into his arms.

"I think I can agree to that." I snuggled up next to him and laid my head against his chest. "I need to shower in the morning as well."

"We'll shower together." He kissed the top of my forehead, and I closed my eyes and drifted off to sleep.

~

I rubbed my eyes and stretched under the sheets. It felt weird to be lying in a proper bed now. Part of me missed the island, but I was happy to be gone. I looked over to the other side of the bed, disappointed to see that Jakob wasn't next to me. I glanced at the clock on the nightstand next to me and frowned. It was only 4:00 a.m. I yawned and wondered where Jakob was, and I realized that the light in the living room was on. I got out of bed to go make sure everything was okay, but as I reached the door, I heard voices.

I paused, since I didn't want to interrupt him, but who was here at 4:00 a.m.? I bit my lower lip and pressed my ear to the door.

"How's Steve, sir?"

"He's alive." Jakob's voice was angry, and I shivered as I thought back to how the scariness of the day before. I'd been so frightened, but I'd known in my heart and soul that Jakob was the one I could trust. "He deviated from the plan," Jakob continued, and I froze. *What plan?*

"I'm sorry, sir, I'm not sure what went wrong. Billy is friends with him. I'm sure he can find out when he regains consciousness."

"He's lucky I didn't kill him for going rogue." Jakob spoke again with a menacing voice.

"I know, sir." The other voice spoke again, and I realized it sounded familiar. I racked my brain trying to think where I knew the voice from. And then I remembered. The blood drained from my face as I realized the man talking to Jakob was the same one who'd worn the mask and pointed the gun at me when I'd been kidnapped. "Did you at least get what you needed on the island, Mr. Bradley?"

"Almost," Jakob replied, and I ran back to the bed.

Jakob was the one who'd kidnapped me. He had set the whole thing up! He had known Steve the whole time. He had purposely put Steve on the island with us. But why?

I ran to the bathroom and locked the door, shivering with fright. Why had the man called Jakob *Mr. Bradley*? I swallowed as I thought back to the beginning. I'd been set up from the start. I looked around the bathroom and spied a phone. Thank goodness for new high-tech hotels. I picked it up and decided to call David. He was the only one who could answer the questions I had.

"Hello?" A groggy voice answered the phone.

"David, it's me, Bianca."

"Bianca?" He sounded surprised. "Where have you been?"

"What do you mean?" My face flushed with anger. "You're the one who set it up."

"What are you talking about?" He hissed.

"The kidnapping," I whispered into the phone.

"Bianca, you should know something." His voice was low and panicked. "My brother, Mattias, was really angry when . . ." he started, and then the phone went dead.

"Bianca?" Jakob's voice called through the door, and I froze.

"Yes?"

"Are you in there?" His voice was low, and I couldn't tell if he knew that I'd heard him.

"I'm just going to the toilet."

"Do you want to have a bath together?" His voice was soft.

"No, it's four a.m." My voice trembled as I looked around the bathroom, trying to figure out what to do.

"That doesn't matter to me."

"I'm tired, and I'm feeling sick. I'm just going to sit in here for a few minutes. Go back to bed, and I'll join you in a few minutes."

"You're sick? Open up the door and let me take care of you."

"It's fine." I bit my lower lip to stop it from trembling. "I tried to call room service to bring me some pills, but the phone died."

"That's the problem with being on an island—service isn't always reliable," he answered, and my face went white. "Let me in, Bianca."

"No!" I shouted, unable to keep the fear out of my voice. Silence filled the air as I waited for Jakob to respond to me. It seemed like minutes had passed, and I wondered if he had just gone back to bed. My heart relaxed for a little bit as I closed my eyes and walked to the door. Maybe I'd be able to sneak through the room quietly and escape from the front.

"You know, don't you, Bianca." His voice was soft and deadly, and I stood still in my tracks. My hand on the handle of the door froze as I realized how close I had come to walking right into his trap.

"I don't know what you're talking about." My voice was nothing more but a whisper, but I was certain that he heard me.

"You heard me talking." He sighed. "You weren't meant to hear that."

"You lied to me." I took a step back from the door.

"I think we need to talk. Please open up." He banged on the door hard, and I could hear him trying to open it. "Please open the door, Bianca."

"You lied to me!" I shouted, and looked around the room for something I could use as a weapon.

"You said you trusted me." He banged the door harder and more frantically, and I felt my insides starting to panic. I had made a mistake. I had trusted the wrong man.

"Who are you, *Jakob*?" I screamed, while looking around for a way to escape. "Why didn't you call the police to tell them we were kidnapped?"

"I already told you why."

"Because those who are meant to help us may do more harm than good, right?" I cried out as I realized what a dumbass I'd been. The reason Jakob had given me the day before for not calling the police was almost the same thing that the man had told me on the phone after the fake police-man had entered my house.

"Open the door, Bianca!" he shouted, and I could see the handle rattling. I could feel myself starting to grow hysterical. The whole situation was so ironic; it had been Jakob himself who told me appearances could be deceiving. I hadn't real-ized that he'd been talking about himself.

"We just made love, Jakob. You told me you were starting to fall for me, but it was a lie, wasn't it. Was this all a ploy to trap me?" I tried to focus on breathing in and out as I felt myself on the verge of a panic attack.

"Let me explain, Bianca."

"So you can lie to me again?" I screamed. "You nearly killed a man." My words were loud and incoherent, and I could hear him trying to bang the door down. "Were you that worried that I was going to steal your family money?" I cried out, my heart breaking.

Everything I thought I knew about Jakob and my time on the island was an illusion. None of it was real, and now I needed to ensure that I survived whatever his master plan really was. I'd made it off the island, but I wasn't sure how I was going to make it out of the hotel room. Until I saw the window. It was large, and I knew I could fit through it if it opened all the way. The only problem would be if there was somewhere for me to go once I made it out of the window.

I grabbed a bathrobe from the back of the door and pulled it on, fumbling with the window latch as I hurried to open it. I looked outside and breathed a sigh of relief as I saw the balcony. Clambering onto the windowsill, I stared at the rattling door one last time before I leaped. The last words I heard Jakob shouting were "To find the truth, one must be prepared to do anything, Bianca. One must be prepared to do anything."

"I don't think so, Jakob." I whispered as I eyed the balcony across from ours. There was only about two feet between the two balconies, and I knew that I had to climb up and jump if I wanted to escape. I climbed up and took a deep breath as I was about to jump. I needed to hurry if I was going to escape Jakob. He'd remember the balcony pretty quickly and then it would be over for me. I needed to jump and make a call. As long as I could call Rosie, I knew everything would be okay. If I got access to a phone, I could tell everyone that I'd finally come face-to-face with Mattias Bradley.

Keep reading for a sneak peek at the next installment
in the tantalizing, heart-stopping Swept Away series
by *New York Times* bestselling author J. S. Cooper

disillusioned

Coming Spring 2015 from Gallery Books!

"Did you really think that I'd let you go, Bianca?" His voice was a muffled whisper to my ear, coming softly through the blindfold tied around my head. "Did you think I'd just give up?" The tip of his tongue trailed from the inside of my ear and down the side of my neck. I shivered in the cool room as I struggled to move my hands. The rope was tight around my wrists and I squirmed in the bed.

"Why are you doing this, Mattias?" I said as his lips pressed against mine roughly. I ached for his touch, even as I resisted it.

"Because I want to." He bit down on my lower lip and tugged gently. "And because you want me to." He leaned down closer to me and I breathed in his scent, wallowing in the smell of his cologne. The first time I'd smelled him I'd been instinctively attracted to him. I could still remember being in the back of the dark car with him the night I'd been kidnapped. My eyes felt heavy as I thought about his betrayal.

How could Jakob have done this to me? How could I have not known he was Mattias?

"You need to trust me, Bianca." His voice was a monotone as he kissed me again and I tried to avoid breathing in his scent.

"You said that last time," I whispered, and my body froze as I smelled him again. Every nerve in my body tingled with shock as the truth hit me.

"I want to make you mine, Bianca. We can still make this work." His voice deepened and I tried not to cringe as I felt his fingers in my hair. I remained tightlipped, scared that my voice would give something away.

"Jakob," I said softly and he froze, confirming what I already knew. "I know who you are." I said again, this time my voice stronger.

"That's why this will be so very enjoyable, Bianca." He kissed my cheek before stepping back. "Let the games begin."

One Week Earlier

"Bianca, open up." I could hear Jakob's voice through the open window as I huddled on the balcony. My heart broke at the sound of worry in his voice. At one time, I would have believed that the concern was for me and my livelihood. Now I knew better. Now I knew that Jakob didn't care about my career. All he cared about was finding out what I knew and scaring me into trusting him—I still couldn't believe he'd masterminded our kidnapping to that desert island. My body shivered as the cool ocean breeze washed over my trembling skin. I held on to the railing and said a quick prayer. The distance to the next balcony was only a couple of yards, but those couple of yards were waiting to pull me down like a dead weight.

"Bianca . . ." Jakob's voice was louder as I heard a loud crack coming from inside the bathroom. Adrenaline kicked in then; I grabbed hold of the side railing and stood up quickly.

"Bianca, stop!" he shouted at me as he poked his head out of the bathroom window.

"One, two, three. You got this," I muttered to myself. I took a deep breath and jumped, arms windmilling through empty space. I screamed as my left foot hit the balcony railing, going instantly numb; I landed on the floor in a heap.

"Bianca, are you okay?" His silky tone almost deceived me as I struggled to get up. I heard him walking onto the balcony and I scrambled to the sliding door that led to the bedroom. The lights were off and my heart was beating fast as I tried to open the door, to no avail.

"Open up, please, open up!" I bit my lower lip as my fingers clenched the handle and tried to pull it open.

"Bianca, please, don't make me come over there."

"Don't even think about it!" I shouted as I turned to look at him. His blue eyes were focused on my face as he stood mere yards away from me.

"You can't get in there." He shook his head. "The door's locked and the room is vacant."

"How do you know that?"

"I made sure of that fact when we arrived." He shrugged. "I didn't want us to have any distractions."

"You mean you didn't want me to find out the truth!" I shouted, anger making me brave in the night air. I stared at his profile as he looked at something in the distance. His face looked so familiar, so ruggedly handsome, so much like the Jakob that I'd come to have feelings for that my heart broke when he turned to look back at me.

"Why are you running from me, Bianca?"

"Do you think I'm crazy?" I shook my head and tightened the bathrobe belt around my waist. "Do you think I'd stay with you after what I heard?"

"What do you think you heard, Bianca?"

"What do I *think* I heard?" I repeated and screamed. "Help me! Somebody help me!"

"Bianca, calm down." He grimaced as he stared at me. "Take some deep breaths and stop panicking. Let your common sense control the situation, not your fear."

"What?" My eyes narrowed as I stared at him, my heart racing fast.

"I was on a deserted island with you, Bianca. I know how your mind works."

"It's a pity I don't know how your mind works, *Jakob*," I said, my fear dissipating as I stared at him. He wouldn't hurt me, would he? He hadn't hurt me on the island. I had to believe he wasn't looking to hurt me now.

But how could I have given myself to this man? I'd trusted him, made love to him, slept soundly in his arms. I could feel hysteria bubbling to the surface as I stared at his naked chest, so familiar, muscular and toned in the moonlight. And then the laughter erupted, flowing out of me with abandon, sounding manic and crazy in the still night.

"Bianca?" His eyes narrowed with worry.

"That's my name, *Jakob*," I said eventually, after my laughter had subsided and all that was left was a dry throat and a heavy heart.

"What is it you think you know?" He leaned closer and I stepped back.

"Don't come over here," I whispered, my voice cracking. "Please."

"Why are you scared of me, Bianca? You know I would never hurt you." His eyes looked sad and I wondered at the fact that he was such a great actor. It was almost ironic, what with me being a movie critic. I'd witnessed the greatest performance I'd ever seen, and I hadn't even known it.

"How could you have made love to me?" My voice dropped and my legs tingled as I thought about the way he had kissed and caressed me just minutes before. My skin felt warm as I remembered the things he had done with his tongue, and I sighed as my senses betrayed me and tried to convince my brain to walk over to him. *Trust him*, my body said. *Let him hold you and keep you warm.* I closed my eyes and took a couple of deep breaths. I needed to focus. I needed to be on high alert. I couldn't allow him to twist the truth and turn me against myself.

"I made love to you because you're beautiful. I made love

to you because I couldn't not make love to you. In fact, I want to make love to you right now." He smiled and then looked at my chest suggestively. "Come, dear Bianca, let's just go back to bed."

"Just tell me two things," I said confidently, and felt a surge of pride running through my veins as I hid my fear. "Did you know the other man on the island—Steve? And were you really kidnapped?"

"Bianca, it's complicated." He bit his lower lip and his eyes narrowed again. His body was tense, his shoulders hunched. His fists were clenched as well and I could see a vein throbbing in his forehead. I took a step toward him.

"Why so worried? Angry that I might know the truth?"

"What 'truth' do you think you know?" He reached out and grabbed my hand in his. His palm felt rough from his time cracking coconuts on the island and carrying wood. His fingers squeezed mine tightly and I gasped at the dart of pain that surged through me at his tight grip. "I'm sorry," he whispered as he stared at me from the other balcony. "I didn't mean to hurt you, Bianca."

"Then let go of my hand." I tried to pull it away from him again, but he wouldn't let go. "Please."

"Bianca." His voice was hoarse. "I can't let you go."

"Why did you lie to me?" I shook my head and stared into his eyes. For a few seconds we were back on the island. For a few seconds, it was just us against the world. For a few seconds, my heart stopped beating and I was caught in the magnetism that had attracted us to each other from the moment we met.

As I stared into his deep blue eyes, I ran the gamut of emotions: pain, anger, sadness, and something akin to love. My heart broke as I recognized the same emotions reflected back at me.

"It wasn't supposed to be like this." His fingers dug into my skin. "I didn't count on falling in love with you, Bianca."

"You didn't answer my questions. Did you know Steve and were you kidnapped?" I couldn't allow myself to think about what he'd just said. Love wasn't a part of Jakob's equation, no matter how much my heart wanted to believe that what he'd said was true.

"You know the answers," he said simply, his eyes never leaving mine.

"Is David your brother?" I asked softly, not even allowing myself to breathe as I waited for his answer. *Please say no, please say no, please say no.* The worst possible answer would be that the man I'd loved as "Jakob" was actually my ex-boyfriend's unbalanced brother Mattias.

"Yes." He nodded. "Yes, David is my brother."

It was then that I saw a sudden movement on the ground below us. A group of people were walking down a narrow pathway toward the hotel.

"Help!" I screamed. "Help me!" I yanked my hand from Jakob's grip and fell backward against the balcony railing. "Help!" I screamed again, desperate for them to hear me.

"Bianca, stop it!"

"Leave me alone!" I screamed, wanting him to know that I wouldn't be silenced.

"Bianca, we had something special. Please, give me the chance to explain."

"We had nothing," I spat out. "It meant nothing. You ruined it all with your lies." I could feel tears running down my face as my shock made the transition from anger to complete and utter devastation.

"I'm coming over." Jakob stood on the edge of the balcony, balancing like an acrobat preparing to leap into the void. I stilled, holding my breath as he stood there.

"Get down." My heart was in my throat as he stood motionless, as relaxed as if he were simply waiting for a cab. "You could fall."

"So you still care." He gave me a satisfied smile as he hopped down, back onto his balcony.

"Why didn't you jump?" I was confused. He could have easily grabbed me if he wanted to. All he had to do was make one small jump. Why hadn't he?

"Have you ever seen *The Talented Mr. Ripley*, Bianca?"

"The movie with Matt Damon and Jude Law?" I frowned at his randomness. Why was he bringing up movies? That was my thing.

"Yes." He nodded.

"Yes, a long time ago. Why?"

"I want you to trust me, Bianca. Everything isn't as it seems."

"Yeah, you're not as you seem, *Jakob*." I paused. "Bradley, right?"

"Yes, my last name is Bradley." He nodded solemnly. "It's not a name I carry with pride."

"I wonder why." I glared at him. "I assume you hate it as much as you hate your first name."

"Life is complicated, Bianca. Sometimes we have to make decisions we don't want to make. It's just what life brings us."

"Like when Ripley kills Peter at the end of the movie?"

"Ripley loved Peter." He sighed. "But he did what he had to do."

"Are you telling me you have to kill me?"

"I would never harm you."

"What do you want from me?"

"I want the same thing you want, Bianca." His face changed and he looked away. "We've both come so far."

"Do you want me to sign away my share of Bradley Corporation? Is that what this is about?" I asked bitterly.

"This is about so much more than that, Bianca." He stretched his arms up and I could hear the fatigue in his voice.

"What is it about, then?"

"You haven't been totally truthful with me either, Bianca."

"What are you talking about?"

"I know about the other letters."

"What?" I stared at him in shock. "What do you mean?"

"I know the secrets you're hiding. I know what your father did. I know the truth behind his guilt."

"My father felt guilty because my mother died and he didn't put the puzzle pieces together soon enough to get justice for her death."

"Do you really think that's the only reason he was upset, Bianca?" His eyes searched mine. "Are you seriously trying to tell me you didn't know about the affair?"

"What?" My jaw dropped as I gazed at him, my mind racing. All of a sudden everything I thought I knew was called into question. All of a sudden I remembered the label on the box that had held my father's papers. All of a sudden Jakob was on my balcony, grabbing my hands and pulling me toward him.

"Don't try and run away again, Bianca." His eyes looked dark as he gazed down on me. "It's not safe here."

"But aren't you the one I should be afraid of?" I whispered up at him.

He said nothing, just leaned down to kiss me roughly.

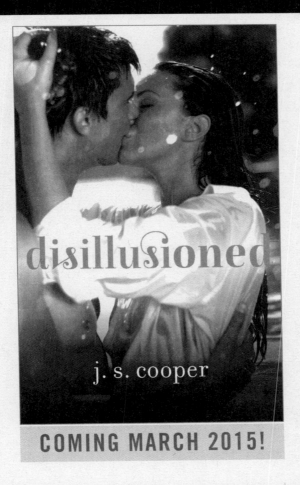